PRAISE FOR
AUDREY CARLAN

"FIVE STAR REVIEW! I recommend this book to anyone looking for a sweet, fierce love story. It takes a lot to write an original story that takes twists and turns you won't see coming."
~Abibliophobia Anonymous Book Reviews Blog

"DAMN! Audrey did it again! Made me smile, made me laugh & made me cry with her beautiful words! I am in love with these books."
~Hooks & Books Book Blog

"A sensual spiritual journey of two people meant for each other, heart and soul. Well-crafted and beautifully written."
~Carly Phillips, *New York Times* Bestselling Author

Enlightened End

A LOTUS HOUSE NOVEL: BOOK SEVEN

Paperback ISBN: 978-1-943893-16-4
PRINTED IN THE UNITED STATES OF AMERICA

Enlightened End

A LOTUS HOUSE NOVEL: BOOK SEVEN

WATERHOUSE PRESS

DEDICATION

Yoga is not just exercise.

It's a calling...a way of life.

A path to an enlightened you.

Namaste

NOTE TO THE READER

Everything in the Lotus House series has been gleaned from years of personal practice and the study of yoga. The yoga positions, meditation practices, and chakra teachings were part of my official schooling with The Art of Yoga through Village Yoga Center in Northern California. Every chakra listed has been personally written by me and comes from my perspective as a Registered Yoga Teacher and follows the guidelines set forth by the National Yoga Alliance and the Art of Yoga. If you want to attempt any standard yoga positions detailed in any of the Lotus House novels, please consult a Registered Yoga Teacher.

Yoga is for everybody and every body.

Love and light,

Audrey

CHAPTER ONE

CROWN
C H A K R A

The crown chakra is found at the very top of the head and/or hovering just above it. This energy source represents enlightenment. It is the seventh chakra.

LUNA

Fear.

Concern.

Anger.

These are the primary emotions battling in my mind as I read the letter I've received from the Winters Group for the second time.

My temperature goes from tepid to boiling as I jump up and pace across my new apartment.

Thank God Dara let me take over her loft above the bakery

when she moved into her home with Silas down the street. It has saved me heaps in rent. Being a full-time yoga teacher is never going to make me rich, but it's my legacy. My mother and her best friend, the previous co-owner, Crystal Nightingale, signed over the business to me. Flat out. The two yogis have served the Berkeley community for the better part of twenty years, and they are moving on in life as two travel-destined hippies in their sixties.

It's my job, my *birthright*, to make Lotus House current and successful and to continue providing for the community's physical and spiritual needs. For some, the classes we offer are therapeutic. Others seek exercise and better health, both on the outside as well as the inside. We have beginning yoga, vinyasa flow, aerial, meditation, and even tantric couples yoga. My mother and her best friend prided themselves on offering the most well-rounded schedule and most diverse list of all the greater Bay Area yoga centers. Heck, we even have *naked yoga* once a week for those who want to think outside of societal norms, challenge their inner demons, and fight off body insecurities.

Now I hold an eviction notice from some big conglomerate business tycoon who is going to come in here and wipe the floor with us. Destroy our building and the community's access to a healthy alternative to a gym membership, along with my legacy.

Oh, and they are generously giving us six months to vacate the premises. Like that's enough time for a business that has been around twenty years!

Then it hits me, and I come to a screeching halt at my wicker love seat. What about the bakery and my home above it? Oh, my God! If Lotus House received a notice that Winters

Group is flattening our building, it's possible Sunflower Bakery, Tattered Pages Used Bookstore, and Rainy Day Café did too! Maybe even the buildings across the street? New to You Thrift Store, the Smoke Shop, Reel Antiques...

Sweet Shiva.

Our entire street is likely at risk. The beautiful hidden gem we've created outside of San Francisco, Oakland, even the main area of Berkeley, will be a haven no more.

"This...this man... What the heck is his name anyway?" I glance down at the notice I'm clutching in a tight fist and scan the bottom. A bold slanted signature stares back at me: Grant Winters, Chief Executive Officer of Winters Group.

At the top of the letter is the company's logo and address.

If this Grant Winters thinks he can just send a piece of paper kicking us out after twenty years, he's got another think coming!

I stomp over to the table, grab my cellphone, and tap the name Dara McKnight in my recent calls list.

"Oh, hell no! Who do these people think they are? Silas is fuming mad and on the phone with his attorney right now!" my best friend states before I can say a word. I'm not shocked to see her badass side coming to the surface.

"I'm assuming you got the eviction notice too?"

"Mmm-hmm. They're going after the entire street on both sides. My mama is fired up too. Says this was the only building we couldn't buy. The Winters Group has owned the land for near on three decades. Guess they bought up a bunch of the land back in the day when it was ripe and cheap. Now it's worth hundreds of millions."

Hundreds of millions.

That number is higher than anything I'll ever see in my

lifetime. Unless the media is talking about the cost of war, I have no frame of reference for that kind of money. It seems so fantastical and out of any realm of possibility that one person or family company could own something that valuable.

"Do you have any idea what they plan on putting here?"

"Nope. But the warehouse across from Lotus has been empty for eons. And that's prime real estate in Berkeley. I've always wondered why nothing was ever put there. Looks like maybe they've been holding off because they already have a plan for it."

I grumble under my breath. "They'll probably put a Starbucks and a McDonald's there. Destroy the private little organic-loving community we've built."

Dara sighs, and I hear a baby coo in the background.

"Is that my godson I hear?" I ask, thinking about their six-month-old son, Jackson.

Dara coos back to her child before answering. "Yes, he's fussy. Needs a nap, but he's trying to stay awake. Never wants to miss a moment." She yawns in my ear.

"Sounds like you could use a nap too. Nursing a six-month-old and taking care of a two-year-old is not an easy task, honey." I don't know from firsthand experience, but I do teach the pre- and postnatal yoga classes at Lotus House. I had to learn a lot of information about pregnancy and the woman's body, before and after birth, in order to teach those classes safely for mommy and baby, which I figure gives me a bit of an edge.

She lets out another tired-sounding grunt. "He's nursing now. When he goes down, I'll catch a nap. Have Silas take Destiny swimming or get her to watch a movie. My little is busy. Always bouncing around with nonstop energy. Just like her father. The solar plexus chakra is fired up at all times. Thank God Jackson is like me. His energy is almost always calm."

"Do you think he's driven by the same chakra as you?"

"Yeah. Even when I was pregnant, I could see the halo of royal blue around my stomach. With Destiny, it was always a bright yellow. I guess I should be thankful the four of us balance each other out." She chuckles.

I giggle too, knowing just how much Silas balances out Dara and little Jackson to his sister, Destiny. A pang of jealousy hits my heart. I wish I had my own man and family to turn to, especially when everything around me seems to be falling apart. My mother is in India with Crystal, meditating and working at some ashram while they study with the monks. She calls on Fridays strictly at six thirty in the evenings because it's bright and early Saturday morning there. This apparently is the least disruptive time in her spiritual journey to check in with me.

My mother and I have a strange relationship. We're best friends in one way but complete strangers in many others. Jewel Marigold likes things to be organic, gluten-free, alcohol-free, and focused on living clean physically, spiritually, and mentally. She does not toss back beers with her friends, whereas that's a pretty regular occurrence for me since half of my friends are guys. *Married* guys, but guys nonetheless. I find I'm far more open-minded about what wellness means to me, spiritually or otherwise. I don't believe having a sandwich with gluten to be harmful as long as the quantity is not excessive. Excess is often the root of things considered problems. People constantly want more, more, more. I'm of the mind that *less* is often truly more.

"What's your plan?" Dara asks, breaking me out of my

thoughts.

I run my hand through my fiery red waves, letting the silken strands slip through my fingers over and over again until there are no tangles. "Well, I think I need to go down to the Winters Group corporate office and give this Grant fellow a piece of my mind."

"A piece of your mind?" Her voice rises, humor coating her tone.

"Yeah!"

"Alone? Meaning you're not going to bring someone huge, like Nick or Clayton? Oh! I know. Call up Viv. Get her husband, Trent, to go with you. The dude is massive, a pro ball player. Then again, Clay is even bigger than Trent. So maybe you should call Moe."

"I'm not calling Monet or Genevieve. I need to deal with this myself. I'm perfectly capable of letting this Grant know exactly what I think of what he's doing."

She groans. "I know, honey, but you look like a fairy princess with skin as white as snow, big blue eyes, and red hair. Plus, your voice is melodic, sweet. You could be a voice actor for kids' animated movies. You're not exactly going to scare some rich, stodgy corporate dude by demanding he listen to you. Ohhh! I know. Take my *mama* with you. She'll scare the pants right off the suit!" She laughs herself silly.

I wait until she gets her laughter under control.

"Seriously, though, babe, you're definitely not going to scare a rich-as-Oprah-type businessman into allowing us to keep our street."

I grind my teeth. For as long as I can remember, I have been put into the sweet-as-apple-pie box. Well, no more! I'm going to put on my fiercest outfit—jeans and a leather jacket.

Yeah, that's what I'll wear. My badass look. And then I'll march into those offices and force some reason into the man. He can't tear down our street. We're iconic. The perfect haven where city slickers come to get a reprieve from the day-to-day rush.

"He's a businessman, but he must have a heart. If he simply sees our street, our businesses, and how we better the area, the town—heck, the entire Bay—he's got to back off."

Dara offers a snort-laugh. "If you say so. In the meantime, I'll be praying but also meeting with our attorney. Be careful, honey. Call me when you get back and let me know how it goes."

"Okay. Will do. Bye."

"Catch you on the flip, Luna."

★ ★ ★

The Winters Group offices are located inside the Transamerica Building, the second-tallest skyscraper in the heart of the San Francisco financial district. What's most interesting about the building is that it's shaped like a pyramid. A friend told me there is a conference room at the top that they use to impress a big client or seal an important business deal. I'm certain I never want to set foot in it.

Interestingly enough, there's a security screening station in place. I move right over to it, my canvas wedges squeaking on the marble floor. I set my purse on the conveyer belt and head toward the officer. Without a word, probably because I didn't set off any buzzers or alarms, I'm allowed to continue through. The security guard hasn't taken his eyes off my chest or body since I walked up. Ignoring him, I make my way over to the table to await my bag.

I notice out of the corner of my eye the guard is still checking me out, only this time, it's my ass as I wait for my purse. When my purse pops out and I toss it over my shoulder, I hear him address the person who was standing behind me.

"Yeah, sir, you're going to need to give me your building ID." His voice is stern and authoritative.

Funny, he didn't ask me for my access pass. I think about telling him this fact but realize if I do, he's going to prevent me from gaining access to Grant Winters, and I *need* to see the man face-to-face. He has to look me in the eye and tell me he's destroying my life's work...my family legacy. I'll have it no other way.

Hustling to grab my purse, I spin on my wedge and head toward the directory. Apparently, five full floors are occupied by the Winters Group. I jet to the bank of elevators and pick the last floor because it has a little placard that says Winters Group Executives next to it. I want to whoop with glee at my good fortune. Then again, the people who come here are usually preapproved, and somehow my bubble-butt got me through. I'll just thank my lucky stars and hope my luck sticks.

When I exit the elevator, a woman in a tailored gray suit glances up at me from the receptionist's desk. Her dark hair is pinned back into a severe bun, her lips stained a cherry red. Her eyes are almond shaped. Interesting. Kind of like a cat's.

"May I help you?"

"Um, yeah, sure. I need to see Mr. Grant Winters, please." I smile my most genuine, cheery smile.

As the woman frowns and clicks on her keyboard, staring at a computer monitor, I'm not so sure my charming smile is going to work.

"Your name?"

"Luna Marigold. I'm the owner of Lotus House Yoga in Berkeley."

The woman's eyes narrow briefly. "And do you have an appointment with Mr. Grant?"

I shake my head and cross my arms over the high bar of the reception desk, getting comfortable. "No. He, uh, sent me this letter, and instead of calling or emailing, I figured it would be best to chat face-to-face. You know, look the man in the eyes while we do business." I pull out the letter they sent. It's crumpled and creased, definitely not flat, white, and pristine like it was when I received it.

I hand her the letter and she scans it. Her eyes widen momentarily. "I'm certain Mr. Grant would rather you email your concerns or any questions you have regarding the eviction of Lotus House Yoga. According to this document, your building is being demolished in six months. There's nothing further to discuss."

I clear my throat and inhale and exhale smoothly, calming myself down. "Excuse me, Miss. I don't mean to be rude, but this is my business. My family, my life. My studio. And your boss is going to demolish it in five months and twenty-eight days. I think I deserve the right to discuss this situation with him *directly*. This is not for you to decide. Now, if you would be so kind as to contact Mr. Grant, tell him I am here, and I'll be waiting in reception over there." I point to a grouping of white office chairs. "I'll wait as long as it takes for him to see me. I'd appreciate it." I offer my cheery smile, even though this woman does not deserve it.

Her lips pinch together, and she cocks her head. She reaches for the phone and presses a button. "Yes, Mr. Grant. I'm sorry to bother you, but a Luna Marigold of Lotus House

Yoga is here without an appointment."

I narrow my eyes, but she doesn't falter. Apparently being bitchy is her norm.

"Yes, I know it's most *unusual* for a person to show up without an appointment... I can tell her to leave if..."

"I'm not leaving until you speak to me!" I say loud enough for the person she's talking to on the phone to hear me.

The receptionist swallows. "Yes, you heard that. She'll be sitting in the reception area when you're finished with your meeting. I understand. Thank you, Mr. Grant."

Her gaze narrows to slits. "Mr. Grant has a meeting now but will call for you when he's done. You're lucky he's being so kind. It's not his usual style." She practically sneers.

"Have you ever taken yoga?" I ask, throwing off her bitchy vibe.

"What?"

"Meditation?" I continue unfettered.

"Excuse me?"

"Had your chakras realigned?"

"I don't even know what you're talking about. Yoga and meditation. Charkas. Pfft." She waves a dismissive hand like I just spoke another language.

"You'd be a lot nicer, much happier, and your face would have fewer *wrinkles* if you practiced yoga and spiritual wellness."

Her eyes widen to the size of saucers.

I dig through my purse and pull out a card. "Here's a free yoga class card. It's good for yoga, vinyasa flow, aerial, naked yoga, meditation—any class we offer, really." I shrug. "You should give it a shot. You'd feel and look so much better." This time I do offer my cheery smile again.

"Naked yoga?" she whispers.

I grin. "Totally. And it's taught by this hunk named Atlas Powers."

"A man teaches it?" She lifts a hand to her chest as if she's shocked.

"Yep, it's co-ed too. It's all about freeing your societal restrictions. Challenging yourself to let go, release everything negative you are holding on to. Even the clothing you wear. Basically, it's designed to set you free."

"Wrinkles?" She presses her fingertips to a tiny line forming between her brows, probably from being so crabby all day at her job. "Yoga gets rid of wrinkles?"

"It can. If you are doing the right facial poses, as well as letting go of stress, getting good sleep, and drinking lots of water."

The woman shakes her head and lifts her hand to take the card from the top of her desk. "Thank you," she mumbles and looks down and away.

"No problem. *Namaste*, friend."

"Friend." She half laughs, as if me calling her friend is funny. I'm not sure why she would think it was so humorous. I'm a firm believer that anyone can turn into a friend, even if they are at first rude. Sometimes people do not realize how their actions hurt others. Everyone makes mistakes, and everyone deserves second chances. This is something I was taught by my mother and father, and I continue to live by that motto. It's served me well over the years.

"Anyway, thank you. Go ahead and take a seat until Mr. Winters calls for you."

"Sounds like a plan. I'll just be over here reading." I pull out my tattered and worn-out favorite book, *The Seven*

Spiritual Laws of Success by Deepak Chopra. Every time I lose my sense of self or my path in the business world or otherwise, I start reading about each law. The lessons he teaches in this self-help book guide a person through finding their own path to enlightenment and success in all things. It's helped me a hundred times over, and I hope it does again.

Right as I finish thumbing through the section on the *Laws of Least Effort*, which refers to acceptance of a situation, taking responsibility, expending energy given through love, and keeping myself open to all points of view, the receptionist calls out to me.

"Mr. Winters will see you now." She smiles softly, stands, and heads my direction. "Through these doors."

Hey, I got the icy woman to smile, a good sign. Maybe my karma is turning around and is about to move in my favor. Though again, like Deepak teaches in his books, I have to be detached from what I want but still hopeful. If it happens, it happens. Be okay with the outcome you receive as it comes.

Right now, however, I'm not okay with any outcome other than this Mr. Winters person agreeing not to bulldoze my dream and my apartment, not to mention the bakery where I have breakfast every morning, the café where I eat my lunch or dinner every day, and the bookstore where I score all my favorites titles.

The receptionist leads me down a long hallway. We pass by a bunch of glass windows where I can see people on their phones or busily typing away on their computers. It's weird, though, because the windows are glass, but they aren't windows to see *outside*. They are windows to see the people *inside*.

A shiver ripples down my spine, and my hair stands up. It's not a good feeling. I wouldn't be able to work in a fishbowl.

As it is, Lotus House is painted with murals depicting a forest, waterfall, and the ocean. I'm greeted by people who want to see me. They come just to see me and take my class and listen to my words and teachings. The thought of sitting behind a desk and being watched from the outside gives me a frightened feeling.

Silently, I send out a bit of soothing energy to the folks who work here, pushing love, light, and serenity their way.

The receptionist stops at a set of double doors at the very end of the hall. She knocks and then, without waiting, opens the door for me. "Mr. Grant. Luna Marigold," she announces but doesn't exactly introduce us. I can't even see the man until I walk past her and through the door.

The office is huge, with a seating area, a bar, and a glass desk with chrome piping. The windows are not exactly floor to ceiling, but they are slanted, so he must have an amazing view of the city. The windows are frosted over, and I don't know if this is a type of glaze or if it's like one of those super-secret type blinds like in the movies. It reminds me of the way light filters through a shoji screen. It actually gives off a very calming effect, even though the rest of the room is black, white, and chrome, lacking any personality.

The big glass desk has a chair behind it, and I can see a head of dark hair peeking over the top, but he's facing the other way.

"Okay, Father, thank you. I'll handle it." He turns fast, slams the phone into the cradle, and his eyes shoot to mine. They are the most piercing shade of sapphire blue. His hair is a dark mess of waves. His chin is slightly squared, with high cheekbones and a beautiful, strong, straight nose. His lips are what steal my attention. They are perfectly shaped with a dip on the top lip I'd like nothing more than to rest my finger against. The bottom lip is full, an elegant crescent shape, which suits his face.

In a word: Remarkable.

His eyes fill with something I can't quite name before he stands, buttons his blazer, and comes over to me. I haven't moved.

He holds out his hand. My goodness he's tall. Well over six feet. Maybe six two or three.

"Grant Winters."

I blink before extending my hand. The second our hands touch, a sizzle of energy so hot hits my palm. I jolt back a few steps and pull my hand away from his hold.

"I must have zapped you. I'm sorry." He smiles.

Sweet Shiva. His smile. Even. White. Brilliant.

"Are you going to speak?"

I open my mouth, close it, and open it again until I manage to mutter, "Um...I'm Luna."

"Luna." His voice is a clear, crisp, masculine tone. Confident. Straightforward.

"Yes. Luna Marigold from Lotus House Yoga."

He folds one arm over the other, and I watch the move as if he's just performed a special dance. Every inch of him is mesmerizing, from the tip of his shiny black shoes, up his long legs, to his broad frame and tanned neck. He's wearing a tailored navy suit, which fits him to perfection. His hair is the only thing a bit wild about him. Everything else is dialed in to the most minute detail.

"Wow," I whisper, not realizing I let it out.

He grins. "I could say the same about you. Redheads are quite unique...special, even. Did you know that fewer than two percent of people are redheads?"

The question hits my sluggish brain and rolls around until something clicks. "Um, yeah. I did know that. Same with green eyes."

Grant walks over to his desk and leans his bum against the surface. He crosses his ankles over one another while placing his hands on the top, fingers curling around the edge. Cool as a cucumber. Casual, almost approachable, definitely cocky.

"How can I help you today, Luna?"

CHAPTER TWO

CROWN
C H A K R A

*The Sanskrit name "Sahasrara" is often used for the seventh
chakra. It can be translated as "thousand petals"
in the form of the Lotus flower.*

GRANT

Her eyes are the color of pure blue skies. Hair a fiery curtain of waves around her pale, effervescent face. She's a living, breathing Disney princess, and I want her. My teeth ache with the promise of her sweetness. And I know she's sweet. I smelled melon the second she entered. Like a ripe, juicy cantaloupe.

She's above average in height, maybe about five foot seven. A good balance to my six foot three. She's long and slim but muscular in a way most women her age are not. I can see through the skin-tight leather blazer that her biceps are well-defined, and the cut of her thighs through her skinny jeans are far stronger than the models I usually date. She's everything I've never had, and I'll stop at nothing to get her.

Only I know the reason she's here, and it's not going to go well. I'm going to have to figure something out in order to get in her good graces, or she'll never date me, let alone allow me to take her to my bed. Repeatedly. And often.

All I can think with her standing before me, practically *quivering*—full of fright, much like a newborn lamb unsure of her footing, of her place in her world—is that I'll happily sweep her off her little feet.

I make my way to my desk and rest against it, prepared for the show, because there will be a show, of that I am certain.

"How can I help you today, Luna?" I attempt a sincere tone, hoping it puts me in a position where I can earn her trust, at least until she's been in my bed and I've had my fill.

But something nags at the back of my neck and throbs at my temples. A warning. She's more.

Better than the women you've dated.

The thought comes to me unhindered and straight from my gut. My gut is never wrong. Not in business or my personal life.

"Well..." She clears her throat and fingers a lock of her red hair. She's nervous. Probably never had to stick up for herself or her business before. "I'd like to discuss the eviction notice you mailed me."

"My receptionist stated this is in regards to the Lotus House Yoga Studio property?"

"Yes. Exactly." She smiles, almost in relief.

"I own the property. It is mine to do with as I please. In fact, the entire street is." I state this flatly, leaving no opportunity for her to mix this up as anything other than what it is. Business. Plain and simple.

She lets her hair go and holds her hands in front of her. "Mr. Winters, we have rented the property for two decades. Almost every business on that street has. Surely that's worth something to you?"

"It is. About two hundred million dollars. None of which your rent or any of the other tenants on that street come close to. The location is prime real estate, and I'm planning to make it profitable again. Very profitable for my company."

She swallows, and I watch the movement in her slender, swanlike neck. God, what I wouldn't give to press a line of open-mouthed kisses from her ear to her clavicle and beyond.

Luna glances to the window unseeingly. I know she sees nothing because they're frosted. I prefer the sun not beat against the glass, disrupting my work, as it sets. "What are you planning to do with it?"

I tip my head and focus on her gaze. Even though she's nervous, her eyes are honest, forthcoming.

"Flatten it and rebuild. High-rise, executive, luxury apartments. It's the perfect location. Far enough away from the city a businessman or woman will feel as though they've left work at work, but close enough to have a great view and the smaller city vibe and still be close enough to get to work within thirty to forty minutes."

She blinks and her eyes fill with tears. "You're going to destroy every business there?" She chokes out the question, emotion filling every word. "I can't believe you'd get rid of everything. Lotus House, Sunflower Bakery, Rainy Day Café... I...I, sweet Shiva, that's horrible!"

Her demeanor is cracking, and emotions are spilling out

too fast for her to maintain her composure.

"You can't do that! You just can't. Mr. Winters, I beg of you."

I beg of you.

The phrase hits my chest like a sucker punch. Hard and unrelenting. I'm surprised by the feeling. It's unusual for me to feel anything other than what's good for business.

"Luna, this is business. It's *not* personal." I attempt to continue, but she cuts me off by stomping right in front of me.

I have to spread my legs and grip the desk in order not to bump into her.

"Everything is personal." She lifts her hand and points at my chest. "You. Me. Lotus House. The bakery. These are people's lives, their livelihood. Don't you understand that? You're not kicking out businesses that will just pick up and find another location and continue as they were. You will be destroying *lives.* Can you live with the weight of your decision?" A tear slips down her smooth, pale cheek, and I cup her warm face and catch the tear against my thumb.

"Luna..."

"What do I have to do? What will make you reconsider this decision? I'll do anything. For my friends, my teachers, my students, my legacy, I'll do anything you ask. Just give us a second chance. Come and see what you're destroying. Give me until the six months are up to change your mind. Whatever it takes."

I push the curl off her forehead and behind her ear so I can see her entire face unobstructed. She's magnificent.

"And what do I get?" I cock an eyebrow.

"What do you want?" She looks at me with sadness and fear in her gaze, and I hate it. Hate it with every fiber of my being. I want to see lust and desire burn in her bright-blue eyes.

"Well, you see, sweet lamb, I never make a wager I don't have a hope of winning." I lower my voice, almost conspiratorially, so she can feel the intensity of the statement.

She licks her lips and my dick notices, stirring from a long nap. Hell, it's been weeks since I've been with a woman. I'm long overdue. Would help with dealing with my asshole father too. Take some of the tension away from our nightmare board meetings and the ridiculous goals he sets, which I'll never for the life of me have a hope of achieving.

"What is it you desire? I doubt there's anything I have that you'd want."

"Oh, Luna. You sell yourself far too short." I grin and run my thumb to her chin, lifting it up so our gazes are locked. "For it is *you* that I want."

Her eyes almost bug out of their sockets. "Me!" Her voice is raspy from crying. I imagine it's close to what she sounds like after a night between the sheets. I can't wait to find out.

"Yes, lamb, you."

She frowns. "I'm not sure I understand."

Ah, she's a smart one.

"To start, for every time you have me come to your little street in the Berkeley hills, for whatever it is you are going to show me, you have to go out on a date with me in return. My date, my choice; your date, your choice."

Luna jerks her head and steps back far enough that I can no longer feel the heat of her body in my sphere of space. "A date? You want to date me?"

"Why does that sound so strange to you?" I chuckle.

Her gaze shifts from left to right, and she bites her bottom lip. "Isn't it obvious? You're...well..."—she holds both her hands gesturing toward me—*"you*. All big-business tycoon, and I'm a simple yoga teacher who runs a studio you're planning to demolish."

"Still not getting what your point is." I cross my arms and lift a hand to my chin, waiting to hear what will come out of her succulent mouth next.

"We don't fit."

The second those three words leave her mouth, I hate them. Hate. Them.

I inhale, deeply and slowly, before raising my eyebrows. "However would you know until you've spent time with me? And I assure you, lamb..." My gaze goes to her chest, where a generous amount of cleavage can be seen, and then along her trim waist, flared hips, muscular thighs, down to her red-tipped toes. She could use a lesson on putting her clothes together; the shoes do not go with the leather blazer and jeans, but I like her quirky flare. More than that, I like her body and want to explore it. Without clothing. "We'd fit perfectly." I finish my thought while continuing to imagine her naked and underneath me.

She lets out a strangled sound from her lips. "You just want to have sex with me."

"Oh yeah." I nod firmly. "That and more. *Far more.* Though I'm happy to court you properly. A woman like you, sugar sweet, compassionate... I'd like nothing more than to have you on my arm."

She sucks her bottom lip into her mouth, and I have to cough back a groan. The moment her lip disappears, I imagine her lips disappearing around my cock. *Fuck.* This woman is bringing out a carnal side of me I have not seen in a long time.

"Let me get this straight." She frowns.

A woman after my own heart. Present the facts, confirm, negotiate, seal the deal.

"For every time you meet me in Berkeley, I have to go on a date of your choosing with you. A date that does not have to end in copulation?"

Copulation.

Definitely smart.

"Exactly."

"And during that time, you realize I'm going to be doing everything in my power to get you to change your mind about demolishing our businesses and building apartment high-rises."

I grin. "Firmly aware that is your intention. Yes." Firmly being the operative word. The longer this woman is close, her fruity scent swimming in the air around me, her music-like voice soothing me, my cock reacts. Soon I'm not going to be able to hide the evidence of my desire for the redheaded princess named Luna. Even her name could be one for a Disney royal character.

"Mr. Winters, this a highly unusual wager."

"Be that as it may, the way I see it, do you really have a choice?"

Her gaze shifts to the floor, and she toes her sandal. "No, I guess I don't. You're on. Meet me at Lotus House tomorrow morning at eight sharp."

"Eight? Lamb, I have work." I chuckle.

She cocks her head. "Didn't you say you were the boss?"

Oh, I like when the claws come out. Still, I don't respond, letting her come to her own conclusion.

"All right, fine. Meet me at six, then."

This time my eyes go wide, an unnatural response if I ever

had one. Usually I'm never taken for a loop. "Six? You teach classes that early?"

"That's my first class. I alternate every day with the meditation teacher. Monday, Wednesday, Friday, Dara teaches meditation first thing in the morning. Tuesday and Thursday, I teach beginning yoga. In order to start, you need to begin with the basics. I wouldn't want you getting hurt." She smirks. "Then how would you run companies into the ground and break dozens of small-business owners' hearts in a single business deal?"

"You make me sound like Superman." I laugh out loud. Another response I'm not used to experiencing, especially while at work. Laughter. And, of course, it's with the pretty redhead I can't get a full read on.

She shakes her head solemnly. "No, Superman saves lives, not wrecks them." On that sad note, she turns around and heads for the door.

Hell, this woman knows how to throw a verbal punch. I swallow down the sudden dryness in my throat and watch her leave.

The disgusting truth is I haven't saved a business in a solid decade. It goes against Father's business model, and since he's Chairman of the Board, he keeps his finger on the pulse of everything Winters Group does. Not just the group. *Me.* What I do. Though I don't know why, I'm never good enough. Always just under the mark, if you ask him.

This business deal is supposed to fix that. I've already got a dozen investors ready to put their millions where their mouths are. The apartments are slated to cost a hundred and sixty million dollars to build a total of eight hundred apartments. The space can fit four twenty-story high-rises without damaging the vistas and clogging up the freeways too much. A group of four high-rises complete with gym, pool, Starbucks, Whole Foods, and other conveniences will make it the most desirable location in the Bay. The profit on something like that is estimated at nine hundred and sixty million. Close to a billion dollars. Which means my investors will each stand to make around sixty-six million apiece. A very nice chunk of change. Anytime a business can make a rich man richer, it's a slam dunk.

My father will have to recognize my ability then. Only thing standing between me, my father's millions, and my achievement is a fiery redhead and a handful of small businesses.

Piece of cake.

I'll get the investors, demolish the buildings, build the high-rises, *and* get the girl.

Walking over to my desk, I take a seat and bring up Google on my computer. I think about it for a moment and type in *men's yoga attire.*

★ ★ ★

I park my Aston Martin in front of the warehouse across the street from Lotus House Yoga. As I look down the street, I can see pots filled with flowers and people milling about in the brisk morning air at this godawful early hour. Sunflower Bakery has its lights on, and a redheaded figure I recognize smiles at someone inside and then exits the front door with two steaming cups of what I hope to God are coffee.

I jog across the street, beeping my alarm as I go. Her gaze meets mine, and even from this distance, her beauty steals my breath. Her figure-molding yoga pants and slouchy shirt, which falls off one creamy white shoulder, give me a great view of the strappy confection she has on under it. The shirt has a giant gold embossed handprint on the front with swirls and dots all over it.

"Hello, Luna."

Even though I'm the man who is going to destroy her business, she smiles at me sweetly and holds out one of the steaming paper cups.

"I got you a latte. Ricardo makes the best. I get one every morning."

I cringe. "Ricardo?"

She smiles softly again and walks toward the entrance to Lotus House. "He runs the bakery in the mornings until Dara, my best friend, gets there."

"Are they usually open this early?"

"No, usually seven, but for me he is." She winks, and an uncomfortable feeling settles in my gut like acid burning a hole right through my stomach lining.

Is she dating the baker? Is that why he hooks her up?

"I-I...hmm..." I stop, incapable of forming thoughts without irritation coating my tone. That's not how I want today to go.

Luna pulls out her keys. "You what?" She releases the lock, holds open the door to Lotus House, and then hustles past me so she can turn off the security alarm.

I'm greeted by the scents of things I don't recognize but which seem to have herbal and spicy notes, like incense and ginger. She walks toward me, and the heavenly fragrance of the studio mingles with her own fruity scent.

"You were saying?"

I shake my head. It would not do any good for me to go off half-cocked about this Ricardo. Next time I come, I'll make sure I'm at the bakery early. Perhaps I'll even check it out when I leave here today. "Nothing. What's the plan? I'm all yours." I hold out my hands for her to scan my body. She does but only briefly...damn it. I had to go deep into the city last night in order to get this crap from a local yoga clothing and fitness store.

She grins and leaves me, heading through another set of doors, using a flower-shaped key card. "This is reception. To the left is the men's locker room, the right is the women's. Down this hall is the doorway to each of the studios. Fairly often during the day we will have four sessions going, but all of the rooms are full in the evenings. We also have a few rooms off the reception area where we hold private lessons."

Private lessons.

"Now that sounds right up my alley." I use my most seductive tone.

She chuckles but doesn't bite. This one's going to be a little tough. Blatant flirting does nothing for her. Guessing I should pay attention in the event there's a quiz, I follow her, at first staring at her perfect heart-shaped ass. Color swooshing across my vision catches my eye. An impressive mural flows down the hallway in every direction, which almost evokes the feeling of standing in a field outside.

"I won't give you a tour of each studio. As you take each of the classes we offer, you'll eventually work your way through each room, so I'll leave them as a surprise."

"I will?" I clench my teeth, and a muscle in my jaw starts ticking with irritation at the mere suggestion of other classes. I love exercise about as much as the next guy in his early thirties, but I'd prefer doing my workout in a gym, with weights and trainers, not mats and calming voices.

She opens a door at the end and, without flicking on any lights, kicks off her flip-flops at the door and pads barefooted over to a platform.

Bare feet.

I shiver at the thought of how many people have walked on this floor. "Uh, how many people's bare feet have been on this wood floor?" There's probably all kinds of funky foot fungus going on.

She giggles, ignoring me, and flicks a switch. Low lighting infiltrates the room through strategically placed lanterns and recessed lights above. The walls of this room are just as ornate and well-painted as the hallway. It has to be the same artist. Here a waterfall is surrounded by trees, and I swear, if I didn't know it was paint on a wall, it would seem as though I could walk right through the forest and touch the rushing waters.

"Incredible work."

Luna looks behind her. "Yeah, Mila Powers is a pretty well-known artist around here. She owns a gallery not too far away, and she and her husband teach yoga here once a week."

"She's an artist who owns a gallery and she teaches yoga?" I snicker. "Is that supposed to be a joke?" I chuckle and wait for her to tell me it's not.

Only she doesn't, and worse, her happy-go-lucky face and attitude seem to shimmer and dim right before my eyes, like a candle being blown out.

"You know, Mr. Winters..."

"We're back to Mr. Winters now? I prefer you call me Grant." I make my request clear and concise. No bullshit. We will be more than Mr. Grant and Ms. Marigold. Much more.

Her lips flatten into a thin line. "Well, I would prefer you be more open-minded. The services we provide here are not only helpful to the people who take our classes. This is a way of life for many, including our teachers, regardless of their station. Mila may be a successful artist and businesswoman, but she also has a passion for vinyasa flow. And her husband, Atlas Powers, who works for Knight & Day Productions as a songwriter and is their head talent agent, teaches here as well. They met here and are committed to sharing their love of the practice and one another with the community. They don't even charge me to teach. They do it because they love it."

Ouch. That hurts. I swallow and straighten my spine. "I'm sorry." I can't remember the last time I apologized for anything. "I misspoke."

Luna nods and carries on with her routine, setting up candles and turning on a machine which mists a calming peppermint scent into the air. She moves to the podium once more and flicks a switch on the stereo. The sound of flutes and calming water flutters through the speakers, creating a different environment. With the mural, I gotta admit it does have the relaxing effect. I can already feel the tension in my shoulders easing.

As Luna approaches, I hear two women laughing at the door, chatting away, dressed to impress in yoga attire. At least I'm not the only one who put an effort into my wardrobe. More people filter in, men and women alike. Quite a lot of people. The room starts to get packed, and I'm stuck standing in front of the riser like a dope who doesn't know what to do. I watch a huge man wearing a baseball cap head over to a closet. He pulls out a couple of black blocks and then picks up a rounded cylindrical-shaped pillow while poking his fingers through the center of a rolled-up orange yoga mat from a basket. He takes his loot to a spot of his choosing and drops it all to the floor.

I take his lead and mimic his process and then stop near where he's set up since he seems to be alone and knows what to do.

"Mind if I pull up a mat?" I ask.

When he lifts his head and the bill of his hat no longer obscures his face, my mouth opens in shock. Recognition hits my mind, and I realize Trent Fox, star professional baseball player for the Oakland Ports, is sitting on the floor in a yoga studio.

"Yeah, man. Go ahead." He nods to the space next to him.

I swallow and nod, speechless. As I set up my mat, not too close to him but not too far away either, maybe four feet or so, I hear him whistle at random.

"Yo, Red." His voice seems sleep-roughened; maybe the guy just rolled out of bed.

I watch in horror as Luna responds to him, spinning around and smiling wide, her arms open as she approaches. "Trent! What are you doing here?"

"Gotta get my head and leg right before practice today. Go easy on the knee, yeah?" He pulls her into a hug and kisses her on the neck. A neck kiss. A very intimate spot to be kissing a woman.

Great. First there was Ricardo, and now Trent Fox. I can't compete with a professional freakin' baseball player. He may not have as much money or clout in the business world as I do, but he's known for his looks and for being a ladies' man. However, I thought he'd gotten married and had a kid. *Aw man, is he a player?* Guy like that, I'm sure he has women bending over backward to be in his bed.

Luna squeezes Trent and pulls back. "You got it. Not too

much on the knee. Where's Viv though?"

"With the kids. You know she doesn't like to miss breakfast with them. Hell, I don't like to either, but field practice has been brutal. Need the stretch on the limbs before I hit the field again. Viv thinks she'll be here for her class at ten."

Viv. I'm trying to place the name. I don't recall his wife's name being Vivian.

"Good. I'll be happy to see her. How's the bump?" She grins wide.

"My wife is a goddess all the time, but pregnant? Shit, men better step off. I get a little territorial when she's got my baby in her belly." He half growls.

Luna slaps him on the shoulder. "You're territorial all the time."

He winks. "Yeah, but you've seen my wife. Hottest woman I've ever met. No offense. You're beautiful, Red, but you know my soul is owned by my gumdrop."

She laughs out loud and adjusts the round pillow under his thigh. "Make sure when we're doing poses, you keep your knee on top of the pillow for cushioning, okay? And rest the side of your knee when sitting. It will help release any pressure that may be stiffening the muscle."

"Thanks, honey. I'll tell Genevieve to plan for some dinner in the future. Our house, with all the kids. Yeah?"

"That would be lovely. Now get situated." She rubs a hand down his back comfortingly. Okay, so maybe they're friends. And his wife is named Genevieve. That name I remember. Guess he's not playing the field on and off. Sounds like a tried-and-true family man.

My opinion of Trent Fox just went up, and he was already up there to begin with.

Luna makes her way to the front of class. "All right, everyone, sit on your mat, close your eyes, and breathe. I want everyone to set their intention for today's practice. What do you want to get out of your life, your body, and your mind? Inhale those good, positive thoughts and let out any negatives. Just let everything else around you go. This time is for you. Make the most of it and breathe..."

I close my eyes and wonder what in the hell have I gotten myself into with this woman.

CHAPTER THREE

CROWN
CHAKRA

White is most commonly associated with the crown or seventh chakra. Often a deep purple or rainbow is used as well. If seen through the aura, it may appear as a white, gold, or sparkling light surrounding the body.

LUNA

The last student leaves my class, save one. The long, toned body of one Grant Winters is still lying flat on a yoga mat in the center of the room. The man who is going to single-handedly ruin my life. And he's *snoring*. Not big, gross snorts of air but soft little rumbles through his mouth on each inhale and exhale. Deep relaxation at the end of class knocked his butt out!

I do my best not to laugh and, instead, pad over to where he rests. A swath of his shirt has pulled up, exposing a tantalizing slice of tanned abdominals and a trail of dark hair at the center of his belly, the hair dipping into his loose pants. Those pants do not hide the sizable package at the apex of his thighs. It is clearly visible even through what look to be high-quality linen pants. His feet are bare, huge with squarish toes, nails groomed neatly with no sign of hair on the top of his feet. *Ugh*. Even his feet are sexy. I almost wish they were nasty. It would make it easier not to like him. I did notice when we started class that he waited until he was on the mat to remove his socks.

Germaphobe.

Somehow his having a bit of a germ issue makes the man seem human, a little more real. Less big-business-rich-guy, and more normal-guy-with-a-good-job. Doesn't change the fact that this particular man is the destroyer of dreams.

Still, he looks so peaceful now, not a care in the world. And he's ridiculously attractive. I decide against torturing myself any further by looking at him until my eyes bug out of my head. I need to wake him. Then I can institute step two of my plan to get him to fall in love with this street and choose not to demolish it and build fancy apartments in its place. Even the thought of skyscrapers on the street I've called home my whole life makes a sour sensation hit my gut.

Inhaling fully and deeply, I let the air out slowly, centering myself. I kneel down next to Grant and place my hand on his shoulder. "Grant..." I shake his body.

He sighs and turns his head toward me but doesn't wake.

"Grant, sweetheart..." I try again to be nice and gentle.

Just as I give another push to his shoulder, his eyes flash open, he jolts up, places his arms around my body, and slams me against him. I gasp and fall completely on top of him. He rolls us both so I'm flat on the hardwood floor, and he's got my body caged in.

I try to speak but can barely catch my breath before his lips are suddenly on mine.

Hard. Soft. Cool. Warm.

His lips are everything at once. Grant hums around my lips and flicks his tongue against the seam. I open willingly, almost desperately. He tastes of mint and man. Delicious. He groans, presses my knees wide with his, and centers his hard body over me to deepen the kiss. The scents of wood and spice, with a hint of jasmine, hit my nose, and I inhale deeply.

Divine.

Before I know it, I've got a leg wrapped around his ass, and he's dry humping me against the floor. The kiss goes from sweet to dangerous in less than a minute. It's as if someone squirted kerosene on our bodies and lit a match. I'm hot all over as his hands slide fiery trails over my skin. One curves around my ass, and he grinds his considerable length against me.

My God, it's been *so long* since I've had a man on top of me, let alone kissing me.

Every touch is better than the next.

Every press of his lips more powerful.

Every thrust of his hips more intense.

Pretty soon we're nothing but moans, grinding bodies, labored breaths, and desperate touches.

I can feel the throb of my clit like a gavel hitting wood. "Sweet Shiva," I cry out when Grant runs his lips down between my breasts, grabbing and squeezing each globe in his hands.

"Christ, lamb, your body is exquisite. I can't get enough." He sucks at the top of the breast he's pushed so far up it's almost spilling out of my tight spandex bralette. His hips are tireless against mine, rotating in dizzying, delicious circles that defy all reason.

The pleasure is out of this world, and I recognize the heat between my thighs, the lava bubbling underneath the surface just waiting to explode.

Only this isn't right. I shouldn't be doing this.

Not here.

Not now.

Not *ever*.

A flicker of sanity hits my mind, and I push against his chest, and he rolls off as I roll on top. I sit up and push at the tendrils of hair that have fallen down around my face. "What are we doing?" I scold him as much as myself.

He grins sexily, his brown waves flopping around his head in the perfect sex-mussed style. Grant grips my body and rotates his fabulous hips, making sure his thick, long erection plays against my most sensitive areas like he's stirring cake batter, only it's me he's stirring into a frenzy of lust and need.

I close my eyes. The moment I remember why this is a bad idea, I jump up and away from him, desperately trying to catch my breath and my good sense. The second his lips hit mine, I completely lost both.

Grant braces his upper body, resting his head in his palm. He smiles wickedly, and I swear the lower half of me takes notice and wants to hop right back on top of him and ride him like a thoroughbred.

I need to get laid.

The little devil on my shoulder gives me the go-ahead to jump him, when my angel reminds me this man is the destroyer of dreams, a fact I cannot in good conscience forget.

"You're an amazing kisser," I blurt without meaning to.

He licks his lip. "I know."

"Humble too, I see."

He chuckles, clearly enjoying this conversation. "Not even a little." He sits, one knee cocked, his package still hard and tenting his pants. An issue he does not seem to be concerned with at all. "Why did you stop? We were just getting to the good part." He grins.

I have to bite my tongue in order not to scream. Straight out, tip my head back, and scream to the heavens that this cannot possibly be my life.

"You surprised me. I got caught up in the moment." I firm my spine and stick to my answer.

He huffs haughtily. "I'll say. The way you were clinging to me, grinding your crotch against my dick..." His eyes flare with lust and desire all over again.

I shake my head.

"You can't deny it, lamb. You were just as hot for me as I was for you."

This astute and completely accurate assessment has flames licking at my chest and neck, making me feel clammy and frustrated at the same time. Because he's right. I haven't been hot for a man in a long while, and when he kissed me, I took advantage, twirled my tongue with his, and kissed him, taking a *deep* drink from the well of his mouth.

I groan, push back my hair, and turn back to the riser to get my things. "Get up. We're going for coffee and pastries."

"Now?" His strained reply comes from behind me.

I ignore his distress and continue shutting down the room and getting my things. "Yes, now," I say over my shoulder.

He responds with an exaggerated sigh.

I roll my eyes. "Big baby," I grumble under my breath. Only I don't realize how close he actually is when I say it until a tanned arm comes at me from behind, curling around my waist and smashing the back of my body to the front of his. I feel his lips against my neck when he speaks.

"Big is right, lamb." He grinds his firm, but no longer *raging*, erection against my behind.

I bite my lip to prevent the moan I so desperately want to release, but just barely. It's unnatural the hold this man's touch has over me. It's like the second he puts his hands on me, I turn into jelly or pudding or any other substance that softens and molds against a harder, firmer object. I grip his arm around my waist and attempt to pull away.

"Why do you call me lamb?" I finally ask the question that has been prodding at my mind since we met.

He runs his nose along my neck, brushing his lips against the sensitive skin and sending a flutter of pleasure through me. "Because the first time I met you, you wobbled on your feet at the sight of me. Your skin is as pale as a lamb's snow-white fur, and you're innocent, Luna. Pure. I haven't met anyone like you in my entire life, and I doubt I ever will again."

Sweet Shiva, that was a nice thing to say.

I swallow and spin around. He keeps me close, his arms wrapping around my waist this time.

"You're ruining my plan," I whisper, admitting more than I wanted to.

He smiles and rubs his nose against mine. "Which was my plan all along."

I shake my head and push against his chest. "Please step back, Grant."

He holds my waist firmly until I look up and into his

eyes. "Is that what you really want?" His sapphire eyes are enchanting, reminding me of the dark waters of the San Francisco Bay on a foggy day.

Grant waits while I pull my thoughts together. "I'd like to take you to have a pastry and another cup of coffee from the bakery next door."

"Is that part of your master plan? Fill me full of sugary treats?" He smiles, letting the intensity of his nearness dissipate a little. Not much but a little.

I nod, unable to form coherent thoughts while in his arms.

He dips his head, puts his mouth to mine, and kisses me softly. A direct contrast to his personality. Nothing about him is soft. His body, his actions, his demeanor. He pulls back and cups my cheek. "Okay, lamb, show me to your bakery."

★ ★ ★

The bakery is absolutely hopping when we push through the door. Men and women in business suits mixed liberally with clients from the class I just taught as well as others who will take the next set of classes.

"This place is a madhouse." Grant's voice has a note of surprise in it.

I smile and urge him toward the line of people waiting to get their treats and coffees. "Yep. Sunflower Bakery has the best baked goods in the Bay Area."

Grant scans the crowd, his lips in a firm line, his eyes focused as he looks around.

"Hey, Luna!" Dara comes in from the back room with a tray of warm cinnamon rolls.

I wave above the crowd and pull Grant along to the

wooden counter divider where the staff come in and out from the back. "Hi, honey. I have someone I want you to meet." I offer a small smile.

Dara's Caribbean blue eyes narrow and her lips purse.

"This is Grant Winters, the CEO of Winters Group."

"Did you really just bring this man into my bakery?" Dara accuses, her tone indignant.

I nod. "Yep. I'm going to be spending the next six months showing Grant everything he's going to be destroying if he demolishes this street and builds fancy apartments."

"Lordy..." Dara waves her hand at her neck. "Fancy apartments?" She shakes her head. "Terrible."

"Yep," I continue when Grant tugs on my arm.

"You realize I'm right here, don't you?" he growls into my ear, which has the opposite effect from what he probably intends. I'm sure he meant it as a warning, but once again, my traitorous body takes it as a promise of sexier things to come.

Sweet Shiva, I've got to get a handle on this attraction.

"So anyway, we'll have a couple of your most awesome baked goods and two lattes. Make us swoon, sister! Our goal is: Wow!" I state with glee, wanting to show her the path I'm taking on this journey.

Dara chuckles. "You got it, girl." Before she turns around, she scans Grant once again. She does this for a solid thirty seconds before he shuffles his feet and crosses his arms over his chest. Likely a defense mechanism or an intimidation tactic he uses in the boardroom. Only that stuff won't work on Dara. She reads auras like regular people read the newspaper.

"Interesting," she comments. "Looks like you're dealing with a lot of insecurities through business and personal relationships. You are undergoing some form of power struggle with a stronger, more arrogant source in your life."

"Excuse me?" Grant's voice is devoid of emotion. Flat.

Dara shrugs. "It's all in your aura. Blinding bright yellow. Means you often shoot from the hip. You mean what you say, and you wield your power like a shield. I get it. Lots of businessmen do that. My husband is driven by the solar plexus chakra too. I call 'em like I see 'em. Stick with Luna. She'll enlighten you."

With her parting comment, she flicks her ponytail off her shoulder and goes to get our treats.

I spin on a heel, place my hands on Grant's chest, and catch his gaze. "She means well. It's impossible for her to ignore her gift. She's always read auras, and I hope—"

Grant cuts me off. "I don't want to talk about it." He wraps a hand around my waist and leads me to a table a couple just vacated.

We stare at one another without speaking. I no longer know what to say or how to do what I want to do. Which is convincing him to love this bakery, Dara, and this street so much he'll leave it alone.

"Grant...I'm sorry—" He stops me by covering my hand with his where it rests on top of the table.

"It's fine. She just gave me something new to digest. Why don't you tell me about yourself?"

I dip my head from left to right as he intertwines our fingers. I close my eyes and enjoy our energies melding, swirling around one another like a vortex. Holding his hand is nice. It feels good. More than good. It feels right.

"Um, I'm a yoga teacher. Have been for ten years and then some."

His eyes widen. "Really?"

"Yeah, my mom owned Lotus House with her best friend, Crystal Nightingale, for as long as I can remember. I used to hang out in the studio every day after school. When I was done with my homework, I'd help out by filing, marking off class cards, picking up the studios after a class. Later, it was how I made my allowance. Then it morphed into me taking every class I could, going to school, and earning my RYT—Registered Yoga Teacher—credential, and registering with the National Yoga Alliance."

He sits back and rubs at his chin, listening intently.

"At eighteen, I took on a load of classes at the studio and never looked back. My mother and Crystal signed the studio over to me last year so they could travel."

"You run the place by yourself?" he asks, sounding interested.

"Yeah. It's a lot of work but a labor of love. There's nothing I want more than to teach yoga, have a family one day, and teach my children the practice."

He swallows and squeezes my hand. "You want kids?"

"Yeah. I always have, and I'm not getting any younger." I laugh.

Ricky walks over with a tray filled to the brim with treats and two steaming lattes. "Hey, sweetness, here's some sugar for my sugar," he says with a flare and a snap before setting down our items.

I jump up and hug him and then kiss him on the cheek. "Thanks, Ricardo."

Grant grins wide. "You're Ricardo?" He smiles.

"One and only. Why? You looking to switch sides? I've been known to turn a man. Hell, I've been known to turn a woman. Not that I don't like those too." He smirks.

"Ricky! Seriously, stop it. This is Grant Winters from the Winters Group."

"I don't care who he is; this boy is fiiiiiine. Wait a minute... Grant whose-a-what's-it." He pinches his lips together. "You the man who's threatening to tear down this street?"

I press against Ricky's chest. "He's the man who's kind enough to give me six months to prove to him how important this street and all the businesses and people who work here are. So cool your jets, He-Man."

Ricky's expression turns into one of disdain as he inhales loudly through his nose and lets it out through his mouth. Then he spins around. "I can't even deal with this today. No way. Nuh-uh. Moving on to hotter buns." He glances over his shoulder. "Okay, maybe not hotter..." He winks.

Ricardo is the world's largest dichotomy. Gay. Not gay. Alpha. Feminine. I can never quite pin the boy down. Then again, that's part of his charm.

I turn around and find Grant taking a huge bite out of a sticky bun.

"Holy hell, this is good," he murmurs around a mouthful of doughy goodness.

I sigh and sit back down. "Once again, I'm sorry about that."

He finishes chewing his bite and then licks his fingers. As each long digit goes into his mouth, I wish it were my mouth licking the sugar off his fingers. Yum. I shake my head and mentally chastise myself for getting sidetracked again.

"It's okay. How's about the next person you introduce me to, you don't give them my last name or the fact that I'm the CEO of the company planning to tear down their businesses?" He lifts a napkin and wipes at his mouth.

"Touché." I lift my latte up and take a sip of the creamy foamy bliss in a cup. When I put it back down, I sigh in relief. Grant, however, is staring at me. He lifts a hand to my face and wipes my upper lip with his thumb, and then he brings the thumb to his mouth. I swallow as I watch him taste the cream.

"Mmm, they make a great latte." He quirks an eyebrow and smiles.

My heart drops right out of my chest and puddles at my feet. I want him to pick it up and hold it close. I have no idea what it is about him, but it's as if my soul is reaching out, trying to hold on to him, and I'm beginning to think it's far more than the need to ensure my legacy and preserve the place I grew up.

"You were telling me about wanting kids." He brings us back to our earlier conversation before we were interrupted by Ricky.

"Uh, yeah."

"How old are you, if you don't mind me asking?"

"Twenty-eight," I state automatically, not at all ashamed of my age.

He frowns. "That's nothing. You've got plenty of time. Me, on the other hand, if I want my own kid, I better get started."

"Why? How old are you?" He doesn't look old. Couldn't be too much older than me.

"Thirty-five."

"You've got seven years on me..." I make a pfft sound, and he chuckles. "That's not much."

He leans forward, resting his elbow on the table and his chin in his palm. "I guess it's not if I find myself a twenty-eight-year-old fairy princess to woo."

I laugh out loud and push at his big thigh pressing near mine. "Shut up!"

He just stares at me and smiles. I have no idea what's on his mind, but I wish I did.

"What about you? Parents, siblings?"

His jaw goes tight, and the easy look in his eyes fades. The lightness around him turns heavy. "My mother left my father when I was five. Up and disappeared and never returned. My father built the Winters Group into what it is today. He's all business, all the time, and raised me to be the same. Speaking of"—he stands up abruptly— "I need to be getting to work. I've enjoyed our morning. Now it's my turn."

I stand up, feeling a little bereft and lost at the sudden change in his playful demeanor of moments ago. "Okay."

"Sunday night, I have a charity event to attend. I'd be honored if you'd attend with me."

"Um...a charity event? Okay, that sounds nice."

He nods but doesn't say anything else.

"What do I wear?"

"It's not black tie, so any cocktail dress will be fine." His voice is lacking emotion, and he keeps glancing at the door like it's going to catch fire any minute and he needs to run through it. "I must go," he says formally again. So different than the man I was just spending time with.

"Okay."

"Give me your phone so I can program my number in."

Numbly I grab my phone out of the front pocket of my hoodie and hand it to him. He punches a series of buttons until I hear his phone ring. He grabs it out of his pants and smashes the button before putting it back.

"I'll have my receptionist contact you with the details." His tone is curt and lacking any emotion.

"Your receptionist?" I cringe, and though he notices my

response, he doesn't acknowledge it.

"Goodbye, Luna. I'll see you Sunday."

Before I can even say goodbye, he's maneuvered himself around the patrons standing in line and is out the door.

What an odd exchange. Everything was going fine and then—whammo!—he turns into the ice-cold business tycoon. Something triggered that response in him. I think back to what we were talking about. My work, family, children, age. Then I asked about his family, and he clammed up. Responded with the fact that his mother had left and his father was a tried-and-true businessman. He didn't say anything positive about either of his parents and nothing about a sibling, so I'm left to assume he doesn't have any. I don't either, so we have that in common. Except, all of a sudden, he's having his receptionist call me instead of making the plans himself.

It's like I flipped some type of jerk-switch. Now I just need to turn it off. And I have until Sunday to figure that out.

CHAPTER FOUR

CROWN
C H A K R A

*Another sign your crown chakra could be blocked is your
moral and ethical beliefs may have been weakened and your
attachment to material things heightened. You may also
feel disconnected from Mother Nature as well
as friends and family around you.*

GRANT

I tossed and turned all night. Couldn't sleep worth a shit.
Worried about how Luna was faring after I iced her out and
pushed her away.

I run my hand through my messy hair. It's all I've been
doing for the last two hours. Pacing my office, stressing about
my redheaded fairy princess. And she is too. Everything I've
never considered a possibility. Women like her—good, kind,

compassionate—hate men like me. Like she said, I destroy lives in the name of business, and I never look back.

Hell, even the women I date leave much to be desired.

A chuckle slips out of my mouth as I stop and look out over the San Francisco Bay. Date is an interesting word. I never really *date* women. Definitely not the model-thin bony bitches. Mostly, I just buy them shit and fuck them for a couple months or so before they jet off to some other rich man with the promise of marriage.

Gold diggers. Every. Last. One.

Not Luna Marigold. She does want something from me. She's trying to save her company. No, that isn't quite it. She's one woman trying to save an entire street from being demolished. And I'm the wrecking ball, yet she continues to treat me with kindness and consideration. Like I'm a good, honest human being.

How is that even possible?

I'm going to ruin her life. Flatten her studio, build luxury apartments, and score a major influx for my bank account and my investors in doing so.

Her smile enters my mind as I stare out over the skyline. Nothing compares to her beauty—even this view. It's nice but not as nice as the gentle slope of her pale, swanlike neck. The glitter of her gaze when something excites her. The pucker of her pink lips after she's been thoroughly kissed.

My intercom buzzes loudly, obliterating my thoughts of sugar plum fairies and bringing me back to the here and now. The cold and harsh world I live in.

I press the button. "Yes, Annette?" I state curtly, not happy my thoughts of a redheaded beauty have been interrupted by a cold brunette.

"Grant Winters *Senior* is on the line for you."

I cringe.

Every time I hear my father's name, the same name he bestowed upon me, I shiver. There was no other option given to my mother. This I've known since I was five, before she left. She wanted to name me Matt. A good, solid name. A name that sounds friendly, approachable. My father had many opinions on the name Matt, all of which he told her, repeatedly. *"No son of mine is going to be named after something you wipe your feet on. He will be a leader. Strong. Confident. There's no name better than my very own."*

I can feel my shoulders tighten of their own accord as I pick up the receiver and straighten my spine, preparing for the onslaught of negativity he'll batter me with today.

"Father."

He speaks without greeting. "The stock on Winters Group is down a quarter of a point. What are you going to do about it?" he barks over the line.

I get these calls regularly. "Father, it's not my first day in business. It's fine. The market is fluctuating, and as soon as we announce the high-rises in Berkeley, stock is going to skyrocket."

"And when are we doing that? You notify the businesses?"

Instead of answering his question, I hammer him with one of my own. "Why didn't you tell me the businesses on that street were thriving and have been there for twenty plus years?"

My father scoffs. The sound of the freeway noise in the background drowns out some of his disdain. "Because it doesn't matter. The time is *now*. The iron is hot, boy. You strike, and you make a billion. I need to know that when I retire, this company is in good hands. So far, you haven't proven yourself..."

I brace against my desk. "Father..." I warn, grinding my teeth, not wanting to hear this crap today of all days. My mood since leaving Luna the other day has been volatile. His voice is only adding fuel to the fire.

"Grant, you need to push those hippies out of there and get to building ASAP. Mark my words...if you don't, I will."

"Now you listen to me, old man. You may be the Chairman of the Board, but I run the day-to-day. I make the decisions now and have for the last eight years. Our stock has skyrocketed every year. Not just once, but multiple times. I've made all of us, investors included, very rich men. You will back off the decisions I make, or so help me, when you're on life support, I'll pull the plug so fast your last breath will be nothing but smoke."

My father's laughter hits my ears like an icepick to my eardrum. "Finally! You have been paying attention. Ruthless. I love it. Glad to hear you're firing on all cylinders, boy! Get the job done. See you at the charity gala tomorrow. Don't be late. Your mother hates that..."

"She's not my mother," I growl into the line.

"You will respect my wife."

"Father, you've had six wives. I can barely remember their names. This one is just another in the long line of women you've taken in and later tossed aside." Out with the trash. Seems to be his motto more often than not. Women are treated no better.

"This one is going to stick."

I laugh whole-heartedly. "Father, she's a gold-digging whore who tried to fuck me at the last dinner you had in your home." The memory of his stick-thin blonde grabbing my crotch and rubbing her skanky body all over me was a thing of nightmares.

"You misread her intention," he grates.

"When her hand was on my dick and she cornered me in the bathroom, pressing her fake tits against my chest? I don't think so...*Dad*." I say the three-letter word as though it was a four-letter word and with nothing but malice.

"Yeah, well, she sucks dick like a goddess and doesn't care when I don't return the favor. I'm keeping her awhile...so do as you're told."

"I'm bringing a date," I say with zero emotion because I don't want him to know how much I genuinely like this woman. If he knows, he'll do his best to ruin it.

"One of your bimbos, I assume." He retaliates for the low blow I made about his wife.

"Yeah, something like that." I wince, hating the thought that I suggested Luna was anywhere near the mindless dates I've brought to events in the past.

"When are you going to impregnate one of your models? Hell, a couple of them would be good. You need a legacy, boy. A child to pass our fortune down to. Carry on the Winters good name." He boasts as though he's proud of what we've built.

Good name. What a joke. We haven't been on the side of *good* since my great grandfather, Gerald Winters, owned the company. Gerry was known by all to be a good man, loving husband, and conducted honorable business. He built things. Beautiful buildings that still stand tall and proud today. He didn't tear down yoga studios and bakeries to make a few hundred million. He'd do what he could to avoid extinguishing something good, a place the community needs. Thrives on.

"...get you one of your long-legged twenty-year-olds.

Brunette would be preferred," he says, continuing his bimbo, baby-making rant.

All I can see is red when he refers to a woman. Red waves and curls for days, falling down her pearlescent back.

"Look, Father, I have a meeting. I'll see you at the event tomorrow." Without waiting for his reply, I hang up the phone abruptly and go back to my pacing.

I scratch at my forearms, the sides of my neck, and then grip my hair and tug on the strands until the roots pull tight, sending a ripple of pain to ease the anger and hostility I feel when talking to my father.

Christ! The man makes my blood boil.

Needing to do *something*, let go of this hate, I pull out my phone and dial her number without even thinking twice about it.

It rings once before her sing-song voice picks up. "Hello, Grant."

When she says my name, it hits me like calamine lotion over a wretched case of poison ivy. Cool, relaxing, a balm to put out the fire raging inside me.

"Lamb," I say, but it comes out practically a whisper.

"What's the matter?" she asks instantly.

I left her the other day, iced her out, and her immediate response to my call is to check in on my well-being. Can this woman be real? I doubt it. I've never met anyone like her.

"I'm better now that I'm hearing your voice." I want to give her a bit of myself. She deserves to know how she affects me.

"As opposed to before you called me?"

"Yeah." I swallow around a wicked case of dry mouth.

"Do you want to talk about it?" she offers, instantly thoughtful.

Christ. Too good to be true.

I don't deserve her kindness. I've done nothing to earn it. Though I'll take it, hold it close my chest, and wallow in it like the schmuck I am.

"No, I don't. I thought I'd call and confirm everything for Sunday." I make up the best excuse I can pull out of thin air as to why I'd be calling her.

She giggles. Christ, even her giggle sounds like music. A melody that digs a hole straight into my chest and eases the beast inside.

"You said you'd have your receptionist call. Annette. She's a lot nicer now that she's taken one of my yoga classes, by the way," she tuts proudly.

Annette is taking yoga with Luna? "Excuse me? Are you recruiting allies?"

"Always!" She laughs into the phone. "Really, though, when I met her the other day when I came to see you, she wasn't very nice. All pinchy-faced and grumpy. So I talked to her and gave her a card for a free yoga session to try. I was surprised, but she came yesterday. Loved it and bought a ten-session card."

"I see." I shake my head and find myself smiling. Only Luna could get the ice queen to loosen up. It's the reason I've kept Annette on. She's a cold-hearted bitch, but she's great at her job. Pretty, though not pretty enough I'd risk breaking our no-fraternization policy. Besides, I don't tend to play in my own backyard. Too many complications with office romances.

"And since she was already here," Luna continues, "we had coffee at Sunflower and talked about the charity event specifics. She's sending a car to pick me up, and I'll meet you there."

"No." The one word is direct and straightforward, lacking any subtlety.

"Huh? No? Do you not want me to go? I'd understand..." She starts to backtrack, her voice taking on a sullen quality I don't like at all. I prefer my fairy princess happy, with joy in her tone.

"No, I'll be picking you up. Not a car. A gentleman picks up his date at her door." *A gentleman?* Where am I coming up with this shit?

Her response is soft. "Oh, okay. I'd like that very much, Grant."

"Good. That's settled. What's your address?" I walk back over to my desk to write it down.

"Just pick me up in front of Sunflower Bakery. I'll be waiting on the sidewalk," she says, back to her cheery tone.

"Lamb, I said, a gentleman picks up his date at her door—"

"That is my door," she cuts me off.

"Sunflower Bakery is your door? That doesn't make any sense." I sit down in my black leather office chair and roll around to face the view once more. The sun is shining across the buildings, rays of light glinting off the windows in a dazzling natural light show.

Luna laughs. "It does because I live in the apartment on top of the bakery, silly. You see, Dara McKnight is my best friend, and her family owns the bakery. She used to live there, but when she married Silas a couple years ago, she let me take over her apartment."

She lives in the fucking bakery.

Luna continues as my thoughts twist, turning darker. "The place is perfect for a single woman, the rent is super cheap, and it's right next to Lotus House."

"You live above the bakery," I remark for no reason. The answer is not going to change no many how times I pose the question.

"Yes." She chuckles. "Why is this not making its way into your brain?"

Probably because it just fucking dawned on me I'm not only going to flatten Luna's business, putting her out of a job, I'm going to be making her homeless.

"Fuck!" I growl, stand up abruptly, and start to pace, phone pressed tightly to my ear.

"What's the matter now?" A hint of worry mars her tone.

Worried about me. Fucking worried about *me*. She needs to be worried about herself, about the fact that I'm personally going to be responsible for destroying everything she has in her life.

Her work.

Her home.

Her street.

"I gotta go!" I clip, grinding my molars together.

"Um, okay. Well, I'll see you Sunday. Annette said the car would pick me up at six. I guess that means I'll see you at six instead."

"Yes," I bite out, still pacing, back to being angry, only this time for a completely different reason.

"I look forward to it. And I hope whatever is bothering you gets better. *Namaste*," she says sweetly before hanging up.

Namaste.

Fucking namaste.

"Jesus!" I roar and toss my phone across the room until it slams into the back of the leather couch and falls onto the seat.

★ ★ ★

A few more sleepless nights, and I'm a fucking nightmare to be around. Annette avoided me all of Friday after I yelled at her when she brought my coffee, because it was too sweet. She argued that she made it the same way she has every morning for the last five years. And she did. Except I don't deserve sweet. The same goes for the redheaded princess I see standing in front of the display window at Sunflower Bakery. The yellow light shines like a halo around her, making her look like a freaking angel.

I park my Aston Martin at the curb, not giving a shit it's a loading zone. Luna gets front-door service. She deserves it.

When I get out of the car, her glossy pink lips form a wide smile. "Wow. You look handsome." Her voice is breathy, and I want to eat that sound right from her lips.

She's standing in a form-fitting, white sequined dress. It's simple, classy, and spectacular. Her red hair is twisted up with curls coming out at the top strategically. There's a whimsical white daisy inserted right at the edge of the twist.

A fuckin' flower in her hair.

Natural. Simple. Beautiful.

The hem of the dress is short, falling about two inches above her knee, gifting me a sexy length of leg. Her legs are bare, and she's paired the dress with a pair of sky-high, gold, strappy stilettos with an insanely thin, four or five-inch heel. Her toes have been painted a soft nude, proving just how elegant she is.

"Lamb...you overwhelm me with your beauty. I love you in white. It suits you to perfection."

She grins while glancing down at the dress. "You like it? I

borrowed it from Dara. I told her this color looks better with her darker skin tone, but she swore you'd love it."

I come close, place a hand at her waist, and tug her body against mine. Her hands flatten against my chest, and she lifts her head, caught off guard.

"I love it," I whisper only a few inches from her mouth.

Her smile turns shy until I dip closer and kiss her. The second my lips touch hers, she's a temptress, her fingernails digging into my dress shirt, her mouth opening instantly, and a moan slipping from her lips. The sound goes straight to my dick. Wrapping my arms around her more fully, I deepen the kiss, tasting mint and peachy lip gloss. The combination is mouthwateringly good. So good, we stand in front of the bakery making out like a couple of lust-drunk teens.

Eventually, her body starts to wiggle against mine, reminding me we are not only not alone, but there is no bed in sight. Then again...she did say her apartment is upstairs.

She tears her lips from mine but keeps her body close. "Hey, big man, I like kissing you; boy, do I ever. You're a really great kisser..."

"Thank you." I cross my wrists behind her, resting them on the top of her ass.

"You're welcome." She huffs. "Nevertheless, I was kind of looking forward to your party. I haven't been to a big event since Knight & Day Productions released a new album, and I wasn't on the arm of a handsome man like yourself. I went with Ricky, funny enough, to make his then boyfriend jealous..."

I press two fingers over her kiss-swollen lips. She stops speaking. "Okay. No more kissing."

Her nose scrunches up, and her eyes turn a strange color. "I didn't say no more kissing..."

I laugh out loud, pulling her close and burying my face in her neck. The scent of melon hits my nose, and I inhale deeply. "Luna, you smell so good."

"Really?"

"Lamb, if we didn't have to go tonight, I'd push you right through that door, walk you up to your apartment, and bend you over your bed so fast you'd forget your name. That's how much your scent affects me."

"Wow. Um, sounds as though you like it a lot."

I snicker and cup her cheeks. "You look sensational. Come on. Time to show you off to all the stuffy businessmen and give some money to charity."

"I love charity work!" she exclaims as I grab her hand and lead her the few feet to the passenger side door. I open the door, and she slides in.

Of course she looks damn good in my car.

When I get to the other side, I hop in and take off toward San Francisco. I glance over at Luna, and she's sitting primly, her knees together and off to the side. Her skirt has ridden up, giving me a great view of her shapely thighs and smooth skin.

"How many classes do you teach a week at Lotus House?" I ask, wanting to know more about her.

"My set week is two classes a day, one on the weekend as we offer a shorter number of classes during the weekends. However, I often sub in as needed, which typically ends up being once a week."

I choke on this information. "You teach fourteen yoga classes a week?"

She grins. "Yeah."

"How are you not stick thin?" I blurt stupidly. One thing all men know is to never comment about a woman's weight.

Whether they are thin or carrying a little extra, or hell, even a lot extra. It's the topic men go to if they want to sabotage a relationship or just to be an asshole. Apparently, I'm the latter, because I have no desire to sabotage anything with Luna that my business practices aren't already going to do on my behalf.

Luna laughs, and it echoes sweetly around the car. "Well, for one, I eat at Sunflower every day." She leans her head against the backrest and looks at me, her gaze turning fierce. "*Every day*. That means a pastry or *two* and a latte. And I love me a latte. All the fat included. Whole milk all the way!" She shrugs and presses her fingers to the thick swoop of bangs over her brow. "Later in the day, I usually have something from Rainy Day Café for lunch or dinner, and they make the best sandwiches on thick focaccia bread. Everything they make is delicious. We'll go there next week."

I realize my fairy princess enjoys her food. "Basically, you're saying you like to eat."

"Absolutely! The more food, the better. You should watch out tonight. I'm going to try every single hors d'oeuvre they have...maybe even twice!" She shimmies in her seat as if she's genuinely excited.

Usually these types of things bore me to tears, but being able to see it through Luna's eyes might just make the evening more fun.

I place my hand above her knee and pat her leg. "Have at it. I'm starving, so I may just keep up with you tonight."

"I'm going to take that as a challenge." She smirks.

"You do that." I squeeze her leg but leave my hand where it is all the way into town and to the valet at the Four Seasons where the event is being held.

"Wow." She gazes out the window seemingly taken with

the beauty of the hotel.

I look at only her. "That's what I said to myself the first time."

"The first time you saw the hotel?"

I run my knuckle down her bare arm. "No, the first time I saw you."

CHAPTER FIVE

CROWN
C H A K R A

If your crown chakra is overactive, you may start to have
feelings of superiority and aggression toward others as well
as a tendency to be judgmental or critical.

LUNA

Grant holds my hand as we walk up the steps of the stunning hotel. I've never been to the Four Seasons—never had reason to. Honestly, I've never been a lot of places. Mexico on a wild weekend with the yoga girls, Hawaii with my mother, Nevada since it's so close to drive to Lake Tahoe and beyond to Reno. That's about it. I've spent the better part of my days, weeks, and years at Lotus House. From the time I could walk and all through my twenties. Now at twenty-eight, I'm regretting that I have not traveled more. Definitely helps me understand why

AUDREY CARLAN

my mom and Crystal would have the travel bug in their sixties.

"Thank you for bringing me." I squeeze Grant's hand, and he cocks his head to the side and smiles.

"Lamb, we just got here. You haven't experienced anything yet." He chuckles.

I run my hand down my skirt, making sure it's perfectly in place after having sat in the car. "I know. It's just, well, I don't get out much. Dressing up is a treat. So thank you for thinking to bring me."

Grant shakes his head, grinning. "You are one of a kind, Luna. Absolutely no one in this world is like you."

I ease closer to his side and pair my steps with his. "As are you. We are all perfect just as we are. Meant to be where we are today. Every step, every decision has led us to this very moment, and right now, I'm feeling very thankful."

He tucks me closer to his side and places his arm around my back, curling his hand on my waist. "As am I. Thankful, that is."

We walk silently through the throngs of hotel patrons, up the elevator, and to the level where the ballrooms are located.

"What's the charity?" I ask.

"Foster care."

I stop where I stand and shove at his chest excitedly. "Why didn't you tell me? My best friend was in foster care. And you raise money for it?"

He glances around and runs a hand through his hair. "Yeah, we do. One of the board members and top investors in Winters Group was a foster care kid. Built himself up from nothing. Attributes his experiences and drive to his time in foster care. He was one of the lucky ones who received good placement with a nice, normal family. However, that is not always the case. He's committed his life to ensuring foster kids get good placement and move on to adoption."

I jump up, wrap my arms around his shoulders, and lay a fat one on him. He isn't prepared for my exuberant attack, so he falls back on one foot but has the strength to hold me securely as we kiss. His lips are warm and soft with a hint of espresso. I nibble on his bottom lip until he opens, where I dip my tongue inside to taste the rich flavor direct from the source. He moans as I flick my tongue against his. He wraps his arms around my waist, smashing my chest against his and holding me close. Everything around us just disappears when our lips touch. My focus is on him and him alone. The little noises he makes in the back of his throat, the way he breathes through his nose, the way his hands can never stay idle and run up and down my back, caressing me into a deeper submission.

For a long time, we kiss, standing in the middle of the hallway. I'm unfazed by where we are, focused solely on being close to Grant in this moment. Soaking up the connection that whispers through my body every time we touch. It's a feeling I can no more define than stop from occurring. It just is. Besides, I'll happily kiss my man anywhere.

My man.

Just as the thought strikes my heart, a loud booming voice breaks through our bubble of building lust.

"Son!" I hear blurted from behind us.

Grant's body goes rigid, and an unease fills the air around his form, clouding our beautiful moment. He clutches at my back, his shoulders rising up. He twirls me around so fast I almost lose my footing, but he's there, tucking me against his side, locking me in place. Which works for me because I'm a little light-headed from our awesome kiss, not to mention the jolt to my psyche.

He's not exactly *my man*, I remind myself. He's a man. The man I keep willingly putting my mouth on, but it's not as if he's mine. Especially if he's going to destroy Lotus House and the entire street. I can't be with someone who would purposely destroy the most important thing in my life and leave me homeless.

Could I?

There are far too many questions to consider at this moment. I need to work out my personal feelings when I'm not tucked to the man in question's side like a boneless Gumby doll. As my thoughts scatter, an older replica of Grant stands before us, a little bit shorter, maybe by an inch or two. His hair is dark brown, with salt and pepper strands kissing the edges of his hairline. His hair is slicked into a perfect gentleman's haircut. His eyes are also blue, only not as pretty, more of a gray-blue than deep sapphire. He's wearing a black suit, which fits his athletic frame to a T. On his arm is a tall, very slender blonde. Her dress is also short, far shorter than mine, just barely covering her bottom, and it's a standout lipstick red. The top is cut in a very cleavage-revealing style, whereas mine is a tank style that cuts modestly straight across the top. It is a charity event after all.

The girl next to the man, who has to be Grant's father, is smacking gum like a cow chewing cud, sloppily and audibly. The woman is so young she looks like she could have just graduated high school. She looks Grant over, seemingly uninterested in anything other than how good my guy looks.

"Father." Grant speaks so low it comes out as a rumble and not an altogether pleasant one.

"Son, say hello to Kiki, your mother."

His mother! No way! I mentally work hard to hold my mouth shut.

"She's not my mother. Stepmother number six," he practically growls before straightening his shoulders and muttering, "Hello, Kiki. Try to keep your hands to yourself this evening," he warns and wraps an arm firmly around my shoulder, making no attempt to introduce me. Which is totally rude, but it's also obvious he doesn't care to introduce me to someone he very clearly does not like.

I shimmy out of his hold and extend my hand. "Hello, I'm Luna Marigold. It's lovely to meet you both."

Kiki smacks her gum and smiles wide. "Hiya. I can totally show you where the bar is. They give you all the drinks you want at these things, and you don't even have to pay. You can get trashed without ever spending a dime on the snot-nosed kids." She beams, and I lose any shred of respect I may have had for her.

Snot-nosed kids? These are foster children she's referring to. Now I get why Grant's tone was clipped and his body language spoke volumes of disdain.

I grind my teeth and firm my resolve. "Not a big drinker, Kiki, but thank you for the tip." I shoot for civil.

Grant reaches an arm back around me just as Mr. Winters takes my hand. He brings it to his lips and kisses it. "Grant Winters Senior. Luna, was it?"

I try to pull my hand back, but he doesn't let it go, continuing to hold it to his face far longer than is appropriate, making me extremely uncomfortable. "Yep. Like the moon. My mother's a hippie. What can I say?"

Grant pulls my arm away from his father's hold with a growl. "You don't have to say anything, lamb. I think I hear them requesting that we take our seats."

"Son, I'm surprised at you," his father says before Grant can fully lead me away. When we stop and look back at him, he continues. "She's a redhead with curves. You don't date redheads. They are fiery. Which can be great in the sack, but hell and damnation out of it."

I gasp, floored that his father would be so bold and so crass, stereotyping me on the basis of my hair color alone.

"No, Father, *you* don't date redheads because my mother was one. She left us high and dry, and you haven't gotten over it. I, on the other hand, have."

His father's expression turns into a menacing scowl. "Boy, you better watch yourself..."

Grant doesn't wait for him to finish his chastisement. "Now, if you don't mind, I'm going to take my *beautiful* date and get her a drink. Come on, Luna."

On his final word, he tugs me by the hand and leads me into the ballroom. Its magnificence momentarily makes me forget the weird meet and greet we had with Grant's father and *stepmother*. The woman is younger than me and probably barely out of college, if she even went to college. If her goal in life was to look pretty and play trophy wife, then she's got her role down pat.

Gold chandeliers glitter over the giant space. At one end, there is a stage with a podium. The charity's banner hangs behind it.

Without speaking, Grant leads me over to one of the bars in the corner. "Scotch neat, two fingers. Lamb, what would you like to drink?" He finally turns to me, his face a mask of professionalism, but I can see the underlying anger simmering there. I run my hand from his shoulder to his elbow.

"A white wine would be great. Thank you."

"White wine for the lady." Grant tosses a twenty-dollar bill into the metal tip jar.

Twenty bucks. Wow. Big tipper.

The bartender is young, and when he sees the twenty, he pours Grant a much larger serving than two fingers—more like three.

Before I can even take a sip, Grant is gulping back half of his. I rest my hand on his wrist. "Talk to me about it. Don't drink your troubles away."

"I hate my father."

"Grant, hate is a very strong word..."

"I hate him. It's all about money with him. All the time. And, of course, the latest piece of ass he up and marries. Do you know he has five women he pays alimony to? *Five.*" He stresses the last word and shakes his head, disgust rife in his features.

I suck in a slow breath and sip my wine, mulling over that bit of information. "Yes, I can see how that would be very trying for any one person to manage."

"He uses women. Hell, he uses *everyone.*" His words say more about his relationship with his father than I imagine he wants to. He obviously thinks his father uses him too, which makes my heart hurt for Grant.

"But we're here..." I use my arm to gesture to the room at large. "A charity event. So at the very least, we can do some real good here. Change how you are feeling about your father and enjoy the evening. Were you planning on making a contribution to the charity tonight?"

He firms his jaw, and a muscle in his cheek ticks. I wait patiently while he breathes in and out. "Yeah."

"A sizable amount?" I confirm.

He sighs. "Yeah, a couple hundred thousand. I've got the check in my jacket." He pats his chest, where I'm assuming the check is. He scans the area but doesn't seem to really be looking at anything. Unless he's making sure he's far away from his father. His eyes look tired. Red rims with purple smudges darken the skin just under those pretty sapphires.

I run a hand down his arm and intertwine our fingers. He glances down the second our hand chakras ignite. He squeezes and lets out a lengthy sigh. "You're so good for me. Just your touch calms the raging fire I want to let loose on my old man."

I kiss the back of his hand. "You're allowed to lean on my energy when you're feeling depleted. I give it freely."

His lips quirk into a half smile. It's a start.

"I see your smile trying to break free. Come on. This is a charitable event, and you have money to donate. Let's go donate it. I'll bet you'll feel better once you do," I taunt.

Grant lowers his head and slides his nose next to mine. He inhales deeply. "Melons. You always smell like fruity melons. Makes my mouth water, lamb. If you're not careful, I could take a bite out of you when you're not looking." He presses his face into the space where my neck and shoulder meet. He sniffs loudly. "Mmm." He presses small kisses against that spot. Gooseflesh rises on my skin, and an intense heat simmers in my gut, warming me, especially the space between my thighs. Once Grant stops kissing my neck, he drags his teeth along the column and bites down, swirling his tongue around where he bit.

"*Fuck*," he groans, and my eyes roll back into my head. My wine sloshes as I lose my sense of self under his magic touch.

"Whoa!" He grips my hip with his free hand. "You are so

responsive, baby. I can't wait to see how you react when I *really* have my mouth on you."

A burst of arousal roars through my body, making my sex feel tight and achy. "Grant...stop it."

Finally, his face clears of his earlier anger and lightens when he smiles. "Stop what? Turning you on?" He leans his forehead against mine and chuckles.

"Yes!" I bite back.

"Never," he teases and nips my lips.

I kiss him back, all too briefly for my liking. When he pulls away, he leads me away from our quiet spot. "Come on. We've got money to give."

★ ★ ★

Shortly after Grant gave the CEO of the charity the check for two hundred thousand dollars, the night went from a shitty meeting with his dad to a dancing-all-night blast! The CEO was beyond thrilled with the very generous contribution and made a big mention of it on the podium, thanking Grant and the Winters Group personally.

After the announcements were made, food was passed out, and I ate my weight in filet mignon, garlic mashed potatoes, and grilled veggies, I found out my big man was a fantastic dancer. He pulled me around the dance floor as if dancing was second nature to him.

After an amazing evening, Grant leads me to his super fly car. It's a shimmery gold metallic that not only looks expensive, it practically growls expensive when he fires it up. "You know, you've really got the moves on the dance floor," I announce happily, back in his car. The new-car-and-leather smell fills the air and mixes with Grant's wood-and-spice scent, creating an aroma extravaganza.

Grant grins and looks at me sideways. "Lamb, I've got *all* the moves. Just you wait and see."

"Oh yeah?" I say coyly, running my hand from his knee to his upper thigh.

"Be careful," he warns. "You don't want to start something you're not prepared to finish." He winks and looks back at the road ahead.

A sense of defiance ripples up my chest and out my mouth in a second flat. "Oh, I can *finish*. Just because you think I'm sweet and innocent doesn't mean I don't get *biz-zee* in the bedroom." I slur a little. "I'll have you know, I'm insanely flexible. I can put my legs behind my head...and I can leave them there for a solid twenty minutes." I pucker my lips and blow a kiss.

"Christ on a cracker!" Grant bites out. "Damn it, Luna. Nothing's going to take that visual away." He adjusts his crotch with one hand.

I smile with smug pride.

"All the yogis I know are very sexual creatures because we each put our body, mind, and soul into each sexual experience." I shift in my seat, focusing all my attention on him as he drives.

Grant drives the vehicle the same way he does everything. With confidence and dedication. It's a very mind-melting quality that has me squirming in my seat as I imagine those long fingers of his no longer gripping the wheel but gripping me...cupping my sex with that same determination. A flutter picks up in my clit as I imagine him working me with those hands.

My mouth opens, and unfiltered words spill out. *Darn*

wine. "I don't know about you, but I think sex is amazing. And I haven't had any complaints, so without being Braggy McBraggerton, I think I'm pretty good at it." Four glasses of wine is making my lips loose. Far looser than I'd normally be on a first real date.

"Braggy McBraggerton?" he queries on a chuckle.

"Yeah. You know, when you brag too much."

"Lamb...I know what you mean; however, you need to get this through your head right now and let it sink in." His midnight-blue eyes focus with the severity of what he says next. "I'm not going to fuck you."

"You aren't?" I frown, and the niggling feeling of being undesirable works its way into my psyche. "Why?" I bite into my lip and try not to tear up. The wine is making me extremely emotional and *horny.* Let's not forget horny. "You don't want me?" My voice comes out so small and shaken I'm surprised he hears it at all.

Grant yanks the steering wheel toward the curb and parks right in front of the bakery. I didn't even realize we were already so close to my place.

"Luna, you've had a bottle of wine go to your head. I'd be no man at all if I took advantage of you in this state. We've had a great night, one I'll never forget. I can't remember the last time I actually had fun at one of these required events. You reminded me what giving to charity really feels like. And it was good. All good, baby. Which is why I'm not going to ruin that by fucking you."

I cringe. "Not if I'm willing! You're not taking advantage of me if I'm willing." I press my hands to his chest and run them down to his rock-hard abs. "And I'm *so* willing."

He grabs my hands and brings them to his mouth. He

kisses one set of fingers and then the other. "As am I, but it doesn't change the fact that I'm not going to do something you might regret tomorrow."

I frown. "That's stupid, you know. I would never regret having great sex, and, Grant, I'm a good lay," I state tipsily with as much confidence as my wine-addled brain will allow.

He laughs heartily. "I have no doubt. And I'm going to very much enjoy the time where you are once again open to that, but lamb, you've had too much to drink, and I'm wiped."

"Wiped?"

"I haven't slept much in two days. Work has been... intense," he says through his teeth, his expression going hard.

Wanting to divert his thoughts away from his shitty work, because it is shitty work if he plans to destroy good businesses and awesome streets in order to make money, I decide he needs to end the night on a really good note.

"Walk me up. I'll give you some essential oil to help calm you tonight so you can get a good night's sleep."

"I don't think that's a good idea..." His gaze moves down to my mouth, and he licks his lips as if he wants to taste me.

Knowing I can't push this right now, I get out of the car and unlock the door to the bakery. I'm entering the security code as I hear his car alarm bleep, and he follows behind me. Once he's in, I reset the alarm.

"Come on. It's through the kitchen and up the back. If we'd gone through the back, we wouldn't have to walk through the bakery and kitchen, but I don't like to go through the alleyway at night."

He places his hand on the back of my dress, keeping me close as I walk through the empty bakery. "Good plan."

I nod and make my way up the stairs toward my place.

"Jesus," Grant growls.

"Everything okay?" I ask.

"Yeah, it's just your perfect fucking ass swaying as you walk up the stairs is like waving a red flag at a bull. Next time, I walk in front of you." He sounds annoyed.

I giggle, thinking about our positions reversed. "Then I would drool over your ass," I state as I reach the landing.

I unlock my door, flick on the lights, and enter my apartment.

Grant stops in the center of the room and spins in a slow circle. "You live in a shoebox." He scowls.

"What! This is huge." I toss my purse on the small island counter.

"Lamb...baby, it's not." His voice is low and strained.

"Yes, it is. It's three times the size of my last apartment, and it's a loft."

"Yeah, which means your bed is in your living room." He glances at my queen-size mattress. The down comforter is fluffy and white. Throw pillows in pretty teal and royal blue and magenta give the bed some pizzazz. The rest of the space is open. I have a small love seat facing an armoire, where I've got my TV and stereo. Plants dot the space, giving the room an earthy garden feel.

"Well, I love it. Don't be snobby."

Grant scowls as he looks around but brings his hand up to his head, pressing his thumb and finger into his temples.

"Headache?"

He nods curtly. "I should go."

"Not if you're in pain and I can help. Take off your jacket, roll up your sleeves, and go lie on my bed."

He lifts his eyebrows in question.

"Relax, big man. Nothing's going to happen. Well, something's going to happen. Me taking away your headache."

Grant looks around the room and puts a hand to his waist as if he's making a decision. Eventually he comes to the right one and shrugs off his suit coat, removes his tie, and sets them over the back of the love seat. He unbuttons a few top buttons, removes his cufflinks, and rolls up his sleeves.

When I see he's doing as I directed, I go over to my essential oil collection and grab the nighttime blend I created. It has a touch of peppermint, lavender, rosemary, and eucalyptus mixed together to create what I consider is the perfect essential blend for nighttime relaxation.

Before I go over to the bed, I hit the restroom and change into my camisole and bed shorts to get more comfortable. When I return, Grant is down to his undershirt, slacks, and socks with the bedspread pulled back and his head on my pillow.

My goodness he looks beautiful lying on my sheets, his big body spread out on my bed.

CHAPTER SIX

CROWN
C H A K R A

Due to its location on the body, the crown chakra is primarily associated with the brain and the entire nervous system. If the chakra is blocked, a person may tend to have headaches, migraines, or a multitude of head, neck, and nervous system issues.

LUNA

"You ready to be wowed?" I ask, padding on bare feet to the bed where he lies.

"I will rescind my initial statement about your apartment. Your bed is fucking fantastic. What am I lying on?" He shifts his legs and wiggles his bum.

"Four inches of high-quality memory foam. Kind of like a

AUDREY CARLAN

Tempur-Pedic only a boatload cheaper."

He pushes his fingers into the bed and watches them sink. "It's freakin' amazing. Seriously, I need to get this for my bed at home."

I grin. "I'll make sure to send you a link to what I purchased online. Now lift your upper body and scoot a bit farther down the bed."

"Why?" He frowns.

"Just do what I say. For once in your life, allow yourself to give up control," I snip smartly but still playfully.

He gives an exaggerated sigh but lifts up and scoots lower on the bed. I slip in behind him with my bottle of oil in hand and cross my legs.

"Lie back and put your head in my lap."

"Kinky." He smirks.

I roll my eyes and grip his head, putting him where I want him. "Now relax." I remove the cap, pour some oil into my hands, and rub them together. The scent floats in the air around us, and I can see his chest rising as he inhales the soothing fragrance.

"Smells good," he murmurs, fluttering his eyes closed.

"Thank you." I press my finger just above his upper lip and under his nostrils, wiping a drop of oil there so he can smell it directly. "Breathe in long and deep, letting the air fill your lungs completely. When you get to the top of the breath, hold it in for a few seconds and then slowly let the air out your mouth. Continue to do this until I tell you to stop."

Grant breathes in, doing exactly what I said. Such a good student. Apparently he *can* listen to someone other than himself.

I run my oil-covered hands around Grant's neck, working

the muscles with my thumbs. His breath falters as I find a sizable knot and massage it out. "Keep breathing in fully and then out at the top of the breath," I remind him, and he follows along.

Once the knot is out, I turn his head to the left and work the length of his neck, running my fingers through the sides of his hair, to the crown of his head, and back down. I circle my thumbs around the occipital lobes at the base of skull where his head and neck meet, removing any tension I find there.

Grant sighs and grunts a little when I press my thumbs into the tightness at his trapezoids, easing the muscles, loosening the grip stress has on his body. Turning his head to the right, I repeat the process on the other side before massaging his whole head.

"Your hands work miracles," Grant compliments. He flickers his eyes open, looking hazy and tired.

I smile, lean down, and kiss his forehead. "I'm not done. Close your eyes and relax. Don't allow the tension to creep back in. Just enjoy."

I slide my fingers through his thick, silky hair and run the pads of my fingers lightly down the lines of his scalp. I can tell when a person is super tense because there is no give in their scalp. Right now, he has no give, so I work my fingers in long lines, giving more pressure than I would during *Savasana* at the end of one of my yoga classes because this is more personal, private. A woman relaxing her man at the end of a hard day.

Those thoughts of him being *my man* start to swirl in my mind again as I circle my fingers around his hairline and back through his hair in long strokes. His breathing is deepening, so I move the tips of my fingers along his forehead and apply pressure down the bridge of his nose, around his eye sockets, and along the side of his cheeks until I get to his temples. Sometimes when I touch the temples first, they are too tender. Usually after I've relaxed the rest of the person's head or body, the temples aren't so sensitive.

His lips puff open as I massage his face and head. He's truly a striking man, though I worry about the dark circles under his eyes. He needs rest. Real sleep, free of worry and stress. As I touch him soothingly, I imagine what it would be like to have this man in my life every day and not just for six months.

He'd come home from a long day at the office, I'd make him dinner, listen to him talk about his day, and then set about creating a home where he wouldn't have to feel stress. Everything around him would be uniquely crafted to ease his tension. Soothing scents, healthy homemade food, my personal affection and care.

It seems so easy, yet I'm twenty-eight and haven't found it yet. I think a lot of men I've dated in the past think what I do is unnecessary and frivolous, but I know with my whole heart I'm providing a much-needed service to people. Helping bodies and minds feel whole.

I love what I do and have never wanted to do anything else. Maybe my mother ingrained this trait in me during the years of watching her run the studio, but she's one of the happiest and healthiest people I know. My father, on the other hand, was a businessman who worked himself to the bone. He always joked that my mother was his reward after a hard day's work. He loved that she was always happy, down to earth, and excited when he came home. Until cancer took him away a few years ago, way too early at only fifty-five. They were beyond happy together. Now she's committed to traveling the world with her best friend. She misses my father terribly, as do I, but she's moving on and living her life.

Healthy and happy.

My father would want that for her and me. It's what I want to find. A man who is willing to take on the brunt of the financial responsibility for our home and needs, have a family, and know when he ends his day he'll have a wife waiting with open arms to greet, feed, and sprinkle love all over him. It may sound old-fashioned, but there isn't any other life I could imagine being better.

My problem now is Lotus House. The more time I spend with Grant, the more I like him, and I don't know if I'm going to be able to convince him not to destroy my family's legacy, my livelihood and those of my friends, not to mention my apartment. The smart thing to do would be to renew my hunt for a new facility I can rent. Consider securing a new location for Lotus House. After a cursory look at the available buildings in the area, the possibility of renting a place big enough to offer four open rooms, two locker rooms, a reception area, and private yoga rooms for a decent rate is slim to none. It also has to be on one level or have an elevator. We insist on being ADA compliant, which means wheelchair access is mandatory.

I sigh and look down at the man who has the power to ruin my life and find he's asleep. His mouth is open, and little snores are coming from his nose, the same way they were when he fell asleep in yoga class a few days ago. He was not kidding when he said he was wiped out. I imagine running a bazillion-dollar company is very stressful. It proves he needs a woman like me in his life to ease the tension. Relieve him of his stress and teach him how to relax.

Enjoying the time I can just look at him without his mouth

getting in the way, I trace his features, running my finger down his long, straight nose. His cheekbones are high and cut. There's a tiny bit of scruff coming in on his square jaw. As my hand floats over his cheek, he turns his head, rubbing against my palm the way a cat would. This tiny, effortless moment of affection rips through my chest and fills my heart with light.

I could so easily fall in love with this man.

Bracing his head straight, I lift it up enough that I can ease out and place his head on my pillow. I survey him. He's resting so comfortably I make a split-second decision. I grab the comforter, pull it over his body, and tuck him in. Then I go to the other side of the bed, pull back the comforter, and slide in next to him. Feeling cold being a foot away, I snuggle up to his form, wrap an arm around his waist, and rest my head on his chest. His arm comes down and locks around me immediately, but he doesn't wake. No, he instinctually curls around me in his sleep and unconsciously locks me to his side.

I smile and close my eyes, wondering what kind of shenanigans tomorrow will bring. All I know is, I hope they include Grant.

★ ★ ★

Juggling two steaming lattes and a bag of fresh warm pastries, I open the door to my apartment. Grant is sitting on the edge of the bed, running his fingers through his mussed hair.

"Jesus Christ, I slept here all night?" he says, his tone not only surprised but edgy.

"Yeah." I maneuver over to my small kitchenette and set the bag and coffees down on the table.

"What time is it?" He looks around my apartment for a

clock.

"Just after eight."

His eyes seem to bulge as he stands up abruptly. "Eight a.m.! Fucking hell!" He groans and looks around the room, my guess, trying to spot his stuff. I placed his shoes next to his dress shirt and jacket.

"Right there over by the couch. Your shoes are sitting there as well. I've got a latte and a pastry for you."

Grant runs his hands down his face and grunts. "I can't believe I overslept. I'm usually in the office by seven thirty and no later."

I move into the kitchen and pull out a couple small plates and then take out the treats I selected. "Sounds like you needed the sleep."

He nods. "Yeah, I guess I did. Haven't slept that well in ages. And it's been forever since I had a full eight hours sleep."

This time my eyes widen as I take a seat at the table. "Really? Grant, your body needs the time to recuperate. Eight hours sleep is ideal for the human body to rest, and the mind needs the time to function properly. It's probably why you conked out so quickly."

He grabs his dress shirt, pulls it on, leaves it open, and walks over to me.

I hold out a latte toward him. "Here. Beauty in a cup."

He caresses my fingers as he takes the latte. "Beauty holding a cup is more like it." His eyes are smiling, but his mouth is still tight. I'll take what I can get.

Grant scans my body. "You're already dressed in your work attire?"

"Because I already taught a class this morning, big man." I sip the vanilla goodness, lifting my feet up onto the chair's edge.

His eyebrows rise up to his hairline and he sits. "You've already been up and taught a class?"

"Yep. First thing every Monday."

He sips the drink and hums. "And you think my job sucks?" He laughs.

I nod. "Yeah, because at least everyone is happy to see me when they show up. They are ready to start their week off in a healthy frame of mind. They don't spend a million meetings planning what company they are going to buy or bulldoze to make a buck."

Grant's jaw firms, and his face hardens into an emotionless mask. "That's what you think I do all day? Bulldoze buildings."

I purse my lips and decide to lay it out there. "All I know is you're planning to bulldoze my building and my friends' buildings in order to build luxury homes for a bunch of high-powered executives who really don't need the space."

"Yes...*creating* new buildings." He stresses the creation part.

"Then why must you destroy before you build? Can you not think of a workaround? A compromise of sorts?"

He sighs and leans back heavily in the chair. "What you're suggesting would cost millions or, worse, the loss of millions."

I put my feet down and sit up straight in my chair. "What you're suggesting would cost many their livelihoods and their jobs. I have four classes running almost every hour of the day, throughout most of the week. I employ almost twenty yoga teachers, all of whom would lose their jobs if I cannot find another location for my studio. Most of those teachers are struggling college students, single mothers, or people like me who teach yoga as their calling. Are their livelihoods not worth those millions?"

And that really is the question.

Grant stands up so fast the wooden chair falls to the floor with a crash.

"I gotta get out of here." He tugs at his hair, turns, lifts the chair, and grabs his coat.

I nod and look down at my chocolate éclair, no longer hungry, when a warm palm curls around my neck.

Grant uses his thumb to lift my chin up. "Thank you for last night and for breakfast. I'm going to take it to go, if you don't mind. I need to get to work...and think. Think about all of this."

Hope springs eternal as I stare at his handsome face. "Thank you for showing me a great time."

He leans down and kisses me so softly I don't even have the chance to taste the latte on his lips before he's pulling away.

"Text me later and tell me what's on for this week. It's your turn, but leave the weekend open. I'm taking you out this weekend."

I smile wide, the idea of going on another date with Grant making me ridiculously happy. Butterflies flutter in my stomach as I nod.

Grant kisses my forehead and releases me to grab his shoes. He slips them on and ties them lightning fast. While he does this, I put the two treats I got him back into the bakery bag so he can take them to go.

I hold up the bag and open the door. "I'll walk you out since the bakery is going to be busy and you'll feel strange walking through the kitchen alone."

He grins and follows me down the stairs.

Once we make it to the kitchen, I run into Mama Jackson.

Oh no, this is not going to be good. Mama Jackson is Dara's mother and the original owner of Sunflower Bakery. She still works the store whenever she feels like it, even though her daughter now owns it, and Mama Jackson does what Mama Jackson wants.

"Moonbeam!" Mama Jackson tugs me into her arms for a big, cuddly hug. Vanessa Jackson is not a small woman by any means, but she holds her weight well and uses it to make her hugs the best ever.

"Child, how you doin'?" She pulls me back and cups my face. Her dark skin looks stark against my super white tone.

"I'm good, Mama Jackson. Uh, this is my friend, Grant." I hook a finger behind me.

Her pitch-black eyes go over my shoulder to the man behind me. "Spent the night, I see. Hmm, didn't know you were dating, Moonbeam." She assesses Grant from top to toe. "Good-looking man. Hope you plan on calling my girl back later on once you've had a chance to relive the goodness you had with my Moonbeam here."

Grant's eyes widen, and he smiles. "I was a perfect gentleman last night, ma'am. I assure you."

Her eyes narrow, and she looks at him and then at me. "You playin' hard to get, child? Mama Jackson likes that. Good for you, sugar." She squeezes my cheek. "Go on, walk yo' man out, but don't be surprised when you get the third degree from Dara."

I grab Grant's hand and tug him along, whispering in his ear. "We just dodged a serious bullet. If she knew who you were, you would be flatter than a pancake on her floor. Seriously, you do *not* want to mess with Mama Jackson." Chills ripple along my arms as I try to escape through the main area of the bakery, ignoring Dara, who's at the register, chatting away.

Just as we make it to the wooden door, Dara's voice rings out.

"Oh *hell* no! Luna...guuuurl, you have some 'splainin' to do," I hear over my shoulder.

Moving fast, I open the wood door and push Grant out. "Go! Save yourself!" I push at his solid form.

He stops and laughs. "Lamb, what are you doing?"

"No, no, you gotta go." I glance to the side and see Dara putting change in someone's hand. "Just go, I'll see you later," I attempt.

Grant holds his place. "I want my goodbye kiss."

My eyes go wide, and I feel her before I hear her. She rests an arm around my waist and tucks me to her side. Her sugary scent tickles my nose, and I drop my head.

Darn it.

"Grant, so nice to see you again, looking all disheveled and well-rested. I see you are wearing a wrinkled suit, and you just came from the kitchen, which tells me you've been enjoying the loft with my best friend and *traitor*, Luna, here." She shakes me a bit, her tone pleasant, but I can hear the accusation underneath. I'm going to have to have a very big heart-to-heart with her and soon.

My guy props one of his hands on his hip, his eyes going hard, his expression turning into steel businessman. The same man I met the first time I visited his office. "What is with the third degree in this bakery? First your mother and now you? Luna is a grown woman who can date any man she wants."

Dara's pretty face twists with an expression of barely concealed contempt. Each of her words is a poison-dipped knife ready to kill. "Not when that man is going to single-handedly ruin her life. I don't know how you sleep at night..."

Grant cuts her off. "Very well, since I was in her bed right next to her warm body."

"You have a lotta nerve."

Grant lifts a finger and points it at Dara. "No, you do. Luna can take care of herself."

Dara swings her body around, cocks a hip, and places a hand on it, attitude flag flying. "Because you know her so well. She's sweet. Innocent. Helps the world every day by shining her bright light on it. And you"—she points her finger at him in return—"are going to burn out that light by taking away what she loves most. That studio!" She points at the wall shared with Lotus House.

"Guys, come on. We don't need to talk about this or do this here. Everyone is watching."

Dara waves her hand. "Let them watch. Let this entire store see the man who is going to bring a big ol' wrecking ball and flatten the first ever Sunflower Bakery. The store I was going to leave to my babies! And their babies! And so on. My parents started this bakery from the ground up. Built their business and have given it to me to pass on to Destiny and Jackson. I may have more stores, but this is the first. The flagship. It's where I work every day. It's where I bring my children on the weekends so they can bake with their mama and grandmama."

I hear the pain in her words. She's losing her legacy too.

Tears fill Dara's eyes, and she stares at Grant, who hasn't spoken a single word.

"Now I can see from your aura that you are upset. The black shrouding your natural energy is a good indication you heard me. And I hope you did, because you need to hear exactly what you're taking away when you flatten my bakery."

Dara's tears fall down her cheeks.

"What in the ever-loving fuck is going on here?" The deep voice comes from the front of the bakery. "Lil' mama, why are you cryin'?" He looks from Dara, to me, and then to Grant. "Heads are about to roll if someone doesn't answer me," Silas announces, his hands turning into fists.

I maneuver around Dara, through the wooden door, and next to Grant. "Silas McKnight, this is Grant Winters, and we were just having a little bit of a heated chat about the situation—"

Si cuts through. "You're the man responsible for the tears my wife has shed every night since you sent us that eviction notice? Twenty plus years of on-time rent, repeatedly refusing to sell the land to the Jacksons, and you have the balls to come in here and show your face? Bro, you must be out of your fuckin' mind."

Grant's body tightens. "I'm sorry the eviction notice upset your wife. It's an unfortunate effect of the business decision my company, investors, and board of directors have made. This is business, not personal."

Silas scowls. "Man, I run Knight & Day Productions. I know what the cost of doing business is, and I know there are always alternatives to those decisions. I suggest you find one." He growls and pushes past Grant by knocking his shoulder roughly.

Grant stands strong and doesn't respond, although I can tell from the tension in his body that the verbal daggers Dara and Silas threw hit their target.

Slowly, Grant eases his body away from mine, turns, and heads out the door.

I spin on a heel, my anger flaming hot. "You did not need to be so harsh! He's working through this decision, and I'm trying to get him to see why he should keep these businesses alive, not give him more reasons to destroy them. You should look at things from his side too. He's doing his job. What everyone is telling him to do. It's business to them, nothing more. I'm doing everything I can to show him it's not just about business, and you just damaged that!" My words are so low and filled with frustration I don't even know what more to say. So I don't. Instead, I chase after Grant.

He's just getting to his car when I fly out of the bakery, my hair flapping around my face as the wind hits it.

"Grant!"

He stops at his car, hand on the handle.

"I don't fucking need this, Luna. None of this." His tone is flat. Dead. "I have a job to do, and I'm going to do it." He opens the door and rests his hand on the top of the window. He shakes his head, and his dark-blue gaze meets mine.

Remorse.

Anger.

Hurt.

Resolution.

All of those things are in his eyes until he lands his final blow. "Move on with your life, Luna. I'm no good for you, and I'm over it. All of this. Deal's off."

With the last parting dagger to my heart, he gets into his car and peels away. I'm not sure if I'm more upset that he blew off our deal or that he set me free from what was building between us.

No, that's not true. I do know. As does my mind, body, and heart, which are crumbling internally.

I've lost him, and I have no idea how to get him back.

CHAPTER SEVEN

CROWN
C H A K R A

*If the crown chakra is blocked, a person will feel
confused and depressed, and experience fear of
success and lack of inspiration.*

GRANT

"Grant... Shit, man. How many bench presses have you done?" My trainer rushes to spot me, and just in time too, because I start to lose my grip, and the weight careens...toward my face.

Clay grabs the weight with no problem and puts the barbell back on the stand, the hundred and fifty pounds are nothing for a man of his strength. "What the hell were you doing? Trying to kill yourself?"

"Death by weight lifting? Yeah, that's the way to go." I groan, plant my feet wide on the ground, and lean over my spread thighs. Drops of sweat fall from my forehead onto the floor.

Fuck. I can't get the look on her face out of my mind.

Hurt. Destroyed. Resigned.

Clay sits down next to me and bumps my shoulder. "Care to talk about it?"

Talk about it?

How do I talk about a woman who is absolutely everything I'm not?

Kind. Compassionate. Honest. Trusting. Loyal. Beautiful.

The broken look on her face yesterday won't fucking leave my mind. I keep seeing it over and over again. In my dreams, throughout my day, while at meetings, on the phone. Her red hair flying in the breeze, her crystal-blue eyes tortured as I told her the deal was off, basically ensuring she no longer had any hope of saving her company or her home.

"What do you care?" I growl and run my fingers through my sopping wet hair.

Clayton grips my shoulder. "Seriously, man? We've been working together for over five years, and you have the balls to say that to me. I thought we were friends." His tone sounds hurt, making him *another* good person I'm fucking over this week.

I look at Clayton's blond spiky hair and blue eyes. "Sorry. I shouldn't have said that. I'm fucked in the head."

"Woman, work, or world?" He says the three words as if they are the be-all end-all. I cringe, uncertain of what he means.

He waves his hand in a circular motion. "Are you like this

because of a woman, something screwed at work, or the world in general?" he clarifies.

I let out a long sigh. "One, both, hell, all three. Take your pick."

Clayton nods curtly and stands up. "All right, then. More workout is not what you need. I'm thinking, a beer, a burger, and a bro lending his ear will do the job. Hit the showers and meet me out front."

I jerk my head back. "You want to go out and have a beer... with me?" I frown at the desperate tone in my voice.

In that moment, it hits me. We've never been anything more than personal trainer and student. I hire him to keep me in shape. He bosses me around the gym, and I pay him well for it. The results are good. Wash. Rinse. Repeat. I never even thought of him as a friend until he called me on it a few minutes ago.

"Yeah. When one of my buds needs me, I'm there. You'd do it for me." He says this as if he knows it to be fact.

Would I?

I guess if he asked me to be, I would. Not that we've ever been in a position to open up to one another. Then again, I've never been in this situation with a woman *ever*. Women have always been expendable. And I've never worried about business decisions in quite this way. And I've not had to completely destroy a street full of thriving companies.

I nod and stand up to head to the showers. "Meet you out front?"

"You got it. And I know just the place to go."

★ ★ ★

The drive isn't long as I follow Clayton from the gym. He pulls up to a brick building with a bright green sign that reads *O'Brien's Pub and Grill,* with four leaf clovers as the apostrophes. I can't remember the last time I was in a pub. Probably back in college. A time when life was about frat parties, girls, and how much beer I could suck down my gullet without throwing up.

Clayton waits at the door as I park my car and jog to meet up with him. I feel odd in my dress slacks and shirt, but I left the tie and jacket in the car, rolled up my sleeves, and unbuttoned a couple buttons. Clayton, on the other hand, is still in his workout attire. A pair of black track pants with a couple white stripes down each leg and a red T-shirt that stretches across his massive chest.

The man is built, to say the least. I have what I would consider a good body. I work hard to stay in shape. Toned muscles, six-pack, and the magic V we all strive to achieve, but Clayton Hart is rock solid. He is toned on an entirely different level.

As we hit a high-top table, Clayton waves at the bartender. "Hey, Cal, how goes it?" he says with a smile. That's the epitome of Clayton Hart. The man is always smiling. At least ever since he got married. Which reminds me, I think he said he'd had a kid not too long ago. Had to miss a few sessions because he was in the hospital with his wife.

"Um, Clay, how's your wife and kid?" I ask, trying to open the conversation. It's been so long since I've gone out with a guy to just hang out and shoot the shit, I'm a little rusty. Most of my dinners with men are business meetings, where they want something out of me or I want something out of them.

"Kids," he clarifies.

"You have more than one kid?" My eyes widen, and I am genuinely surprised.

"Yeah, man. Strangest thing. I got with Moe, and we found out her daughter is biologically mine."

I'm pretty sure my mouth hits the floor. What the hell? "How in the world did that happen?"

Clayton laughs. "Back in the day, when I was working my way through college, I used to donate to a local sperm bank. Years later, Monet and her then-husband picked my boys for the job. I met Moe, hooked up with her, and when it came to her backstory and her kid, two and two were adding up to four pretty quick. Her best friend did a genetic test, and *voila*, the kid is mine."

I whistle and shake my head. "Bet that blew your mind."

He chuckles. "It did. But since I fell in love with Monet, it worked out. Now we have Lily, who's seven, and my son, Knight, who's two. Though I keep hiding her birth control pills, so I'm hoping for another." He snickers.

"You're kidding?"

He laughs and shakes his head as a waitress finally comes up. Slow moving around here, but the place is nice, seems really low key.

"You boys want something to drink...eat?" she asks, leaning her hand on the table.

"Beer. Cold. Whatever Cal recommends," Clay responds.

"Whiskey, neat. Two fingers." I hold up two of my own fingers.

"And we'll also take a couple of Cal's famous burgers. Yeah, Grant?"

I shrug. "Sounds good to me." I don't admit that I can't remember the last time I had a burger. Again, most of my dinners are out at fancy restaurants or a casserole I can heat up stocked in my freezer by my house attendant.

When the waitress leaves, she hustles back with our drinks far quicker than it took for her to make her way over initially. As she sets the drinks on the table and walks off, Clayton levels me with a pointed stare. "Lay it on me. What happened?"

I take a sip of my whiskey, letting it burn a fiery trail down my throat. Maybe the burn will coat the words, making them seem less damaging. I'm not sure I want Clayton to know how much of an asshole I really am.

"Grant, no judgment, man. Just a friendly ear," he encourages.

I sigh, set my drink on the table, and run my finger around the rim. "There's this woman, a yoga teacher..."

His eyebrows rise up to his hairline. "Yeah, yogis are hot man. My wife does yoga regularly. Can't say I don't enjoy the benefits of that practice, plus I take a bunch of classes myself."

This surprises me. He seems like a loyal member of the gym brotherhood.

He notices my expression and grins. "Yeah. I prefer aerial. My buddy Nick teaches it. Stretches out my muscles in a way I can't do at the gym."

I nod. "Well, here's the problem. I own a span of land on which I'm planning to build high-rise luxury apartments. This is a couple-hundred-million-dollar project that's going to return close to a billion in revenue for Winters Group and the other investors."

"Okay, I'm following. So what's the problem?" Clay sucks back a swallow of his beer.

"Doing so means I have to evict about seven thriving businesses. One of which is a yoga studio."

"No shit. Are you telling me the chick you're going for works at the studio?"

I shake my head.

Clayton playfully wipes at his brow. "Whew...I figured you were going to be in a world of hurt if that was the case."

"She owns it. And lives in an open apartment on top of one of the other businesses I'm going to flatten."

Clayton's face pales, and then he lifts the beer and gulps back almost all of it. I match his sentiment by killing my whiskey. It hits my gut and warms my entire body instantly. Something of a blessing. I've been cold for days.

"Dude, that's fucked. So what are you going to do?"

I run my fingers through my hair and glance behind me. The bartender lifts his head, and I raise my glass and point to Clay's as well. We're going to need a lot more alcohol for this.

"Not much. The process is already started. Technically, the renters have less than six months to vacate the street."

Clayton whistles. "Damn. What about the woman? The yogi?"

"She hates me."

"I'm seeing you don't hate her. Now you're worried about her business and her being homeless."

"Yeah. I know I can't fix what's happening, but shit, I want to so bad." I huff out a frustrated breath. "Even told her I'd give her six months to change my mind if she dated me for the six months. We'd each get a turn showing the other our side of things. Then it just got too much to handle."

"You reneged?" His voice is strange when he asks, almost a deep grumble.

The waitress comes up and switches out our old drinks with fresh ones.

"Kind of, yeah."

"Why?"

"That's the billion-dollar question, isn't it? Luna's beautiful, man. Nothing like any of the women I've ever dated. She makes me feel...I don't know. Fuck. More. Just more."

"Luna?" Clayton sits up straight, his arms pressed out to brace against the table.

I grin. "Yeah. Said her mom is a hippie. Named her moon."

"Fuck. This is bad, dude." Clayton's expression turns hard.

"Why?"

"You're talking about Luna Marigold, pretty redhead, sweet body, white-ass skin, the owner of Lotus House?"

This time I sit up in my chair, the hair on the back of my neck standing on end. "How the fuck...?"

"I'm friends with her. Hell, I'm friends with *all of them*. My buddy Nick I mentioned, he works there. As do several of my friends. That's the studio I go to. The same one my wife goes to. And you're flattening the street? Fuck, dude. Sunflower Bakery? Rainy Day Café?" He runs his hands over his face and then braces his elbows on the table. "Man, you have to find another way."

"Clay, I just told you...this venture is set to profit by nearly a *billion dollars*. The rent these businesses have been paying for the last twenty years is nothing."

My buddy runs his hand across his chin. "I get it. I do... but... Dude, this street is special. You need to spend some time there."

I slam my hand down on the table, my whiskey almost sloshing out of the glass. "That's what I was doing, until I spent the night with Luna and got sidelined by her friends who own the bakery. They despise me, and I get it. I truly get it. I'm ruining something they love, but it's just...*business.*" I grind my teeth on the last word.

Clayton inhales, deeply and slowly. "It's not to them, though. That street is iconic. It's one of the most chill and comfortable places to go. It's a secret gem in the area. And the businesses, they've been there twenty years or more."

I nod and suck back a slug of whiskey, letting that fire burn...wanting it.

"Looks to me like you've got some soul searching to do. What about your time with Luna?"

"It's over." With those two words, pain squeezes my chest in a death grip. I rub at my heart, trying to soothe it.

Clayton's jaw goes hard, and he runs his tongue over his teeth. "She's a friend. And you just said you spent the night. You look like a man who's had his balls kicked and his dog run over. Obviously, she's more to you than a quick fuck..."

"I didn't fuck her! We slept. Just slept together."

He cocks a brow. "You mean to tell me, you had Luna Marigold in a bed, and you did not take a piece of that?" Clayton laughs. "Better man than me. I mean, if I wasn't ass-over-dick in love with Moe and have a serious thing for flexible Asian hotties, I would have considered Luna a huge win."

I bite down on my molars and hold my jaw firm. The simple thought of Clayton wanting Luna makes me insane. Fucking *certifiable.* "Don't," I warn through clenched teeth.

Clayton lifts his hands. "Hey now, happily married man here. I'm just sayin' I know her and she's beautiful. She's going to make some man very happy one day. And from what I understand, that's really all she wants."

"What do you mean?" I ask right as the waitress brings our burgers.

The second the plate touches the table, my mouth waters. I haven't eaten all day, and I worked every muscle in my body beyond fatigue. I grip the burger and watch the juice run off onto the plate before I take a monster bite out of it. The meat, cheese, and sauce flood my taste buds, and suddenly, I'm ravenous.

Clay shrugs. "What I understand, she's a bit old-fashioned."

I chew and swallow before responding. "Luna is the farthest thing from old-fashioned. She's as new age as they come with her yoga, breathing, oils."

Clayton shakes his head and finishes his own bite. "Not in that way. Moe told me Luna wants to get married, have a couple of kids, and teach yoga. Take care of her kids and her man, make dinner, clean house. Kind of like a hippie June Cleaver." He chuckles.

The vision of Luna moving around my apartment, cleaning house, making us dinner, taking care of our children...a boy and a girl. A legacy. A home. Not something I've ever had, nor did I think I would have. The beauty of that simple vision hits me like a two-ton boulder along with a deep-seated desire to make that vision come to life.

Except it never will. She hates me.

I haven't even truly tasted the woman, and she hates me. "I'll never get another chance with her," I whisper, not realizing I said it out loud.

"Not true. If you want her, *truly* want to be with her, see where it leads, then go back to her. There is nothing a woman likes more than a man who apologizes, means it, and is man enough to admit it."

"Just apologize. That's your sage advice?" I pop a fry into my mouth. Damn, even the fries are world-class. Seasoned to perfection with a hint of paprika, which tingles against the tongue.

Clayton grins. "Betcha it works. And if she tries to let you off the hook but not bring you back into the fold, push your way in. Show up in her world. Everywhere she goes, you go. Make yourself a nuisance."

This time I'm laughing out loud. "Is that how you wooed your wife?"

He grins. "No. I offered to help out a mutual friend of mine, ended up watching her kid, and never left. She'd been physically hurt by her ex, as in a hundred stitches running down her back, so I moved my ass in."

I jerk my head up from focusing on my heavenly burger back to my friend. Friend. It feels good to think that and know it's true.

"You just moved yourself into her house?"

He nodded. "And her life. She was meant to be mine, man. Knew it straight down to my marrow she was for me. I found an in, and I took it. Best decision I ever made, pushing my way into her life and heart. Now she's mine for good, and I thank the man upstairs every day for the blessing."

I wipe my mouth with my napkin. "Your advice, then, is to..."

"Push yourself on her. Make yourself a nuisance if you have to, but make sure you apologize first. Luna's got a mind of her own, but she's sweet. And if you're into her, *really* into her, then you have to take a chance."

"What about the fact that I'm going to be obliterating her

business and her friends' businesses?"

"Find a way to make it work. Get around it. Build somewhere else. I don't know. Only you know what your business can take and what you're willing to sacrifice. All I know is a woman like Luna deserves a man who will bend the rules, break his back, fall down on his knees to worship her. The question then is, are you that man?"

I sip on the whiskey and swirl it in the glass, watching the amber liquid spin a beautiful vortex. "I don't know; I'd like to be."

Clayton pats me on the shoulder. "It's up to you how you're going to respond. The way I see it, the way you look right now, all down and out, seems like the woman means a lot more than the potential profit."

I want to tell him it's more than just profit. My father, the investors, they are relentless, ruthless in their desire for more wealth. These plans were already in place before a fairy princess walked through my office door and brought me to my proverbial knees.

Then there's the aching need to settle the score with my father. Prove I'm every bit as good a businessman. Better even than he was. Finally show them all I've got the chops to grow Winters Group far beyond what they even hoped for. This project was the start of all that. It would show my father and his cronies I have what it takes. Perhaps once in my entire godforsaken life, I might see pride in my father's face, maybe even an *atta boy* tossed my way.

It's ridiculous that a thirty-five-year-old man would need that kind of recognition and acceptance from his own father, but it's true. I've strived to impress him my entire life, and all he's ever said was how I missed the mark. Came close, but close was for second place, not winners, not leaders.

"Luna is not something I planned for..."

Clayton slaps his thigh a few times. "Women never are, God bless 'em. All I know is I'd be lost without Monet. She owns my soul, and I'd walk through fire to ensure her happiness. When you find the one you're meant to be with, you'll do anything to make her happy. I live for her. Plain and simple."

He lives for his wife.

The sentiment seems so foreign to me but not unpleasant. It's hard to imagine because I've never felt anything like it, but I'd like to. Boy, would I like to.

★ ★ ★

The wind blows against my face as I stand outside of Lotus House the next morning. Clayton was right. I need to mend the rift with Luna. I haven't been sleeping well, thinking only of her and how I need to fix things between us. Remembering her lips on mine, the way her fruity scent coated my body for an entire day after I slept in her bed. God, I miss her smell.

The second hand of my watch lands on the twelve, and out walks a dream.

My dream.

Luna waves at someone inside the bakery and turns, smiling. Her steps falter when she looks up and sees me waiting by the door. The smile falls and disappears completely as she makes it to where I'm standing.

"Why are you here?" Her voice sounds weak and reed thin.

"It's your turn," I state lamely. It's the only thing I can come up with.

She tips her head. "But you said it was over and the deal was off. You made it very clear..."

"Deal's back on." I swallow around the thickness entering my throat.

She shakes her head. "You can't do that. I can't go through that again. Grant, you hurt me..."

Fear ripples up my spine, and I lose all rational thought. I can't hear her reasons why she won't let us have another chance, not when I need her. Need her body against mine, her taste on my tongue. Without a second thought, I grab her around the waist, and her body slams into mine. Before she can say another word, I'm kissing her. I cup her cheek and tilt her head, opening my mouth and licking her lips. She opens on a moan, and it's all the invitation I need.

I take from her lips. Take her sweet mouth in a searing hot press of lips until she's kissing me back with as much passion as I have for her. She's *starved* for it. Her body wiggles against mine as she tries to get closer, pressing her soft tits against my chest.

I hold her close and devour her mouth. Eventually, we need air, so I pull back but keep my forehead pressed to hers. "Lamb, give me another chance. I know I don't deserve it, but I want it. I want another chance. Please." I grip her body tightly to mine.

Her breath comes in little puffs against my wet lips. She opens her eyes, and her gaze breaks my heart. In them, I see her hesitance, her fear and anxiety, but more than that, I see her hope. It's flickering a mile a minute in her gaze, and it wounds me, the knife of that desire cutting deep.

She thinks I'm going to save her.

How does she not see she's the one saving me?

CHAPTER EIGHT

CROWN
C H A K R A

*If we immerse ourselves in the energy from our crown chakra,
we will find a state of blissful union with all that is and all that
is meant to be. Essentially, spiritual ecstasy.*

LUNA

It was the last *please* that got to me. Not just his minty breath puffing against my face or the sorrow and remorse he's clearly showing in his sapphire eyes, but the word itself, which wounded me in a very deep place.

Please.

A plea. I would venture to bet this man has never begged for anything in his entire life, and here he stands, wearing his emotions on his sleeve for me to see, touch, and feel.

A bone-crushing ache starts up in my chest. "Grant...I

want to. I really do, but I'm scared," I whisper, my head still tilted down, my gaze focused on nothing, even though my heart is pounding a harsh rhythm in my chest.

Grant lifts my chin and keeps my body wrapped tightly against his. "Don't be scared. Don't *ever* be scared of me. I'd never hurt you."

I swallow around the lump in my throat. "Don't you see, Grant? You *are* hurting me."

He shakes his head. "No. We're going to give this a second chance. You're going to show me everything you want to save, and I'm gonna..." He lets out a labored sigh. "I'm going to find a way to make it all okay. I don't know how exactly, but right now, I want nothing more than to be standing right here. With you. On your street, in front of your yoga studio, holding you close."

My heart squeezes, and my mind fills with a million stray thoughts. Could he really be suggesting that he's going to try to find a way to save the street?

"What does that mean?"

His lips flatten into a thin line. "Lamb, I don't have the answer just yet. For now, just give me a second chance. Can you do that?"

I close my eyes, and the answer is so simple. There really is no other option. When it comes to Grant Winters, I lose all reason and fight.

"Yes. For you, I will."

His lips form an ear-to-ear smile. The beauty of it is blinding, and I love that it's pointed at me because of something I said to him.

"You're not going to regret this. I won't let you regret this." He nods as if he's making a deal with himself.

I cup his cheek and run my fingertips from his temple to his jaw. "Your second chance still comes at a price."

He cocks an eyebrow. "Everything comes with a price, baby."

"Every single week you are going to meet me here for a class of my choosing. No complaints, no get-out-of-jail-free card, no negotiations. I want a solid commitment."

He runs his tongue over his front teeth. "If that's what it takes to be near you and get a second chance, then I agree to your terms. You still have to go out with me once a week as well."

I frown. "Technically it's you asking me for a second chance, so really, I shouldn't have to do anything," I remind him.

He chuckles and wraps his arms low at my waist, keeping me close. "Are you telling me you don't want to go on dates with me? Get to know me better in my world?"

I do. So much it fills my heart with joy and my body with butterflies. I tip my head as if I'm considering it. "Well...when you put it like that..."

Grant laughs out loud, nuzzles my nose, and kisses me softly. His lips are warm and velvety. I could kiss him for a lifetime and consider myself blessed. When he pulls away, he grins. "I figured you'd see my side of it."

I shrug and spin out of his arms. "I think it's time you start your second chance right now."

He glances down at his pristine suit. He looks absolutely edible in the charcoal-gray suit and light-blue dress shirt. The hue of the shirt makes his eyes look even brighter.

"Not exactly dressed for yoga today, lamb." He smirks.

I purse my lips, cross my arms, and tap my foot. "If you

really want to get back into my good graces, it shouldn't matter what you're wearing. Besides, for the class we're going to take, you're dressed perfectly fine."

He cringes. "Why does this feel like you're setting me up?"

I glance over my shoulder, unlock the door to Lotus House, and push in to shut off the alarm. "Because you don't trust anyone?"

He clears his throat, and his eyes pierce mine as he responds. "I trust you."

I smile huge. I can't help the happiness that flows through my form like healing balm. "Then come in. Class will start in twenty minutes, and it's always completely full. You'll want to get a good spot up front."

He follows me into the building. I chance a glance over my shoulder, and as expected, his eyes are on my bubble-butt. Heat picks up around my neck, probably staining my cheeks a bright red. I sway my hips as I walk, wanting to give him a bit of a show, hook him deep.

I can't believe he came today to ask for a second chance. When I saw him standing by the door to Lotus House, my stomach dropped and my heart squeezed. It was as if everything inside me went perfectly still. I was afraid to breathe in case he'd disappear. Perhaps I was seeing a mirage, but the hope inside my soul sprang to the surface, and I knew it was real. He was there waiting for me...ready to beg for a second chance.

Grant leans against the reception desk as I stow away my things. The door opens behind me, and Atlas Powers enters alongside his wife, Mila. They met here and have taught a couple classes a week to keep up with the practice that brought them together.

Atlas has a mess of curls flopping all over his head as

he hooks an arm around his wife's shoulder. She's looking stunning as usual, her honey-toasted Latina skin tone making my glow-in-the-dark self envious as always.

"Luna, babe, how goes it?" Atlas shuffles up to me, lets his wife go, grabs me by the shoulders, and pulls me up to the desk so he can lean over and kiss my cheek.

I ruffle his curly hair. "Did you even bother brushing it this morning, or did you just roll out of bed ready to come teach?" I laugh.

Grant watches from the side, his expression one of serious contemplation.

Atlas laughs and runs a hand through his hair, the curls flopping all over the place.

"Curly doesn't care what his hair looks like." Mila purses her lips and sets an arm on the desk to lean in. "I keep telling him he should cut it off, try something a little more business-like, but what do I know?" She levels a fiery glare his way.

Atlas jerks his head back, and a horrified look crosses his chiseled face. "Wildcat, don't you dare lie. You know I'm never cutting my hair." His voice dips low, and he palms his wife's neck, bringing his face much closer to hers. "Because my sexy-as-fuck *wife* turns into a tigress the second I get my mouth on her and likes to run her fingers through it and hold on for dear life. So no, I'm not cutting my fuckin' hair. Get that shit outta your head...right"—he kisses her forehead—"fucking"—he kisses her nose—"now." He lays a deep kiss on her, wrapping one arm around her waist and plastering her to his chest while he takes her mouth.

I step back and move over to where Grant is standing. He instantly claims me by hooking my waist to his. "Those two newlyweds?" he whispers.

I laugh lightly and shake my head. "No. They've been married a while and have a three-year-old daughter."

"Damn..." Grant breathes, awe coating his tone while he watches the couple.

The crazy-in-love duo stops making out when the door opens and patrons start filing in. They break away from one another but only far enough that they can walk side by side.

"Hey, guys, who's got Aria?" I ask about their daughter.

"Genevieve. She's going to bring her here after class before she teaches prenatal. I'm going to take that class too," Mila says, smiling.

I open my mouth in shock. "Are you?"

Atlas spins around a beaming smile on his face. "She finally let me knock her up again!" He fist-pumps the air like he's a quarterback who just made a touchdown pass at a football game before kissing his wife's temple sweetly.

Chills race down my arms, and I rush around the desk to bring Mila into a hug. "My goodness, I'm happy for you both. And little Aria will be delighted to be a big sister."

Mila hugs me, her eyes filling with tears. "Yeah, she will. Thanks. We haven't really told anyone but Moe yet. We're only ten weeks, so we're keeping it on the down-low," she whispers and glances around.

I put my fingers to my lips in a shushing gesture and bring her into another hug.

"Wildcat, we need to get ready. They're coming in droves. Two by two. Today's class is going to be so much fun with couples. I've been dying to teach this forever! Thanks for letting me, Luna." Atlas clasps my hand and squeezes it.

"Of course. And I'm going to be taking it today too." I glance at Grant, who's leaning casually against the end of the desk, looking quite dapper in his bespoke suit.

Atlas looks over my head to where Grant is standing.

His eyebrows rise to his hairline, and he grins sexily. "You're taking my couples yoga with the suit over there?"

Mila makes no bones about maneuvering herself around me and walks over to Grant. "You seeing our girl Luna?" She tilts her head and rests a hand on her hip, attitude flying without even trying.

Grant stands straight and puts his hand out in greeting. "Grant Winters, and if by *seeing* you mean *dating*, then yes. We're dating." His eyes flash to mine and dare me to contradict him. I don't because I like the idea of dating Grant Winters, even though it should be all kinds of wrong.

Mila ignores his hand and squints up with her accessing brown eyes. "You don't seem like her type," she blurts with zero tact.

"Mila!" I warn.

She scowls and looks him up and down, even though that's pretty hard to do since she's just barely over five feet to his six feet plus.

Mila continues undaunted with her assessment. "Fine as hell. That part fits. She deserves a hottie. Though you seem pretty stiff," she carries on, and I sigh.

Grant smirks. "Not for long, seeing as I'm about to take a yoga class."

Ooh! Point for Grant. Mila is a tough cookie on a good day. She does not trust easily, although she's been getting better since becoming a wife and mother. Still, she has a guilty-until-proven-innocent system with new people.

Atlas finally cages his wife by putting an arm around her chest from behind. "Wildcat, leave the poor guy alone. He's just dating Luna; he's not a terrorist."

Mila puts a hand up and points at Grant. "I'm watching you, suit. You better be good to her. She deserves the best."

Atlas grabs her wrist, tucks it to her chest, and kisses her neck before speaking to us. "Sorry. She gets like this when she's pregnant. On a good day, she's feisty. Pregnant..." He sucks in a breath through his teeth. "Super protective. I think it's the mama gene coming out full force."

Mila cringes and spins around. "Do you want me to chop your balls off and serve them to you for dinner, curly?" She makes a face and deepens her voice, mimicking him. *"She gets like this when pregnant."* Her eyes widen. And she lifts a pointy finger and pokes him in the chest.

"Ouch, baby." Atlas pouts and goes for the finger.

Her voice rises to a threatening pitch. "I get like this when I see my friend with a man I've not seen before, and he's all sexy-suit-wearing-rich-guy to my Zen-loving, granola-crunching, yoga-teaching bestie! One of these things is not like the other!" She growls and spins back around.

I step in, knowing how Mila gets when she's pregnant, which is far beyond protective. I think it has a lot to do with her hormones changing and the lack of blood relatives in her life. Her friends have become her family, and she holds us all close to the chest.

I place my hands on Mila's biceps and rub them up and down in a soothing gesture. "It's fine, honey. We've been dating for the past couple weeks. I know what I'm getting myself into. You have nothing to worry about."

Her brown eyes water, and she bites her lip, nodding. Then she pulls me into a hug. "I'm sorry. I don't know what came over me. I'm not usually like this..."

I rub my hands down her back. "I know, honey. Baby makes you a little protective, but it's endearing, and I love you even more because of it."

Mila nods and lets me go. "Um, sorry, Grant." She sniffs, and Atlas brings her into the safety and comfort of his arms. Mila looks up at her husband. "I don't know what got into me."

He lays a hand over her belly. "Wildcat, it's okay. Baby loves his feisty mama, and so do I." He kisses her. "Now come on. I'm itching to teach this class for the first time."

She grins and nods.

"See you in a bit. And uh, sorry again."

"No worries. See you in a bit." I wave and then move over to Grant and place my hand on his chest.

"That was...intense."

I grin, happy that my crazy pregnant friend didn't freak him out too much. "My friends are all different kinds of beautiful crazy."

He smiles. "I'm looking forward to meeting them all."

"Good. Now we've got to go because the class will be starting in a few minutes." My heart picks up a fast rhythm as I realize which class we're about to take.

"Bring it on," he says, wrapping an arm around my shoulder. "So...granola-crunching?"

Warmth fills my chest as he nudges my temple with his forehead. It's an intimate gesture, one I've not had for a very long time.

I shrug. "I do like granola in my yogurt and my cereal and as a snack."

"Fascinating. And I took you for a cheeseburger and fries kind of girl," he murmurs against my hairline, the rumble of his voice seeping into my chest, sending a bout of arousal through me.

"Oh, I'm that too."

"Really? I was just introduced to a great pub. Maybe I'll take you there." His voice is warm and panty-melting, which isn't going to matter in a couple minutes when he realizes what type of class we're taking. Panties are absolutely not needed. I cannot wait to see the look on his face when he realizes what he agreed to.

"I love pubs. And burgers. And beer."

"And yoga and tree-hugging and making people happy..." he adds.

I smile and squeeze his waist tighter. "That too."

★ ★ ★

The lights are low in the room when we enter. Atlas is at the riser with Mila, setting out their mats, side by side, only two inches apart. A tingle of excitement ripples through my body as I realize what I'm about to do.

"Grab two mats, will you?" I gesture to where couples are picking their mats, a variety of colors to choose from. I always find it interesting what color people will choose. It typically ends up being whatever color charka is driving them that day.

Shockingly, Grant comes back with two in a deep-fuchsia color. In the color wheel of chakras, the color represents the seventh chakra, the crown, connoting enlightenment.

I'm pleased with his choice but surprised by it. He doesn't seem like the type of man who would feel a sense of enlightenment at this stage in not only our weird relationship, if I can even call it that, but in his world. Perhaps he needs to be enlightened. I imagine that's what my friend Dara, the aura reader, would say.

Atlas claps his hands together, and both of us turn to see what he's going to say.

"Since this is our first couples' yoga class, I've got my beautiful wife, Mila, with me." He glances at her adoringly, and lightness starts to fill the room with a palpable happy energy. "What you need to do is place your mats next to your partner's, about two to four inches apart. I hope you chose your partner well, because you are going to be touching one another a lot. Sweaty can be sexy...and slippery." He winks at his wife, and she rolls her eyes. "Be careful when you do the more advanced poses, and remember, if there is something you're not comfortable attempting, just stay at the first level. I'll be starting each pose with a beginner's pose, then intermediate, and move to advanced poses in some cases. Take the phase that suits you best."

I grab Grant's hand as he stands, looking completely out of place in his suit. "Don't worry, we'll start small and work our way up if you're feeling good. Okay?"

He nods, and then his eyes meet mine. "I trust you, Luna."

I smile. "Good." I say the word but wonder if it's going to hold true when he realizes what we're about to do.

"All right, class..." Atlas grins. "You know what to do. Take it all off. There are cubbies in the back to store your stuff."

Grant's eyes flash to mine, and his jaw hardens. "What the fuck is he talking about?"

Instead of answering, I swallow down the anxiety, cross my arms over my waist, grip the hem of my tank, and pull it over my head. His lips flatten and his nostrils flare. I continue, repeating the move this time with my sports bra in hand as I tug it over my head, my bare breasts bouncing back into place.

"Jesus Christ." His gaze is all over me. "Luna..." His voice is a low growl.

I cock an eyebrow, put my thumbs in at my yoga pants, and push them and my panties down in one fell swoop.

Grant steps forward and plasters his body to mine. "What the fuck are you doing?" He positions his hands over my ass as if to protect me from other curious eyes.

I giggle into his neck and kiss him there. "Look around, big man. What is everyone doing?"

He turns his head and takes in the other couples in various stages of undress.

"I don't..." He swallows, and his voice is grittier, like a box of rocks being shaken.

"It's naked yoga. Now strip." I push away from him, and he just barely lets me go.

"You expect me to remove my clothes?" His eyes run the course of my body, and he grinds his teeth, puts his hands into his hair, and tugs. "Fuck, you're beautiful."

"Your turn," I taunt. "Otherwise, I'm going to have to ask the gentleman who came alone to be my partner. Rub my naked body all over his during the poses..."

His gaze turns murderous. "The fuck you are." He shrugs his jacket off until it hits the floor. He yanks at his tie viciously until it separates from its knot, and he rips it off. He unbuttons his shirt unbelievably fast while toeing off his shoes and socks.

My mouth goes dry as I wait for any bit of skin to be revealed.

Grant opens his shirt, and nothing but golden tanned skin greets my eyes. My goodness, he's gorgeous everywhere. He lets the shirt hang open as he undoes his belt, flicks the button on his dress slacks, pushes them down, and steps out of them.

A pair of skin-tight, black boxer briefs covering a pretty large bulge greets me.

He steps closer to me, and my hands move as if they have a mind of their own, in search for warm golden skin to caress. My fingers and palms make contact, and I sway on my feet at the unbelievable warmth and firmness of his chest. I run my hands from his brick-like abdominals up to his defined square pecs, pushing the shirt over his shoulders and off so my gaze is no longer hindered by fine cotton. It falls to the floor in the heap at his feet.

Grant's body is trembling in my hands. "Are you frightened?" I look up, curving my hands around the lip of his underwear, teasing the skin there with my fingers.

His eyes are the darkest midnight as he dips his head. One of his hands rests against my hip, the fingers digging into the flesh there. The other hand curls around my nape, his thumb lifting my chin. "No," he growls. "I'm just doing my best not to get hard as a rock."

I chuckle lightly. "There is an awful lot of naked flesh to gaze at in this class."

His fingers twitch against my body, and he shakes his head. "Can't see anything but you. Your pearl-white skin. Rose-tipped breasts, which are the perfect goddamn size for my hands...my mouth. The red curls a teasing triangle like a fucking arrow pointing to heaven. And your ass..." He moves both hands down to my booty and cups both cheeks, pressing his hardening length against my belly deliciously. I can't help the soft moan that slips past my lips.

"I could write erotic love poems about how much I want this ass." He runs his nose along the side of my face, his breath skating across my ear. "You drive me insane clothed. Naked...

fuck, lamb, all bets are off."

I lock my arms around him and force his face up so he can see mine. The fact that he is hot for my body makes me bold and brave. A feeling I'm not used to but appreciate all the same. "Big man, *you* promised our deal was on, and your deal is to experience a class a week. Right now, you're going to experience couples' naked yoga. Now remove your shorts and show me what I have to look forward to."

Grant licks his lips, and I practically swoon where I stand, my knees feeling week, my heart pounding, my sex softening and aching with every breath he graces me with.

"As you wish." He loops his fingers into his boxer briefs and pushes them down his legs.

I practically faint with need when I see his thick penis, long, hard, and flushed with desire, standing proudly at attention. And all for me. I made his body respond like this.

"You're more than I could have dreamed of," I admit, my voice quavering. All I can think about is how good it will feel to have his hard edges pressing into my much softer ones.

Grant stands straight before me, his manhood a powerful, virile display of his masculinity and desire for me. "Lamb, you are my living dream come true."

CHAPTER NINE

CROWN
C H A K R A

*Since the crown chakra is connected to a power greater
than our own, a person driven by this chakra will live
fully in the present because the spirit is in
harmony with our body and will.*

GRANT

No man on this earth has been presented with heaven and
expected not to touch, kiss, caress, fuck, and own what stands
before him. I can't take my eyes off her perfect body. What
seems like miles of pearly white skin, absolutely unmarred,
stands before me. She's a natural redhead in every sense of
the word, and I'm fascinated by her hair falling in waves over
her shoulders, teasing her breasts the way I want to tease them
with my mouth.

I grip my hands into tight fists and grind my teeth. There is nothing I can do right now but try to calm the fuck down or lose my shit by lifting her over my shoulder and carrying her to the nearest flat surface. Forget flat. I'll take a wall at this point, even a goddamned utility closet as long as it's private.

Fuck!

I run my fingers through my hair as she sits down. Dear Lord, give me strength; her face is at exact eye level with my hard cock.

She glances at my dick and licks her lips.

Licks her fucking lips.

It takes herculean effort not to thrust my hips in her direction and demand those beautiful bow-shaped bits of flesh suck me in.

Luna lifts her hand and clasps mine. "Sit down on your mat, face the teacher, and wait for your instruction." She bugs her eyes and makes a face, gesturing around the room. I chance a look away from her beauty and find I'm basically the only one standing up, losing his ever-loving mind while the most stunning woman I've ever met is sitting naked, eye level with my dick.

How is anyone functioning right now?

Doing what she says, I make my way to a seated position and cup my hand over my erection, hoping the fucker will go down. Looking around, I see that a few other fellows are having the same problem, including the teacher.

Atlas, the curly haired guy, smiles at the class. He's got one hell of a spitfire for a wife...who happens to have a bangin' little body now that I can see it fully naked. "For those of you who are new, welcome to naked yoga. This is our first ever couples' yoga. Which means, ladies, don't be surprised if your men get a bit excited. And gents, it's perfectly natural to be aroused by your woman's naked body. Delayed gratification can work wonders for the libido." He grins wickedly.

I grind my teeth together and look sideways at Luna. She's sitting on her ankles, her knees held tightly together, her back a bit arched so her breasts are pointed forward in what I would consider a scintillating offering. Only she's not facing me. The beast within roars with irritation, needing to make sure everyone around me knows this woman is *all mine*, and they can keep their fucking hands and eyes to themselves, I wrap my arm around her waist, making sure it's obvious she belongs to me. At least as long as she'll allow it.

Luna takes in the move and doesn't say anything, but her lips give her away when they curve into a small smile.

"First position I want you to get into is lotus position, but I'd like your knees facing one another and touching. Close your eyes and place your hands on one another's knees, keeping the connection to your mate stronger. We'll be doing most of our positions today while touching your mate intimately, so the two of you can share and feed into one another's energy."

Luna turns, opens her fucking legs, and sits crossed-legged. I twist around to copy her and realize her legs are spread wide, and I can see straight into the heart of her. I swallow around the need in my throat to push her back, put those legs over my shoulders, and taste my fill. She smirks, places her hands just above my knees, and closes her eyes.

I can't move. Not when her pussy is spread open, so pink and pretty with those tight red curls framing it delicately. I groan and wiggle on my ass, my cock punching the skin of my belly as I curve forward and breathe.

Bad idea.

Her melon scent mixes with something rich and earthy. Like cinnamon over hot apple pie.

My hands are in fists at my sides, my knuckles aching with how tight I'm squeezing. I breathe in for a few beats and let it out, feeling like I'm running a marathon when I'm doing nothing but sitting.

Luna's eyes open, and she frowns. "Big man, put your hands on me," she whispers.

I shake my head. "If I touch you, I can't be held responsible for my actions."

Luna giggles lightly, and it reaches my chest and pounds against my ribcage. She comes up onto her knees, her breasts swaying as she places her hands on my shoulders and glides them over my biceps and forearms until they reach my fists. "Give me your hands."

I do as she asks. Hell, I'd do anything she asks right now.

She eases back on her bottom, and I do my best not to stare at the beauty between her thighs. My mouth waters, and the blood in my veins boils with arousal at the spicy scent billowing between us.

Luna places my hands just above her knees and then mimics the gesture on my body. Her touch feels like molten lava, searing straight through to the bone.

How the fuck am I going to make it through an entire hour of this?

"Now, class, I want you to pair your breathing with your partner's, curve your spine toward the wall behind you on the exhale, and then lift your chin to the sky, arching your back on the inhale."

Luna winks at me, closes her eyes, and inhales. Her breasts now point at me in offering, an offering I sure as hell want to take but stop myself from doing so. I watch as she curves her spine, dipping her head down toward her legs, using her hands to press against my knees and lift back up, inhaling and exposing her swanlike neck and chin to the sky.

"You're magnificent." She's unearthly serene. I want to grab ahold of her, wrap her up in silk, and never let her out of my sight.

"As are you." Her gaze flicks down to my cock.

I grin with pride, enjoying the fact that she seems to like my dick. At least her eyes do. I could assure her that my dick likes her as well—more than a little, in fact, if the tension I'm starting to feel in my balls is any indication.

"Follow along like a good little student," she teases.

I mimic her movements, pairing my breathing with hers. With each inhalation and exhalation, I can feel the tension starting to seep out of my shoulders, loosening them, my grip on her knees no longer so intense.

"Place your hands in front of you against your partner's, like so." Atlas's voice breaks through, and I glance at what he is doing with his wife. They make a stunning picture of a loving couple, hands pressed together in front of their chests.

"Use the pressure of your partner's hands and swiftly breathe in, lifting your hands above your head, stretching them out and in a circular shape. Pair with your breathing and find the speed and pressure that suits you and your mate."

My mate.

I'd like nothing more than to make Luna my mate. I just don't know what kind of life I can give her. My world is not one of Zen and compassion. It's of business and ruthlessness. Cutting-edge technology, fast-paced deals, and money. Ridiculous amounts of money changing hands.

As we breathe and stretch our arms above our heads, I close my eyes, allowing the peace of the movement to settle and soothe me. I'm sitting naked next to the woman who has held all of my attention for the past couple weeks, yet I'm becoming calm. Stress is leaving my body with every breath, and the view I've got of Luna is unparalleled in its graceful elegance.

"Okay, class, I want you to ease to a standing position," Atlas says. "Rest your chests against one another's, allowing your heart chakras to align."

Luna smiles softly as she places her hands on my waist delicately and flattens her body to mine. Just when I thought I'd gotten my dick under control, we're touching from tits to toes.

"Stretch your arms out in a T and rest your hands along one another's wrists, hands, forearms, whatever you can reach. Use the friction to push against one another and look up to the ceiling, arching your lower back. Firm your buttocks so that you don't put any strain on your lower back. And *breathe*. This is a variation of *Tadasana* or Mountain Pose. Only we're hugging the sky, lifting our hearts, and sharing it with our partner."

The second Luna arches her body and her perfect handfuls press against my chest, I lose focus. I glance down, and all the breath in my lungs pours out at the visual of her white skin glued to mine. She's a porcelain goddess, and I want to put my tongue all over her skin, starting with her breasts. God, do I want to put my mouth on her.

Luna lifts my hands with hers out into a T following along with the rest of the class. "Pay attention," she scolds, but there is no malice to her tone, only a playful reprimand.

I dip my head enough to lick a line from her clavicle, up

her velvet soft neck to her ear. "You're a tasteful distraction."

Her body stiffens, the muscles in her arms contracting and tightening against my stretched-out arms. My cock hardens further, and I adjust to give him top billing against her soft-as-silk stomach.

She groans and dips her head, resting her forehead to my chest. "You're not playing fair." Her lips brush against my chest, and I have to close my eyes and hold her wrists, keeping her spread. Instead of following the rules, I leave her arms out and run my hands along her limbs, down past her pits, to the side of her rib cage.

Luna shivers against me, her chin resting against my chest, her crystal-blue orbs swirling with desire. I glide my fingertips along her rib cage, to her waist and around her back and down to her juicy ass. I grind my cock against her belly while holding her to me.

She bites into her lip and closes her eyes. "Grant..." Her voice is but a whisper, a plea if I've ever heard one.

Before I can react to it, Atlas calls out the next instruction. It acts like a bucket of water poured over the both of us, instantly putting out the fire that was raging a moment ago. Only I don't suspect it will last, because my body can't help reacting to Luna Marigold. She's my wet dream incarnate, every man's fantasy wrapped in a purity I want to taint, over and over, until she's just as filthy as I am. Preferably while lying sated underneath me after having given her a handful of orgasms in penance for dirtying her up.

Luna blinks a few times and steps back.

"This position is going to test your resolve." Atlas grins wickedly. "But it will also stretch your partner in a body lengthening move, which will adjust her spine and deepen her stretch. We'll start with the women first. Ladies, watch Mila go into *Adho Mukha Vrikshasana*, most commonly known as downward facing dog."

I watch in equal parts fascination and horror as Luna bends over, her ass facing me, while she maneuvers her body into the shape of a triangle with her hands and feet on the mat.

"Christ on a cracker..." I rub at my forehead, close my eyes, and then open them again. Her rounded ass is lush and so damn bitable I have to clench my teeth and fist my hands in order not to reach out and take a bite. Sweat mists against my hairline as my body overheats with need.

Luna giggles, which has the taunting response of an ass wiggle, right in front of my face. That's nothing compared to her next move, where she stretches her legs and feet out to shoulder width apart. This has the inevitable effect of creating a steel pipe between my thighs as she presents me with a perfect view of her pink slit and shadowy pucker.

I step up behind her on autopilot, ready to claim my woman. I place my hands on her ass. I can't help it.

Thank God, Atlas does the same, only shockingly, he doesn't have a hard-on. Which is insanity because I'm so hard my dick might break off if I don't get to press it into the sweet heat of her body.

Not following the rules, I cup her sex possessively.

Luna jolts with a surprised squeak but holds her position.

"This is mine," I growl, leaning over her back, not putting any additional weight on her while she holds the pose. "I'm going to take this pussy so deep, you're going to feel me knocking against your navel...from the *inside*," I grate through my teeth.

Luna's entire body quivers.

"Hold on to your partner's hips and pull them back so they can stretch their spine fully," Atlas says to the class.

I ignore him. Instead, I push two fingers deep into her heat, guarding the view with my body by standing in front of her ass and pressing close, my hand wedged between us so I can play.

"Oh, my God." She gasps low in her throat.

I glance around and notice that *every* fucking man is focused on nothing but his woman's backside. Which is good, because I'd lose my goddamned mind if anyone saw what I was about to do to my woman, but hell, she's positively *begging* for it.

Couples' fucking naked yoga.

Stretch me out while bending over and showing me your sweet cunt.

Fuckin' bullshit. And she's about to find out I'm not the kind of man who takes this shit lightly. No way. No how is she getting out of this without some part of my body inside her.

I thrust my fingers in and out a few times as her body rocks back against mine. Leaning over her once more, I whisper, "This is going to go one of two ways, lamb. I either make you come in front of a room filled with other couples, or you stand up, we both grab our clothes, sneak out of the class, and go straight to your apartment, where I make good on my promise."

Her body shudders in my arms, and I place a series of kisses along her spine. Since she doesn't answer right away, I finger fuck her harder, easing my other hand around her body to pinch her clit.

Luna gasps, pushes back hard, and wiggles free. When she stands abruptly and spins around, her entire body is flushed, her blue eyes darker, filled with an intensity I haven't seen before but recognize instinctively. Lust.

Pure. Unhindered. Lust.

Not wanting to waste a minute, I grab my dress shirt and wrap it around her shoulders. She presses her arms into it. I find her panties and open them for her to slip into. She does. I don't bother with my clothes other than my slacks. I cover the important parts, cradle our clothes in a ball against my body, and take her hand in mine.

"Take me the back way to your apartment."

Luna doesn't say a word, her eyes wild, her chest heaving with exertion. She's gone. Lost to the hunger between us, the need I'm going to fill in about two minutes when she gets me through the studio, around the back of her building, and up to her apartment.

We walk barefoot through the yoga studio, half-dressed, and I couldn't give one flying fuck. Luna leads me to a back exit, which she pushes open.

I follow her down the back sidewalk to a door that's separate from the back of the bakery. "Dara had, um, a door put into the back so I can get directly to my apartment without going through the kitchen or bakery, but I don't use it at night. It's safer going out the front," she says randomly as if she needs to talk, to say something.

I grunt and nod as she opens the door and beats feet up the stairs. I take them two at a time, eager to get her to her comfy-as-fuck bed where I can gorge on her goodness.

The moment she opens the door, I unbutton my pants and let them fall, my erection already straining.

She glances down at the hard length between my thighs and my naked body and unbuttons the few buttons she did up on my shirt. It falls from her shoulders as I kick the door shut and twist the lock without even looking.

"Keep going." I open and close my fists, readying to pounce on my little lamb the second she's naked, but I'm trying my damnedest to keep my shit in check.

Luna bites her lips, hooks her thumbs into the scrap of lace covering her lower curls, and shimmies out of them.

I lick my lips, so damn hungry. "You know what you did in there?"

She shakes her head, her red hair falling all around her pretty shoulders and erect nipples.

"You woke the beast, and I'm hungry, lamb. Starved for your body."

She swallows visibly, and I take a step closer. Luna takes one back. We do this dance of her backing up, me stalking forward, not saying a damn thing until her legs hit the edge of her bed and she gasps.

I gesture to the bed. "Get on the bed. In the middle. Spread your legs out wide for me. Show me what you've been torturing me with."

"Grant..." My name is coated in honey and just as sweet. So sweet I want to lick it off her lips, but I have something else I need to get my mouth on.

"Do it, Luna." I lift my fingers to an inch apart. "I'm this close to losing it. Seeing you naked, smelling your pretty cunt. Dipping my fingers into that heavenly heat...*Jesus*. I'm going crazy talking about it. Now get on the bed and spread your legs so I can make you scream my name so loud you remember to never again test my patience. You'll find I don't have a patient bone in my body when it comes to you."

Luna's eyes fill with more heat. She trembles where she

stands, but I know the moment her decision is made. Her shoulders come up, her spine straightens, and she crawls onto the bed. She gets to the middle, her knees held tightly, before she smirks sexily and drops them both to the sides.

A pink heaven awaits.

I practically fly to the bed, fall to my knees at the side, grip her ankles, and tug her to the edge.

When her cinnamon-and-apples scent hits my nose, I inhale it deeply, planting the memory in my subconscious forever. My dick jerks, wanting in on the action, but not just yet.

"Good choice. Now lie back and let me rock your freakin' world," I say right before I use the flat of my tongue and lick her from pucker to clit in one long, succulent taste.

Her hips rise instantly, and her hands go straight for my hair as I expected. I love a woman who gets into being eaten.

"Grant!" she cries out as I suck hard on her bundle of nerves, torturing the reddened bud as much as she tortured me in that class with her lush curves and spicy-smelling pussy.

She tastes like a caramel-coated apple. Thick, sugary sweet, with a hint of spice. I delve my tongue deep into her slit, flicking against the walls of her sex until she's twitching. Moving my hands up her thighs, I spread her lips so nothing gets in the way of tasting her deep. Her arousal coats my lips, chin, and mouth as I pull back up to play with her clit.

She raises her hips as I work her into a frenzy. "Grant, I'm going to—"

"Come all over my face. Yes, lamb. Yes, you are."

On that note, I double my efforts by inserting two fingers into her heat, and the walls of her sex lock down around the invasion. I can't wait to feel my dick receive that grip. My own body jolts at the sensation, my balls drawing up. I wrap one fist around the base of my cock to stave off my own impending orgasm. Just getting her off is filling me to the brim with unreleased sexual tension. I push the tendrils of my own need aside and focus on my woman.

Luna is mewling and sighing as I finger her fast and hard, but it's not until I wrap my lips around her clit, flick it a dozen times with the very tip of my tongue, and then suck hard, that she finally lets go. Her entire body flushes pink, and she cries out to the heavens.

Hell yes!

"Grant, Grant, God, Grant!" Her body arches almost unnaturally as I extend her pleasure as long as I can. Removing my fingers from her pussy, I dip my tongue in to get a taste and find that her orgasm makes her even sweeter. I gorge on her as if she is chocolate-dipped strawberries and I haven't eaten in a week. Nothing will ever taste better than her sweet cunt after I've wrung an orgasm out of her.

I hum around her flesh and jerk my cock a few times slowly until she eases her body back down to the bed, and I imagine her mind is slowly coming back to planet Earth.

I stand up and stroke my dick, watching her hands move restlessly over her heated skin. Eventually, her eyes flicker open but only halfway. Her gaze goes straight to where I'm tugging on my cock.

I'm excited to find out that my sweet fairy princess can be dirty as she glides her hands over her breasts and squeezes the mounds. While I watch her hips stir over the bedspread, her thumb and forefinger go for her nipples, where she pinches both until she cries out.

"Take me," she whispers, her voice sounding deeper, sex-roughened.

A burst of pride shoots down my spine. "No condom?" I keep stroking my dick, just enjoying the view of her touching herself.

"I'm clean and I'm on the shot," she says, moving her hands from her tits down her belly. I watch with rapt fascination as her hands trail down to where she's wettest. "Are you clean? Been tested recently?" Her words are a weighted sigh, thick with the rising hunger once more.

I nod. "Never taken a woman bare before. Test last month. Clean bill of health." My own voice is unrecognizable as I grunt through my reply.

"Then what are you waiting for?" She runs her palms down the insides of her thighs until her hands frame her glistening slit.

"I don't have a fucking clue!" I growl before hitching a knee on the bed, lifting her ass up to center my blistering hot dick to her entrance, and plow home.

Jesus!

Fuck!

Christ!

So good!

I chant as I wedge my fat cock as deep as I can go into her body. She's hot and tighter than I could have ever imagined. Once seated, I hook an arm under her back and lift us both up to the top of the bed, scooting her body so that her head rests comfortably on a pillow.

"My goodness you're strong," she gasps, her fingernails digging into my biceps where she holds on.

"Lamb, you haven't seen anything yet. Just lie back and enjoy the ride!"

CHAPTER TEN

CROWN
C H A K R A

The crown chakra is noted to be the chakra that connects us to God...the divine. Guidance from the divine through this connection helps lead us through our life.

LUNA

I've never experienced a moment more profound, more life changing than when Grant and I became one. When he was rooted deep, one hand on my right cheek, his thumb tracing my bottom lip, eyes to mine, time stood still. There was nothing but the two of us.

Connected.

The moment was so powerful I knew right then and there I'd remember it for the rest of my days. Grant swallowed, his lips coming open as he dipped his head down and kissed my lips over his thumb.

He still hasn't moved, his manhood twitching inside me. I blink and run my hand through his dark hair.

Grant closes his eyes and rests his lips against mine, not in a kiss, just touching in every way possible. Bodies, hands, lips.

"Nothing could ever be this perfect," he whispers against my lips, his words seeping through my skin and straight down to my very soul.

I run my fingers once more through his hair and cup his cheek. He eases back, and his eyes are on fire. Midnight blue like the very base of a lit match.

"No. I don't think it ever could."

He closes his eyes, nods, and then shifts his hips back and thrusts forward. A burst of pleasure ripples from between my thighs and through every one of my pores all the way to my fingertips. Each plunge of his thick penis takes me higher.

Takes *us* higher.

I expect Grant to take my body with the same ruthless confidence and drive he exhibits in his business dealings, but that is not what I am experiencing.

With every touch of his fingers, he focuses on my pleasure. Watches my eyes as I respond to him. Each kiss he bestows is a promise of more to come. Every breath he takes against my neck, my mouth, my breasts, he worships me in a way I've never felt in my life.

Grant wraps his arms around my back and plunges deeply, his body shaking. Mine is wound tightly, readying to release, and right there he consumes my heart and soul through his kiss.

Together we reach the light, a height so intense I gasp for

air. I have no need to strain, for Grant is there, breathing life back into me with his kiss, as together, we start our descent.

He eases in and out of me softly, working his length until he is spent. Grant runs his lips over my neck, my collarbone, between my breasts, where he takes each nipple into his mouth and sucks briefly. It's as if he is making every inch of my body tingle with aftershocks.

Once he has kissed his way down to my belly, he licks a circle around my navel and then continues down where he places a closed-mouth kiss on my curls and then moves to each hip, where he nips and teases until I giggle.

He's not done with his journey. He moves down my thigh with a long line of kisses until he reaches the knee. Then he switches sides and repeats the gesture. On my shin, he licks a long line down before nibbling on my ankle.

"Grant!" I laugh when he makes it to the end of the bed, where he steps off, naked as the day he was born, lifts my feet, kisses the tops of each, and then places a closed-mouth kiss on each big toe.

I pull my feet out of his grasp, laughing hysterically.

"Bathroom over there?" He hooks a thumb in the direction of the frosted blocks in the corner with the single door. It is the only closed-off room in the entire loft.

"Yeah." I turn onto my side.

"Be right back with a cloth." He turns and gifts me a spectacular view of his toned bare ass, back, and thighs.

Wow. Grant is handsome everywhere. I sigh and close my eyes, enjoying flashbacks of our lovemaking.

His mouth between my legs.

I shiver.

His body pressed flat against mine.

I moan into the pillow.

His penis, thick and hard inside me.

I mewl with renewed desire.

"You starting round two without me?" Grant's laugh hits my dreamlike state, and I sit up fast, pushing my hair out of my face.

"What?"

"Lamb, your legs were rubbing together, and one of your hands was squeezing your breast." He chuckles. "I totally caught you starting without me. Which I one hundred percent approve of because it means I get to watch the show and then join in."

I cringe. "I was *not* starting without you. I mean, I've already had two incredible orgasms."

"Baby, you were too."

"Was not!" I scold and watch while he crawls along the bed, one arm on each side of me.

"Lamb, you were. Now open your legs so I can clean you up for round two." His expression is filled with cockiness, and as much as I want to call him on it, I would much prefer round two, so I do as he asks and spread my legs.

He uses the cloth and cleans me thoroughly. Then he produces a second cloth and doubles up on the job.

"Two cloths?"

"Yeah, the first to clean the bulk of my mess, the second to ensure a pristine pussy."

"Oh, my God!" I toss my body backward and yank the comforter up and over my naked body. "Do you always talk about this stuff so directly?"

Grant gets off the bed and goes back to the bathroom, where I hear the water running, and I assume he's washing his hands...again. The man really does have a germ issue.

He pads back on bare feet, grabs the comforter, and flings the entire thing off the bed.

"With you, I'm direct. Yes. I don't want you to ever think I'm not telling you the truth. And when it comes to sex, there's nothing you ever need to hide from me. Not this sexy-as-fuck body"—he runs a hand from my neck down over my breasts, belly, and between my thighs, where he cups me like he did before in the studio—"and especially not with this perfect pussy. I want no bullshit between us. I deal with liars and cheats every single day. With you, I want full disclosure."

I like that. Full disclosure. Gives me hope that he'll be completely honest with me about what he decides regarding my building and my friends' buildings.

"What are you going to do to my building?" I ask.

Grant's shoulders slump, and he lies next to me, elbow to the mattress, head in his hand. He uses his other hand to trace figure eights around my breasts.

"Honestly, I don't know yet. The plans are already in the works, money has already changed hands with the investors, contracts signed. I'm still thinking about it."

I nod and watch as his eyes change color.

"You have the loveliest skin." He glides just his fingertips down the center of my chest to my belly, where he lays his palm. "What do you want out of life, Luna?"

The air around our little bubble shifts into more serious territory, so I turn sideways. It doesn't change his touching me, but he's moved to the dip in my waist and swell of my hip.

I inhale fully and deeply and rest my head against the pillow so I can watch his eyes change color while we talk. He may be a hard man to read, all big-business tycoon, but his eyes give him away. I can tell he's feeling something very deep, and I have a feeling it's all about me and the love we just made.

"Well, I've always taught yoga. My mother is a career yogi, as you know. I love the practice, and I believe in what I do, how my teaching helps people. I'm never unhappy at the end of the day, always filled with positive energy and the knowledge that what I do is making others feel better."

Grant traces a line from my shoulder all the way to my hip. Gooseflesh rises along my skin, and he smiles as if he has created magic with his touch.

"What else do you want?" His eyes flicker a deeper blue while he watches me respond.

"I want to be a wife and a mother someday. Raise a couple children, teach them the art of yoga, share the beauty of nature and the earth."

He chuckles and curls a hand around my hip. "You are a hippie." He grins.

I shrug, smiling. "Yeah, I guess. It's what I know. I had fun dressing up for your charity event, and dancing with you and donating the money to the charity were the highlights."

His gaze turns pointed, colder. "Do you think you could handle going to one of those types of events every week, along with at least one or two business dinners?" His voice is rough with a dagger of seriousness I wouldn't have anticipated while lying naked in bed after a couple awesome orgasms.

I cup his cheek, using my thumb to pet his bottom lip the way he did mine. "If it meant being with you at those events and those dinners, I believe I could not only handle them, I'd enjoy them. Because I enjoy spending time with you, learning about the things that matter to you."

His voice softens as he cups my neck. "Luna, you're too

good to be true. I don't deserve a woman like you in my life, but I *want* you. I want you so fucking much."

I smile wide, push at his chest, and straddle his hips, laughing. I place my hands on his chest as he holds on to my hips. "Don't you see, my silly big man, you already have me. When you begged me for a second chance today...I was yours."

Grant curls his hand around my neck, tugging me forward until I'm flat against his chest. "Come here."

He kisses me hard, wet, and so deeply, I'm squirming all over his naked body, ready to get started on round two.

When Grant finally lets my lips go, I ease back, leaving about six inches between our faces but not our lower bodies. I move my hips up and back, glorying in the fact that I've made him hard as stone, while I coat his length with my arousal.

Grant groans, lifts his hips to control the movement, but I lock my thighs against his side. "No way." I press my fingers to his lips before he can comment. "My turn to play."

Both of Grant's hands leave my hips, and he cups my face. He holds my cheeks and stares into my eyes. "There isn't another woman on this earth I want more than you. I'm going to find a way to keep you. Mark my words, lamb. You're mine."

★ ★ ★

Later that afternoon, we walk hand in hand down to Rainy Day Café. A sexually sated Grant is, not surprisingly, a happy Grant. I glance over at him as he swings my arm back and forth while we walk past Sunflower Bakery and Tattered Pages Bookstore down to the café.

"You're smiling a lot more than usual," I remark, even though I can feel heat color my cheeks.

He smirks. "Lamb, we just spent the last five hours fucking. My dick is worn out from how tight your little body and mouth can squeeze it. What man wouldn't be on cloud nine after a day like that?"

I cringe. "You don't have to say it like that. I mean, have you ever thought to call it making love instead of, you know..."

"Fucking." He says the word so loud I swear everyone on the entire block can hear him.

I tug his hand and force him to a stop. "Yes," I hiss. "You don't need to say it so loud."

Grant pulls me into his arms, his hands on my booty. "You are so damn cute!" He kisses my nose. "Do you ever cuss?"

I glance around to see if anyone is looking. "Of course, I do. Perhaps not as liberally as you..."

"Your man."

"What?"

"You do not cuss as liberally as *your man* does."

A flush of arousal and excitement roars through me at his words. I place my hand over his heart and look up at him. "You want me to call you my man." My voice is but a whisper, but he hears it.

He dips his head until we're eye to eye. "Abso-fucking-lutely. I am your man, and you are my woman. We are together."

I smile. "As in, we're in a relationship. Grant and Luna."

He swallows and purses his lips. "I can't say that I've ever been in a 'relationship' before." He uses air quotes before he grins. "Huh. Yes. I'm okay with it. We're in a *relationship*."

"You know that means you're my boyfriend." I continue to poke and prod at him, making sure he understands exactly what he's saying.

He grins. "I am aware of societal titles for when a man and

a woman agree to become a couple."

"Ohh...a couple! I like that even more." I place my hands to my chest and clap with the tips of my fingers.

"Jesus Christ. Fuckin' cute."

"You know, you really don't need to be so profane."

One of his eyebrows rises up toward his hairline. "I'm pretty sure you enjoyed my profane abilities back in your apartment. Did you not?"

I smack his chest. "Grant!"

He hooks an arm around my shoulder. "Come on, I'm starving. Besides, I need to fuel up."

"Fuel up?"

"Yeah, for round a hundred and six," he says as if he's dead serious.

"You can't be serious. You can't want to have sex again today."

He runs his hand down to my ass and squeezes the cheek hard. His head cants, and he curves against my body, placing his lips on my neck, where he proceeds to skate his teeth up the column. A bout of intense arousal flutters through my body, soaking my panties with renewed excitement. He sucks at my neck while squeezing my ass.

"Oh, my God." I grip his form and hold on as my body reacts in what feels like a million pleasurable tingles.

"Case in point. If I put my hand down your pants, you'd be slick and ready to take me. So yeah, I need to fuel up because my woman is insatiable, and as her man, I need to fill every last one of her needs."

He bites down on the edge of my earlobe, and I jerk in his hold, my hips thrusting against him.

He chuckles. "Still hungry?"

I nod dumbly.

"For food?"

"No."

He laughs out loud, turning me toward the café and opening the door for me. "Lamb, you are too fuckin' easy. Now get your ass in there so I can feed you." He smacks my booty hard enough to sting.

"Owee!" I rub at my sore bum.

He comes up behind me, resting his body against my backside. "Don't worry, there's more where that came from."

I'm wide-eyed and lost in a sensual haze as we enter. Coree, one of the owners, waves. I smile and offer a wave of my own while Grant leads me to the counter.

He scans the board, and I just look at him. His profile is exquisite. Dark hair, cropped at the sides, the top layers falling longer to frame a chiseled face. His nose is long, strong, and straight. His lips are beyond kissable, like soft little pillows I can't get enough of.

Grant turns his head and says something, but I don't hear it; I'm so focused on how attractive he is.

Eventually he smiles and cups my cheeks. "Lamb, you awake?"

"Um, yeah." I shake off the simmering desire sitting right on the surface. It's as if we opened Pandora's sex box, and now I can't get enough.

"I asked what you wanted to eat for dinner. We skipped lunch altogether. Not that I'm complaining." He smirks.

My cheeks heat and I glance at Coree, who smiles wide, looks at me, and then looks at Grant and back. She lifts her hand and gives me a quick thumbs-up. Now my cheeks are flaming. I know they must be bright red.

Grant notices, of course, and runs his thumbs along them. "Lamb, you're getting hot. You okay?"

I swallow and nod. "Yeah. I'm fine. It's uh, warm in here. I'll have the turkey club with a cup of cream soup. Whichever you have today." They always have a vegetable, cream, and meat soup of the day, and they're always fabulous.

Grant orders a heated ham and cheese on rye with a cup of soup and drinks for both of us. Once he pays, he puts a hand to my lower back and leads me across the space to an open table.

After we take our seats, he looks around. "Place is interesting. And packed. It's four o'clock. You'd think it would be dead in here."

I shake my head. "It's always packed. More so at other times, of course, like lunch and brunch times and then again at dinner. A lot of people take it to go, too. And, of course, as you may know, they were going to expand to the small store next door and open it up so there was a patio area. Extend the rainforest feel but leave it fully covered so that, even when it rains or it's cold, they can warm it up and still have the indoor-outdoor vibe."

Grant nods. "Interesting clientele."

I grin as I notice what he notices. "They're mostly a bunch of suits, and the rest are yogis."

"Yeah, seems like it." He tilts his head as if he's assessing the crowd.

"You putting that business mind of yours to work, big man?"

He grins, and his eyes flash to mine. "Trying to figure out a way to make you happy and keep my father and our investors off my ass at the same time."

Grant's shoulders seem to stiffen at the mention of his

father.

"You and your dad have a very tumultuous relationship," I declare rather than question.

He sighs. "Most of the time, I despise him." He shakes his head. "In business, though, he's the chairman, and I want..."

"To impress him."

Grant lifts his head and winces before shrugging one shoulder.

I reach out to cover his hands on the table. "It's okay to want to make your father proud of you. You've taken over the helm of the ship, and you want to prove you are a good captain. I get it. I want my mother to be proud of me when it comes to Lotus House. She worked her bum off to provide this legacy, and it's my job to continue it and show my appreciation. Except my mom tells me all the time how much she loves me and how well I'm doing. I get the feeling your dad doesn't give you many pats on the back."

He sits back, releasing my hands, and laughs out loud. "My father has never once told me I've done well, even though the company has seen skyrocketing profits since I took over. He just adds to the never-ending pile of shit I should be doing better."

"Grant, you aren't responsible for making him happy. He doesn't seem like a very jolly man to begin with."

"He's not," he says flatly.

I rub my arms and twist my fingers together, wanting to ask about the one person he's never brought up.

Coree walks over and sets down our plates of food, soup, and iced teas.

"Looks amazing. Thank you," Grant says before picking up his sandwich and taking a big bite.

I suck in a deep breath, the smell of the food making my mouth water. "Will you tell me about your mother?"

Grant stops mid-chew, sets down his sandwich, and leans back, putting as much distance as possible between the two of us. For a few seconds, I sit with fear, thinking he's going to ice me out again. When he doesn't want to talk about something, he turns cold, frigid in his body language and word choices.

It seems like I wait forever until he firms his lips and reaches his hands out. I unlock my fingers and grab for his touch as fast as I can, needing to know that I haven't stepped over some imaginary line.

"Luna, I will tell you about my mother. Not today though. I don't like talking about it or her in general. You're going to find it's a hot-button item for me. Eventually, we'll discuss it. I'm asking you to give me time to prepare for it and leave it alone for today. We're having a great time. The best fucking day of my life. I do not want to ruin it with thoughts of the woman who abandoned me. Okay?"

I nod quickly. "Okay, yes. I'm sorry." I squeeze his hands, and he returns the gesture and smiles softly, his face turning warm once more.

"My lamb hasn't touched her food, and there's one thing I know about my woman: she likes her food."

I laugh, lift up my sandwich, and take a huge bite. So big that bits of lettuce fall onto the plate.

Grant cracks up and shakes his head. "I am so keeping you, Luna Marigold."

I finish chewing and swallowing before I respond. "Good. Because I'm keeping you too, Grant Winters."

CHAPTER ELEVEN

CROWN
CHAKRA

The crown chakra can represent your attitude, beliefs, values, conscience, faith, courage, and humanitarianism.

GRANT

Life is good. No, it's *great*. I walk into Winters Group with a swing to my step and a lightness in my heart. Clay was right. I'll have to send the man a case of the finest whiskey. He was there when I needed a friend and gave solid advice that actually worked. Though nothing worked as well as just being honest, apologizing for the errors of my ways, and hoping she'd give me a second chance. She did. And boy, it was better than I ever could have imagined.

Luna is light, energy, and kindness wrapped in a sinful body and a pure soul. Everything I could ever want and never hoped to find. But I have. In her.

With thoughts of her filling my mind, I pick up the phone and call my architect.

He picks up on the first ring. "Walters."

"Hey, Brando, it's Winters."

"Grant, I didn't expect to hear from your ass for another five months. What building do you want to tear down now?" He chuckles.

His question sends a direct shot to my already tender psyche. Although, in his defense, he wouldn't know that I've had an epiphany, which came at the hands of a redheaded fairy princess.

"Brando, this time I've got something new to throw your way. It's going to be challenging. Unbelievably expensive, and my board of directors is going to hate it. Which means you have to come up with something I can sell to them in order to get full approval."

"Shit, man, what are you planning?"

"You know the Berkeley four we're planning to build?"

"Yeah, of course. Soon as the tenants move out, we flatten and rebuild the four towers. Are you telling me this plan is changing?"

I grin and spin around in my chair to survey the San Francisco skyline. "Yeah, the plans are changing. I want you to find a way to incorporate most, if not all, of the businesses currently on the street but still find a way to build most, if not all, of the towers. Can you do that for me?"

"Uh...are you fucking kidding?" His voice is strained—not a good sign.

I grind my teeth, knowing this request is not only unusual but a burden to my architect and the plans we've already put in place. It's a good thing I've used him for the past decade on all my builds, or he'd be in the poorhouse. Now he's one of the best-known architects on the West Coast. He owes me, and he knows it.

"Brando, are you telling me you can't handle a challenge?"

"No, I'm telling you we already had this laid out. For *months*. Materials have been commissioned, guys' contracts set to work."

"And none of that should change. Just look at the street and find a way to keep the local businesses there and incorporate them into your design. Whatever you have to do. I need Lotus House, Sunflower Bakery, and Rainy Day Café to be saved."

"And the other side of the street? You know that's where the major overhaul has to be done underground. And it's a smoke shop, an antique store, and a fucking thrift store, man. Not the type of market we're selling to. The yoga studio, the bakery, and the café fit. Hell, even the used bookstore, but the others don't."

Luna hasn't mentioned being extremely attached to those other businesses. "Look, do what you can to incorporate the studio and the bakery. My woman..." I wince, realizing my slip of lip.

Brandon, better known as "Brando" to his old lacrosse buddies back in college, clears his throat on a cough.

"Um, I'm sorry. Did my ears deceive me? Did you just say *your woman*? Since when the fuck do you have a woman, and better yet...why is she involved in this two-hundred-million-dollar build?"

I clench my teeth and think about lying, and then the image of her innocent face, those blue eyes, red curls, and sweet, sweet lips kissing me goodbye, telling me to have a good day at work... *Fuck*. I can't get her honesty out of my mind.

"Yeah..." I sigh. "Look, this is between you and me and a twenty-one-year-old bottle of Macallan I'll have Annette send directly to your office."

"Hoo-wee, looks like this ought to be good. I'm sitting down. Okay, lay it on me, Winters."

I let out a rumble from deep within my chest. "The owner of Lotus House Yoga is my girlfriend."

"I'm sorry...did you say girlfriend?" he queries.

I suck in a harsh breath. "Quit fuckin' around. I'm serious."

"So am I. I have never, not *ever* heard Grant Winters utter the word girlfriend, and I've known you more than a decade. She must be really fuckin' special to nail down the un-nailable."

I furiously rub at my temples with thumb and forefinger. The bastard knows me too well. "Be that as it may, she is important to me. Very fucking important, and Lotus House is her studio. Her family legacy. Not to mention, Sunflower Bakery is owned and operated by her best friend. Who...get this...also happens to be a *McKnight*. As in Knight & Day Productions. I do not need shit getting out that my team and I single-handedly destroyed the flagship Sunflower Bakery."

"Jesus, man, when you go big, you go fucking *big*. Did you think it would be a good idea to start something with the woman you were kicking out of her property?" He groans. "Let me think. Fuckin' hell. You're rich. Just buy her and her friend another building somewhere else they can run. Problem solved."

"Not good enough. She's committed to that street, not to mention she lives in the loft above the bakery."

Brando busts up laughing, so loud I have to hold the phone away from my ear until his chuckles fall away. "Dude, you are a piece of freakin' work. Not only do you get hooked to a woman whose building you're demolishing in five months, but you're also making her *homeless*. You could always just ask her to move in with you..."

He says the words, and instantly, the thought of coming home to Luna every night, to a warm house and a smile from my own personal fairy princess, pummels my chest like a barrel of bricks landing on top of me. I rub at my suddenly aching chest. The idea has some serious merit, but it's far too soon. I haven't hooked her deep enough yet. And even though she doesn't know it, she's definitely hooked me good. There is nowhere I wouldn't go to get to her. I can't explain or define it. I just want to be near her. Wallow in her beauty and the calm she brings to my soul.

"Look, I'm not asking you to figure out anything but how to save those few businesses. Look at your plans, do what you can, and call me back when you have something."

"Even if it's going to cost you."

I huff. "Brando, anything worth doing costs me. This will be worth the price. Just do it."

I slam my handset down on the receiver and stand up to pace the room.

The phone on my desk buzzes, and Annette's cold tone comes through. "You have a surprise visitor."

My heart starts to pound, and I smile, imagining my lamb stopping by. But it's strange since I just left her. "If it's Luna, send her in."

"It's not."

I frown. "Who is it?"

Her voice dips low. "Strangely, it's Honor Salerno. You would know her as Honor Carmichael."

"Carmichael? As in Timothy Carmichael on our board of directors and one of our top investors?"

"His daughter, sir." Her words are clipped. She knows a visit from a board member's daughter is not going to make me happy or put me in a positive mood.

"Fuck!"

"My sentiments exactly. Should I send her in?"

"Yes, absolutely. Send her in." I put the phone down and sit back in my chair. Honor Carmichael, the sole heir to the Carmichael and Gannon fortunes, is mysteriously paying a visit. The Carmichaels and Gannons are old money and have a lot of it. More than even my father.

Annette taps on my door and enters with an angelic woman. Blond hair so light it's almost white, pale skin, and see-through gray eyes, she looks like an angel incarnate. She's pushing a double stroller occupied by two sleeping children with dark hair who couldn't be more than two or three.

She's wearing a flowing white dress with a red belt cinched at the waist. She looks like a young, vibrant mother in her twenties. Her clothes are top-of-the-line, but she's nowhere near dressed up. Her hair is pulled back halfway so most of it falls over her shoulders and down her back, but the rest is out of her face.

She parks the stroller off to the side so she can still see the children from my desk. As she turns around, she smiles, and it's as if I'm being smiled upon from the heavens above.

"Honor..."

"Salerno, previously Carmichael." She holds out her hand, and I shake it.

"I'm sorry. I don't believe we've met." I scan through my memory bank.

"No, we haven't, though we've been to many of the same events."

"I think I would have noticed you," I say, and even though it could come off as flirting, it's more a compliment to her true beauty.

Her cheeks redden, reminding me of Luna. "I was good at hiding in the background. I am here to talk about business."

I gesture to the chairs in front of my desk, and she takes one, sitting up straight, as prim and proper as I would expect from a woman of her upbringing.

"How can I help you, Mrs. Salerno?"

"My father has informed me of your plans to obliterate Lotus House Yoga and all of the businesses on that street in order to build luxury apartments."

I sit back in my chair and cross my ankle over my knee. "And you would like to buy an apartment?"

She shakes her head and smiles. "No, I'd like to know how much money it will take for you to leave Lotus House Yoga alone. As you know, I'm very wealthy. Money is of no importance to me."

"And what is of importance to you?" I fire back, getting right to the heart of why she's here.

Honor glances at her children. "My husband works at Lotus House Yoga, and many of our friends do as well. The McKnights are personal friends, as are the Powers, the Foxes, and the owner, Luna Marigold."

"You know my Luna?" Again, I want to bite off my own fucking tongue. It seems, when it comes to my lamb, I can't keep her to myself.

She grins. "*Your* Luna?"

I swallow and focus on her pretty face. Not as pretty as

Luna's, but if they had similar hair color, they could be sisters, with their pale skin and light eyes. "Yes, I'm in a relationship with Luna Marigold," I admit, my chest rising with pride.

Honor beams right before my eyes, her beauty becoming effervescent. Wow, her husband must be enchanted, because making this woman happy is a sight to behold.

"Well, that's magnificent! Then you're obviously ending the plans to destroy the street." She smiles wide.

I lean against the desk, a moment of defeat filling my conscience. "Unfortunately, no. As your father may have told you, I'm stuck. Contracts have been signed. The board has already signed off, as have all the rest of the investors. Right now, I'm trying to figure out how to save what I can."

Honor glances down and away. "Well, I'm willing to help in whatever way I can."

"You said your husband works there?"

"Yes, a couple times a week. Teaches aerial yoga."

Fucking aerial yoga. Clayton mentioned he took classes from his buddy Nick who taught aerial yoga there. Small damn world.

Honor continues speaking. "Even though we have Sal's Boxing Gym & Fitness Center, which keeps us hopping."

"You run a gym with your husband?" I'm intrigued by the fact that a socialite the likes of a Carmichael/Gannon would need to work at all.

She nods, the light coming out of her once more at the mere mention of her work. "I bought into the business, and we've expanded it exponentially. We're considering looking for another location, actually."

"Really? Hmm, I'll bet an entire floor of a luxury high-rise would give you some great clientele who would pay top dollar, not to mention if you had a word with your father about the area and how you believe in keeping it quaint."

Her gaze flashes to mine. "My father owes me dearly." Her gray eyes turn as cold as ice. "I will not go into details, but if you need leverage against him, I can assure you you'll have it. Just give me a call. I'll leave my contact information with your receptionist."

"That would be lovely." I stand up and button my suit jacket, a clear sign our chat has come to its conclusion. "Thank you for stopping by, Honor. I hope to see you again sometime."

She grins. "Oh, I'm sure you will." Her tone is conspiratorial. "Once my Nick finds out you're dating Luna Marigold, you may have a face-to-face visit with a rough-around-the-edges Italian." She runs her hands through her blond hair rather timidly. "He means well, but he's protective of the women at Lotus House." She shrugs. "Comes from a family with five sisters."

"Are you warning me that your husband is going to seek me out?" I jerk my head back and cross my arms over my chest in defense.

Honor walks over to her children, tuts over them like any good mother would, making sure they are sleeping soundly before moving behind the stroller to push them along.

"I'm surprised he hasn't already. He must not know yet. Which is super fun for me." She grins. "I never know anything first."

Honor Salerno is sweet but kooky. Must be the lack of sun. My Luna has the goofball gene and is as white as snow too. Lucky Nick. After yesterday, I sure as hell know exactly how lucky I am to have Luna's beauty in bed.

Honor pushes the stroller toward the door expertly.

"Thank you for seeing me. And feel free to call if you need anything. Like I said, I want my friends' businesses to stay. If you can find a way to make that happen, I will be grateful as well as *generous* with my pocketbook."

Of course she would. She has more money than she could ever spend in her or her children's lifetimes. I find it interesting that she chose a boxer/yoga teacher as her mate and runs a gym alongside being a mother. Just proves money cannot buy true happiness. Happiness is found in the most peculiar places.

"Understood. Thank you for stopping by."

She wiggles her fingers, and I press the button that automatically opens the door. As she leaves, I fall back into my chair.

"What could possibly come next?"

★ ★ ★

When she exits the studio, I watch her lock the door and then turn on her sandaled feet until she sees me leaning against my car. Her smile could light up an entirely dark street.

"Hey, big man. I hoped I'd be seeing you this evening." She takes her time walking over to me. I don't move until her body is close enough for me to reach out and grab her hips and plant them against mine before taking her mouth.

She smells of melon and tastes of chamomile tea. I drink from her lips, sucking her tongue, flicking my tongue against hers until my dick starts to stir, wanting a far different taste.

I pull back and cup her cheek.

"I missed you today." Her shy admission is not only lovely but gives me an incredible feeling. Her honesty fills all the holes a long day puts into me.

I rub my nose along hers, and keeping with my goal of full disclosure, I return her gesture. "I missed you more."

She grins against my mouth and kisses me, this time closed-mouthed but hard.

"You hungry?" I ask, knowing she is. The woman taught three classes today. She must be starved.

"Yes." She locks her arms around my neck and presses her body tighter to mine.

"For food?" My voice is husky, deeper than usual.

"No." She runs a finger from my temple down to my mouth, where she presses it.

I kiss her finger and then push her back with my hand on her belly. "Go pack a bag. I'm going to feed you, and then you're going to stay with me at my place."

Her eyes widen, and she literally bounces on her feet. "Really? I can't wait to see your place!" She flips around so fast her fruity scent accosts me as she rushes to the bakery door at a full run.

I chuckle and pull up my phone and notice a text from Clayton.

Did you make yourself a nuisance?

I grin and shake my head. Who would have thought my professional trainer would become a friend? I guess he'd always thought we were friends, and perhaps we were. Until I met Luna, I think my eyes were closed off to seeing other connections with people. It's as if she's opened my eyes to the beauty of friendships and other types of relationships. I mean, I have Brando, an old college friend, and we meet every few months or so for a drink. However, I was never the one to seek him out. He would always contact me. Just like Clayton did now.

The truth of the situation is that I'm not a very good friend, even though I have two men and now a woman who think of me as important...personally. Not professionally. Although, technically, I'm in business with Brando. He makes a lot of money off me, as does Clayton. Each provides a service I pay handsomely for. Yet, they are the closest things to best male friends I have.

The concept is sobering as I stare down at the message. My natural inclination is to wave off the text, tell him to mind his own business, but I don't think that's how true friendships work. Not that I really know the difference.

What would Luna do?

I smile, thinking about her fun and quirky personality. She'd probably call the man and get into an hour-long conversation and tell him her life's story. There is no way in hell I'm doing any such thing. Though I imagine she'd definitely respond to his message. He is obviously reaching out and being considerate in doing so. As with my commitment to Luna, I decide to, at the very least, give back the respect and respond with honesty.

I hit reply on my screen and tap out my response.

All is well. She has forgiven me, and we are together.

I read the message a few more times, not realizing Luna has returned until her scent entices my senses once more as she looks over my shoulder down at the phone's display.

"No way! You know Clayton Hart? I'm friends with his wife, Monet! I've even taught him in a few classes in the past, though he prefers Nick's aerial. I didn't know you were friends with him." She smiles, not at all concerned about the content of my reply.

"He's my personal trainer. Has been for several years. And he's my friend." I roll the word friend around and like how it sounds.

"Cool! So where are we going for dinner?" Her blue eyes seem to sparkle under the streetlight and the warm glow of the bakery behind her. Even at this hour, the place is packed to the gills with people picking up sweet treats to take home.

"Ah, I see my lamb is hungry for actual food, not just her man." I laugh and wink at her.

She hums in the back of her throat, and I swear my cock reacts with a punch to the front of my slacks.

"Oooh, both!" she admits freely and with exuberance, laying her hand flat on my chest and lifting for a kiss. The woman has not a care in the world about this thing between us, even though I could easily destroy her world as she knows it. Instead, she's honest and open with her feelings, happy to see me, and has no issue with showing it.

Another woman, a woman with a hidden agenda, would hide her desire, use it against me to get what she wants. Which is usually my money and the hope of becoming the first Mrs. Winters without the burden of a prenup.

Luna doesn't have a wicked nature or an ulterior motive. In the beginning, when she came to my office, sure. She was hoping to save her business, but I know with my entire being she's not *with me* in the hopes of saving herself or her friends. She's with me because she can't deny the connection between us, which is building stronger with each kiss, every touch, hell, every fucking breath we take.

I snuggle her against my side, enjoying her standing next

to me after a long day.

"I'm thinking Italian?"

She licks her lips. "I love pasta."

"What don't you love?" I chuckle, move her aside, and bleep the locks on my Aston Martin, opening the door for her to get in.

"Hmmm, I'll have to think about it."

Of course she would have to think about something she doesn't love. I swear the woman was put on this earth to spread joy and happiness. Everything she touches practically turns to gold. I know I feel richer in her presence, and that's not something I've felt since the day my mother left. She always made me feel special, loved, wanted. And then she left.

A knife-like pain digs into my heart as I walk around the car.

Would Luna just abandon me? The thought simmers inside my gut, growing, building, filling my stomach with acid. If I can't save her building or those of her friends in a professional capacity...what happens to us personally?

Would Luna leave me too?

CHAPTER TWELVE

CROWN
C H A K R A

The quality of awareness that comes with the
crown chakra is universal, transcendent.

L U N A

Grant went cold again, and I have no idea why. Before I got in the car he was fine. Joking, happy, smiling. Then, all of a sudden, he changed. His mood turned icy and his face rigid with tension.

The car is silent as he maneuvers through Berkeley and toward San Francisco.

"You live in the city?" I ask, trying to cut the tension in the car.

He nods but doesn't say anything.

I put my hand over his thigh and just leave it there, sharing my energy and my warmth, in the hope he'll work through whatever issue is plaguing him.

"Where do you see us going?" Grant says abruptly, his words devoid of any emotion.

"Uh, to an Italian restaurant?" I chuckle, and for a moment, his lips twitch. I rub his thigh. "What's wrong? You were happy a minute ago."

He places his hand over mine, lifts it to his mouth, and kisses each fingertip and then my palm before placing it back down over his thigh, where he continues to hold my hand.

His hand chakras start spinning, and I can feel our energy colliding, weaving together. I squeeze his hand in mine.

"I mean, where do you see us going in our relationship?"

A laugh bubbles up and slips out.

His eyes flash to mine, and they are serious as a heart attack. It's not at all the response, or the question, I'd expect from him. It's far too telling for a man like him.

"Big man, what has got you so fired up? You were fine a moment ago."

"I just...need to know where you think this is going. What future you think we have."

"Okay." I swallow the sudden dryness in my throat. "I hadn't exactly thought too far ahead since we've only been a couple for all of forty-eight hours."

He scowls. "Feels much longer to me."

I smile. "I like that."

His brows furrow. "You don't feel the same?"

"What is this all about? One moment I'm kissing you, packing a bag, and preparing to have yummy pasta and then even yummier sex, and now we're talking about the future?"

His features change, and his words are hard when he

responds. "Do. You. See. Me. In. Your. Future? It's a simple question." His jaw is tight, firm in a way that emphasizes my response means something to him. Something very important.

I think back to earlier today when I was teaching classes, and my mind would wander to Grant.

Sex with Grant.

Eating with Grant.

Holding hands with Grant.

Sexy yoga with Grant.

Laughing with Grant.

"Well, today I spent the day thinking of nothing but you and how much I wanted to be with you. How thankful I am that I've found a man who wants me."

He scoffs. "Every man *wants* you. You're gorgeous, innocent, have the most kissable lips, the prettiest eyes, and your body is made for sin. Besides, you're gorgeous."

"You already said gorgeous," I whisper.

"It was worth repeating twice," he deadpans.

A flurry of butterflies builds in my stomach at his admission. This time, I lift his hand and bring it to my lips. "I think you're gorgeous too. So handsome that every woman notices. Confident. Arrogant. And protective in a way that makes me feel safe. I see nothing but happiness in a possible future with you. As long as we're together, anything is possible. Don't you feel it?"

He swallows and closes his eyes for a mere second before focusing back on the road. The chilliness in the air seeps out, and the warmth resumes inside the car. His wood-and-spice scent permeates the air around me, and I want to cuddle in it. Breathe it in for eternity.

"Thank you." His words are coated in emotion, but I can't

place which one.

"For what?"

"Your honesty."

I grip his hand tighter. "I'll always be honest with you."

He glances at me, his eyes sad but with a renewed hope flickering behind them. "I'm counting on it."

★ ★ ★

Dinner tasted like sawdust on my tongue. Grant noticed within ten minutes of receiving our food that I was no longer in the mood to eat. I was set on pushing my food around the plate, waiting for him to share with me the reason behind the weird conversation in the car.

Why would he ask me about our future so soon?

We've only dated for a couple days. I guess you could say a little over a couple weeks if you counted the time since I walked into his office ready to battle it out.

As expected, Grant took charge, called for our bill, paid, and had me back in the car, racing toward his apartment. Which, not surprisingly, was in a skyscraper. The same skyscraper he apparently works in.

I cringe as we step into the elevator. "Why do you live where you work?" I ask him but continue to stare at the red numbers climbing up each floor as we pass it.

He leans toward my ear. "Funny question, seeing as you live above Sunflower Bakery, a half a breath from your own workplace."

I purse my lips. "You've got a point."

He chuckles, the first I've heard since we stood outside his car. "Come." The door opens to the same floor he works on.

The reception desk has a soft light above it.

"Why are we at your office?"

"Because that door"—he points to the opposite side of the room and a set of double doors—"is where I live."

"You literally live on the same floor as your office? I mean, yeah, I live close to Lotus House, which is convenient, very convenient since I don't have a car, but you actually live *in* your office. Blech. At least I get to walk the street a little, take in the smells and sounds of the outdoors, walk down to Rainy Day, the bookstore, or sit and chat with my friends in the bakery before I walk up a set of stairs that lead to my super-duper cool loft."

Grant loops his arm around my waist and clucks his tongue. "You shouldn't assume something isn't super-duper cool…" He whispers my words against my ear. A shiver ripples down my spine at his nearness and the seductive tone when he continues speaking against my skin. "Unless you've seen it with your own eyes."

He presses his hand to a panel next to the door. It scans his hand, turns green, and the lock clicks on the door.

"Okay, I gotta admit. That was way cool! Can I try it?"

He smiles. "You could, but it wouldn't open."

I frown.

"I'll have my security team for the building scan your hand and give you unlimited access to the building and my apartment."

"Really? That sounds suspiciously similar to giving one's girlfriend a key to his apartment," I taunt, thinking he'll laugh along with me.

He doesn't. Instead he stops at the threshold of his home and takes my coat from my arms. "That's precisely what I'm doing. And I shall expect a key to yours in return."

"Um, I'll have to ask Dara about that," I admit right off the bat, even though I know it's not what he wants to hear.

He presses his hand to my lower back to lead me into a totally different space. It looks nothing like an office building but a lush and open apartment.

"Wow." I glance around and notice the sunken-in living room, where a large black sectional couch sits atop a white carpet. No comfy throw pillows grace the couch. He could use those. Across the large space is the kitchen, black granite countertops, white cabinets, and gleaming silver appliances. Nothing of interest to be seen on the counters. No clutter or stacks of mail. The only thing I can find with color is a fruit bowl—which boasts a couple apples, a few bananas, and a couple oranges—on a gleaming glass kitchen table with mirrored legs.

"This is where you live?" I'm horrified by the lack of warmth. Everything is so cold and monochromatic. I mean, I've been to all my guy friends' apartments, and none of them were this austere. It makes me sad to see that he lives in a world so devoid of color. Heck, I look down at my purple leggings tucked into a pair of black suede boots. A tan tunic with a black leather belt wrapped twice around my waist, my wrists and neck filled with chunky multicolored beaded jewelry, and it slams into me... I'm the most colorful thing in this entire place.

He sighs and leads me to the kitchen. "Yes. Now why would you have to discuss giving your boyfriend a key with Dara?"

I can't help but glance around at the sheer nothingness surrounding me. It makes me want to take my clothes off and throw them on the floor just so I can see something vibrant in the room. "Um, yeah..." I lick my lips, still shocked by how he lives. "Dara owns the loft. The keys to the loft and the doors are the same as the bakery. Giving you a key to my apartment means giving you a key to her store. I don't know if she'd approve of that choice at this time."

Grant scowls, spins on a shiny black shoe, and goes to his wine fridge, where he pulls out a bottle of white wine.

"Wine?"

"Sure." Hell, just placing the yellow bottle on the counter would make me feel a bit cheerier.

"Why were you upset at dinner?" His tone is questioning, but I can hear the hint of unease.

I shrug. "Why were you so weird in the car?"

"I wasn't weird." He frowns.

"To me you were." I keep my tone low and unassuming. I don't want to push him, but in order for me to figure out how to help, how to understand him better, I need to know where these mood swings are coming from.

He waves a hand. "It doesn't matter now. I got over it after you agreed we had a future."

That is not at all what I said in the car, but I'm not going to fight with him since he's being open.

"I guess I was just surprised you were worried about it."

He opens a cabinet and brings down a pair of wineglasses. In the drawer near where he stands, he finds the corkscrew and sets about uncorking the wine.

"This may come as a surprise to you, but I do not have a lot of experience being in a relationship."

I grin. "No?" I say this sarcastically but with a playful edge.

He cocks an eyebrow and tugs out the cork. "I told you the

other night I was keeping you, and you said you were keeping me too. I just wanted make sure that hadn't changed."

"In a day?"

He cants his head and pours the wine. "When you say it like that, it sounds silly."

I smile wide and come around the counter and wrap my hands around his waist, tucking my face against his shoulder. "Because it is silly, my big man. Why do you continue to feel the need to place labels on our relationship? We've already agreed we're together. Is that not enough?"

He sighs and leans into the counter. "When it comes to you, I'm not sure simply being together will ever be enough. I want you too much."

I spin him around until I can plaster my body to his. He wraps his arms around me. "What do I have to do to prove you have me?" I run my hands down his chest and back up.

"I don't know. I guess I'm always going to be waiting for you to leave."

Slowly, and with my intention very obvious, I unbutton the first button of his shirt and then place a kiss to the open space. The second button receives the same treatment, and the third and fourth and fifth, until I've opened his shirt and untucked it from his waist.

I look up into his sapphire gaze and am floored with the heat I see burning there.

"Then I think I have some work to do, to show you how very..." I unbuckle his belt. "*Very...*" I undo his pants and unzip them. "*Very...*" I let his pants fall to his knees. "*Very* much I like being exactly where I am." I palm his large erection before pulling down his boxer briefs and sinking to my knees.

One of his hands instantly goes into my hair to pull it

away from my face. I know what he's doing because, during our sexfest the other day, I found out a tiny fact about Grant Winters. One that turns me on beyond all reason.

My man is a voyeur. He likes to watch me touch and taste him. Which works for me because I like his eyes on me and only me. They're like a gift bestowed onto me—one I'll never forsake.

I run my hands up his muscled thighs and scratch my way back down. He shifts, his large penis nearing my mouth, taunting me with its rich, musky scent. I close my eyes and nuzzle my nose at the base of his cock, letting his length rest against my cheek. I breathe him into my lungs, searing his scent on my memory.

"Christ, you really are my own personal fairy princess."

I grin and kiss the base of his penis, letting my lips drag along each inch, teasing with my tongue when I feel like it.

He closes his eyes but opens them right as I swirl my tongue around the plush tip. A drop of his arousal beads there, proving how much he desires me. His fingers tighten in my hair, but he doesn't move me. No, he holds my head with reverence, as if he's honored to have me on my knees about to worship him, when in reality, I'm the one who's blessed.

After flicking the tip, I suck the knobbed head, swirling my tongue around it with the added benefit of suction until he rocks his head back and groans fully and deeply. The sound ricochets straight into my body, sending the flames of arousal to flicker and spark along every one of my nerve endings. I squirm in my position, wanting to touch myself but remembering this is for him and him alone. This is me showing him my affection, my determination to be here with him and loving every second of it.

He moves one hand from my head, and he grips the counter, bracing his body to allow me to work. I inhale fully through my nose and then take him as deep as I can into my mouth. He's too big for me to take him all the way, but I do my best. As I reverse my position, I lay the flat of my tongue along his length to give him maximum pleasure while I suck hard. I know he likes it when I use more force, because his fingers dig into my scalp before he realizes his error and softens his touch.

What he doesn't see is that I like when he's more forceful with me. We have time. He'll figure it out as the days turn to weeks, and weeks turn to months, and months turn to years.

Grant's body arches as I take him in and out of my mouth, sucking with wild abandon.

"Jesus fuck, you're so damned good with your mouth." He hisses and pumps his hips, losing his inhibitions along with his reason.

I love every second of it. My chest tightens as heat builds between my thighs, throbbing and ready for him to take charge, but I'm determined to take him to the very end of his release.

I double up my efforts, cupping his balls and squeezing gently as I bob back and forth, fluttering my tongue along the sensitive underside, dipping my tongue into the little slit before repeating the process. When I get him as deep as I can go, I wrap my other hand around the base and jack him along with my movement.

"Lamb...oh, God. Fuck, Luna, I'm gonna blow." He humps my face, lost to his passion. My own desire swirls and fires through me as I suck and jack him, humming around his cock until he lets my hair go, grabs the counter behind him, thrusts his hips, and cries out. "Yes!"

Shots of his essence coat my tongue over and over, and I

swallow it all, working him down the same way he works me down when his head is between my thighs.

Eventually, he puts one of his hands on my head and runs his fingers through my hair. He cups my cheek as I give him one last goodbye suck to the sensitive tip. He trembles, and I smile sexily, letting his penis go. I lick my lips, making sure I've got all of him off me, and am shocked to see his manhood jerk, hardening once again.

My eyes must show my surprise as he bends over, lifts me up, and sets me on the counter. "You just gave me the best fucking head of my entire life." His eyes are swirling with surprise and intrigue.

I shrug and wipe at my lip with my thumb, even though there's nothing there. He grabs my thumb and sucks the digit into his mouth, swirling his tongue around it before letting me go.

"You didn't do that the other night."

"If I remember correctly, I barely got my mouth on you before you hauled me up and took me again. Besides, a girl's gotta have some surprises in her pocket to keep her man happy."

He curls one of his hands around my face and runs his thumb along my bottom lip. "Everything you do makes me happy."

I smile wide. "You're just saying that because you got a blow job."

He chuckles and dips forward to kiss me but instead speaks against my lips. "You think so?"

I wrap my arms around his shoulders and neck. "I hope so." I wink.

He shakes his head. "You have two choices to make right

now."

"Again with the choices. What is it with you and options?" I rub my forehead against his.

This time, he shrugs. "I don't know. Just work with me."

"I thought I just worked you." I smirk.

He closes his eyes. "Lamb, you are going to bring me to my knees."

"Yes, please," I admit, immediately imagining him returning the favor by going down on me in the kitchen.

Grant laughs, and his laughter feels good against my face.

"You can either let me return the favor, right here, right now, or you can allow me to fill your glass with wine. You can share a glass with me, and we can take a bath together in my large tub, where I will make you feel very good and clean...and then I'll return the favor in my bed."

I pucker my lips and tilt my head. "How big of a tub are we talking about?"

CHAPTER THIRTEEN

CROWN
CHAKRA

The crown chakra shares great knowledge,
deep understanding, inner wisdom, and embodies
liberation of the spirit and mind.

GRANT

"Huge," I answer, because the tub is ridiculous in size. It could fit two three-hundred-pound humans with room to spare.

"I don't have a bathtub," she murmurs, her lips close to mine, one of her hands tracing my face.

When I kiss her lips, she sighs. I love that about her. The way she loses herself the second my lips touch hers.

"I know."

She pouts. "You don't play fair."

"How do you figure?" I frown at the mere hint of her dissatisfaction.

"I was looking forward to you going down on me in the kitchen." Her pout turns into a beatific smile so wide I can see all of her teeth in their stunning white glory.

Pure fuckin' honesty. No bullshit. No lies. Just truth. All the time.

I love her.

The three words hit me so hard in the chest I have to grip my hands into fists and bite my tongue to not react by telling her right away. Love is such a foreign concept for me and not something I remember feeling in thirty years. Exactly thirty years. The last time being the day my mother left.

I back away from her body, and her arms fall to her sides. Without looking at her, I pull my pants up, leaving the button undone and the belt open. I run my hand through my hair and then over my chin, trying to think, to figure out what I'm supposed to do with this onslaught of feelings and emotions I don't fucking understand.

"Grant..." Her voice is thin, somewhat frightened.

Fuck, I didn't mean to scare her by moving away so quickly.

Knowing if she pushes me, I'm going to cave and say something I shouldn't before I've had the chance to think it over, I move back to her body, hold her beautiful face in my hands, and cover her mouth with my own so I can't speak. I can't say the words or tell her about the emotions bubbling up from my soul.

She wraps her arms around mine once again, and her focus is lost to passion. No longer is she worried about my sudden response. Easing her back down on the counter, I pull down her leggings and go to town on her sweet cunt. She tastes like heaven and smells like apples and spice. Nothing will ever be so sweet in my life...until the day she returns those three little words to me.

Only right now, it's too soon, so I'll gorge on her body and fill my heart and soul with more of her in the hopes that someday soon, she'll experience the same epiphany I have.

★ ★ ★

A full week of nothing but joy slips by as I spend my days working to handle the plans for the street Lotus House is on and my nights wooing a fairy princess.

I may sound like a fucking idiot, but my time with Luna has been magical. She's everything I could ever want in a woman. Honest, beautiful, energetic, humorous, sweet, and a tigress in the sack. She has zero qualms about telling me exactly what she wants in bed or going after it herself. The best part of sleeping with her is waking up next to her warm, fruity-smelling body.

Before sleeping beside Luna, I couldn't remember the last time I'd had a good night's sleep, and now I've had a week of it. Not only am I feeling at the top of my game at work, but my body and mind feel better. Then again, I've avoided my father and his cronies all week, which I'm sure has helped.

I park at the curb across from Lotus House and hop out of the car with a change of clothes and a garment bag, which includes a suit for tomorrow. It's easier for me to stay with Luna during the week since she doesn't have a vehicle and works where she lives. Even though that adds a twenty to thirty-minute commute to work for me, it's really a straight shot, and I enjoy the time to think about the day ahead before stepping out my door and being in my office. Besides, I genuinely enjoy being surrounded by Luna's things. She's eccentric, to say the least, but everything she owns and has in her space is comfortable. To sit on, look at, lean against. There are no hard edges. And her bed...by God. Her bed is definitely magical. I fall asleep instantly and don't wake with pains and aches in my neck and back.

Jogging across the street, I make my way into Lotus House.

I smell her melon scent the second I walk in. She's at the desk, her head tipped back with laughter. A man waves his hands in the air, telling her something funny.

She notices me and smiles wide. "Hey, big man. I've got someone I want you to meet."

"Do you now?" I pass the man without so much as a glance, my eyes on nothing but her. She has her red hair piled on top of her head, curls escaping in every direction, looking unbelievably adorable and utterly fuckable. A green tank offsets her white skin, making her glow under the track lighting.

I curve an arm around her waist and dip my head right to her neck, inhaling her lush scent where it's the most intense, breathing her in and letting go of my day. I place a series of kisses there as she laughs and pushes at my chest. I pull away and smile, looking down at her happy face. "You look beautiful."

She stands on her toes and kisses me, the man before her lost to her desire to touch me. The primitive male in me rejoices that she so easily forgets everything else around her when I enter a room. It's the exact same for me.

Finally, she pulls back with a hum, pats my chest, and glances over her shoulder, turning her body toward her friend.

"Nick Salerno, this is my boyfriend, Grant Winters. Nick

is teaching the class we're taking today."

I turn to the man and take him in. All of him. And there's a lot. The narrowed eyes, the furrowed brow, the tight jaw that should have been shaved days ago but probably makes the ladies swoon. His eyes are sea-green and shooting daggers my way. He crosses his arms over his chest, not seeming friendly in the slightest, more like an enforcer straight out of the Italian mafia.

"So you're the suit who's dating my girl Luna." His tone is threatening, and I don't much care for it.

"Nicky..." Luna starts, but I hold my hand up and ease in front of her, taking a protective stance.

"First and foremost, Luna is *my* girl. Second, I don't care for your tone."

"I don't care for your face," he fires back instantly with a scowl. "Smug." He looks me up and down in a second flat. "What makes you think you're good enough for my *friend* Luna here?"

At least he had the decency to correct himself on the friend part.

"I'm not good enough for her," I state matter-of-factly. "I suspect no man will ever be. I can only strive to be worthy of her affection." I say the words, meaning every single letter. I'm not, nor will I ever be good enough for her, but I don't care. She's mine anyway, and I'm going to do everything in my power to keep it that way. If it pisses off her friends, so be it. No man or woman is going to get in the way of what we're building together.

Nick's scowl turns into a sideways grin. "Good answer, bro." The man holds out a muscled arm, offering me his hand. "Nick Salerno. I'm the regular big brother around here. No one messes with the ladies of Lotus House under my watch. *Capiche?*"

I blink numbly at the change of demeanor and his now friendly gesture.

Luna nudges my shoulder. "He's trying to shake your hand, Grant. It would be wise to do so."

I shoot out my arm and take hold of his hand. He squeezes mine much harder than is necessary, but I don't back down, returning the force.

"I understand you're Honor Carmichael-Gannon's husband?" I state, attempting to make conversation and find a level ground with the man.

Wrong fucking thing to say.

Nick snarls. "*Salerno.*" He grinds through his teeth. "Honor Salerno. What do you know about my wife?" His tone is back to being threatening. Jesus Christ, this man goes hot and cold more than a heating and cooling unit.

"Not much, man. Although she came to visit me a little over a week ago."

"The fuck you say?" He growls. Fucking *growls*.

"Your wife, Honor, used to circulate in the same circles as my family. She came to visit me to see what she could do to assist in saving Lotus House and the businesses along this street."

Nick leans on the reception counter, his bulky frame and dark features taking on a rather menacing air. "You're the douchebag who's going to rip apart the street?" Then Nick points accusingly at Luna. "And you're with this joker?"

Luna rushes to interrupt. "Nick, you don't understand, and it's not any of your business."

"The fuck it is. This is your *home.* A home away from home

for a lot of us. Sunflower is where you lay your head and where Dara makes the world a little bit better through her sweetness. The bookstore, the café? Man, what the hell are you thinking?"

As Nick's voice rises, the door behind him opens, and a blond male and a girl-next-door-type brunette enter hand in hand.

"What's going on here?" the blond male says, the woman tight to his side.

Nick snarls but doesn't so much as turn around. He must know the man behind him, because he speaks his disdain freely. "Dash, this is the guy who's planning to destroy Lotus House and the street. And guess who he's conveniently dating...all of a sudden?" Nick's voice drips with suspicious accusation.

I shake my head. "Look, there is nothing nefarious going on here. Luna and I are together. A couple. There's nothing you or your friends can do about it. I am, however, working on a plan for the street. I can make no promises, nor have I promised anything to Luna."

"Is this true, Luna?" The blond man, whom I assume is Dash, clocks Luna with his gaze. The brunette sidles up to his side, a shiny wedding band on her finger. Probably his wife.

Luna hooks her arm around my waist. "Yeah, it is. We're together, and Grant is doing what he can to help us. He isn't single-handedly ruining everything. He's trying to make things better for us and continue the work his company, board of directors, and investors already planned out for the property. The entire street is owned by the Winters Group."

She takes a full breath and continues. "We rent. The downside to renting a building is that you could be asked to move at any time. For the last twenty or so years, we've been lucky. Very lucky to have affordable rent and allowed to keep our street the way it is. That could change...but we don't know the outcome." Her voice rises and falls with her irritation. "What I would suggest you do is not be so judgmental, Nick, in your instant dislike of someone who is also in a difficult position."

Nick's shoulders fall before my eyes, and Dash slaps him on the shoulder a few times. "You protectin' the women again, brother?"

Nick huffs. "It's what I do."

The brunette looks me up and down. "He doesn't look that threatening to me. And the way he's holding on to our Luna shows he's definitely into her. Plus"—her green cat-like eyes meet mine—"he's very attractive."

Dash gives me the once-over. "Yeah, Luna baby, it looks like you caught yourself a live one." Dash holds out his hand. "Dash Alexander. I teach Tantric Yoga here. This is my wife, Amber."

Her cheeks pinken as she waves, glancing between Luna and me with a big smile on her face. "We'll have to do dinner," she offers rather shyly.

"What my wife means is, I'll have to cook dinner or we'll meet you out. *Dr. Alexander* thinks she has this open schedule, when in reality, I rarely see her." He chuckles and hooks his arm around her, kissing her temple.

Amber smacks his chest. "Hey, I try, but the kids need me at the hospital."

"Little bird, how am I ever going to plant *my kid* into you if you're never home?"

Luna's arm locks around my waist. "Are you guys trying to get pregnant?" Her voice is filled with excitement.

Amber nods, and Dash smiles.

"Finally! Jesus, Mary, and Joseph! It's only been forever since you two hooked up!" Nick claps, once more turning into a friendly guy by hugging Dash and patting him roughly on the back and then pulling Amber into his arms, lifting her off her feet. "I'm trying to get Honor to agree to another baby too. She's leery about taking time away from the twins. Besides me, they're her entire world and she dotes on her boys." His chest lifts with pride.

"Let me down, Nicky," Amber scolds, but Dash just looks on with amusement at the mafia guy man-handling his wife. They do seem to be a close-knit group. "And you shouldn't be spreading that info around the family, Dash. You'll get their hopes up, and we just started."

"Like I said, if you'd work a tad less, I'd have you pregnant in no time." He smirks.

She sighs and looks up at the ceiling. "Lord, please help me with this man."

"Well, I'm stoked for you guys. I can't wait to tell Honor. She'll be thrilled," Nick puts in.

"Seems like something's in the water around here." Luna grins. "First Genevieve, then Mila, and now possibly the two of you adding to your clans. So much to be excited about."

I lock my arm around Luna and imagine her telling her friends she's carrying *my* child. The idea is not unwelcome. If she was the mother of my children, they'd be perfect. Hopefully, just like her.

Dash cups Nick's shoulder and glances back to the two of us. "I think you owe someone an apology for being a bit overprotective."

Nick winces and cracks his neck before focusing on the two of us. "I'm sorry, Luna. Grant. I'm a little high-strung about this issue with the street, and Luna's happiness and well-being is important to me. To all of us." He looks at Dash and Amber, who both nod in agreement. "I shouldn't have gone off all half-cocked. I tell you what... Do you box?"

I'm trying to keep up with the conversation. "As in fight?" I wasn't sure I should answer that type of question.

"Yeah, man." He proceeds to show me a one-two punch and fast feet.

"Uh, no. I have a personal trainer. Your friend Clayton Hart, as a matter of fact."

Nick's eyes widen. "You're friends with Clay? Shoot, man, if you'd told me that, I wouldn't have been so hard on you. Clay's a great judge of character."

On this we can agree. "He is. And a great friend too." I make the statement with confidence because Clayton and I have been building our friendship.

"Well, if you don't box or need a gym membership, I'll bring Luna a case of my family's wine. You drink wine?"

"Yes, but you really needn't worry. I'm happy Luna has men around her who care to protect her best interests."

Nick shakes his head. "Nah, man, my bad. I was harsh, and I'm man enough to admit it. I'll bring a case by, yeah?" He directs the question to Luna.

"That would be lovely, Nicky. You know how much I enjoy your family's wine."

"Doesn't everyone?" He chuckles and glances up at the clock. "Need to get hoppin'. My class starts in ten, and I want to make sure the silks are locked in tight." He puts his hand out toward me again. "We cool, brotha?"

I nod. "Yeah, I... We're cool." I shake his hand and notice his grip isn't nearly as firm as it was before.

"Rockin'. Dash." He squeezes the man's bicep. "Amber. Get on that baby-making. I want a little Alexander running around with my boys soon."

The Alexanders both smile and agree to try.

"Trying's part of the fun." He winks and enters the hallway toward the classes.

Amber and Dash head in the same direction after waving goodbye to Luna and me.

"That was strange," I murmur.

Luna plants her head on my chest. "It was. I'm sorry. Nick is like a big brother, and I'm pissed he was such a..."

"Dick?" I offer. "Cad?" I continue. "Overbearing brute?" I finish.

Her shoulders slump, and she rubs her nose against my chest before resting her chin and looking up. "At least he admitted he was wrong."

I wrap my arms around her and hug her close. "That he did. Though I no longer have a desire to take his class. Early dinner instead?"

Her eyes go half-mast. "Food isn't always going to get me to do what you want," she threatens, but it's one hundred percent empty. Food always gets her to see my way.

"Mmm-hmm. What are you in the mood for?"

"Thai!" she exclaims like it's the best food on God's green earth. I swear, if I didn't know how good she is at being a yoga teacher, I'd suggest she start culinary school. The woman is obsessed with her meals.

I chuckle. "My lamb wants Thai, she gets Thai. I know a great place not far from here, just on the edge of the city."

"Do I need to change?" She gestures down to her plain black yoga pants and green tank. "I've got boots and a sweater

I can grab too."

"Then you're fine. Besides, I love your ass in yoga pants."

She snorts and bends over, gifting me an awesome view of said ass as she grabs her purse and sweater hanging over the back of the chair. "Every man likes a woman's ass in a pair of yoga pants. That's why they are so versatile."

She's got a solid point. All of the women I've seen here at the studio, whether bigger or smaller than my woman, all looked good in their yoga pants. It's quite the phenomenon.

"This is true, but your ass"—I palm it as I lead her out of the studio—"is exceptionally fantastic."

"Says the man who has to love it because he's not getting anyone else's." She sways her ass while walking to my car.

"With zero complaints on all fronts," I assure her.

She grins and hops into the car before I can make it around to open the door for her.

I sigh, get in, and buckle up.

★ ★ ★

The Thai restaurant is one of my favorites, and the owner and staff know me. This secures us an excellent table by the window with a full view of the restaurant.

We place our order for spring rolls to share and pad thai for Luna, because the woman eats everything whether it's healthy or not and doesn't gain a pound, at least not that I've seen since we met. I order the chicken in coconut soup and a round of Mekhongs over ice.

"What is this drink?" Luna sips the amber liquor and tilts her head as if deciding whether or not she likes it.

"It's a Thai whiskey."

Her blue eyes seem to widen as she takes another taste. "It tastes like rum."

I smile in approval. "It does. Spicy and sweet, with hints of ginger and honey, vanilla, and floral notes." I take a swallow myself, appreciating the distinct taste along with the familiar warmth the whiskey brings. "The most interesting fact about this particular whiskey, besides not tasting like whiskey"—I chuckle—"is that it's made with about five percent rice."

Luna purses her lips. "That is neat. I like it."

"You like everything," I tease and then lean over, steal one of her spring rolls, and take a big bite out of it before putting it back.

"Hey!" She smacks my hand, grinning.

"Sharing is caring." I laugh out loud but feel a prickling on the back of my neck. To the left of us is a table with a couple. A pretty brunette with dark-blue eyes is staring at me.

I glance back to Luna and continue poking fun at her, trying to steal her noodles from her pad thai and enjoying her snark when she pretends to be mad at me.

Once more I feel the tingle at the base of my neck and look over at the couple to find that this time, both of their eyes are on us. The man has dark-brown hair and brown eyes. I don't recognize him at all, but from the way they are staring, they recognize me. This is not unknown to happen because of the many events and circles I work in for business, but it's incredibly rude of them to keep staring.

I frown and suck back a gulp of my drink, trying to ignore them.

"What's the matter, big man? You got caught stealing and you're pouting. Don't worry... Punishment won't be too harsh. I'm thinking a couple orgasms tonight ought to free you from your troubles." She smiles wickedly, and I lay my hand over hers.

"Duly noted, and the punishment absolutely fits the crime." I wink. "What's strange, though, is that couple keeps staring at me. First it was the woman, and now it's both of them."

Luna's smile is heartwarming as she squeezes my hand. "Grant, honey, you're hot. As in, women everywhere you go want to have sex with you. No-questions-asked kind of hot. Then they see you with me, you in a suit and me in workout attire, and they stare, thinking maybe they have a chance. They don't, but I can hardly blame them." She tags more noodles with her fork and spins it like spaghetti before shoving it in her mouth.

I shake my head. Leave it to Luna to compliment me while I'm feeling uncomfortable. "Lamb, that's very sweet... and incorrect. Any woman within a ten-mile radius can see that I'm taken by my own personal fairy princess. They would never stand a chance against your beauty. Or your body. Or how insanely good you are in the sack." I wink and grin.

"Aw, words of love to live by," she jokes, and I snap my teeth in jest.

"Only that's not it. Look to your right in a few moments and see if they are still staring."

She giggles and covers her mouth. "That's so silly."

"Just do it. For me."

She rolls her eyes and nods. I sip at my drink and stare at her face and then bug my eyes so she'll make her move. I watch as she raises her hands in the air, stretching and yawning as if she's tired, before turning her head to the side.

Subtle.

Not.

I can't help but laugh at her cuteness.

Her expression is serious when she turns back around. I glance over to find the woman still staring and not even trying to hide it.

"They totally *are* staring!" she whispers. "What are you going to do?"

I stand up and set my napkin on the table. "Confront them, of course."

"Grant..."

I walk the twenty or so feet over to the couple's table, and neither one of them hide their curiosity at my approach. They were caught several times and are owning up to it right away.

"Can I help you?" I ask, tucking my hands in to my pockets.

"Um...no." The woman glances down and back up. Her blue eyes are red-rimmed, as if she'd been crying or was really tired. Her skin tone even looks a little ashy up close. Not someone I recall.

"We know you," she states. "Well, we know *of* you." Her voice shakes, and it sounds familiar, kind of like a long-lost memory, but I'm not sure why. Her face, bone structure, and the color of her eyes offer a glimmer of something, as if I've seen them before.

"Through work or my professional contacts?" I assume.

She shakes her head but doesn't respond. The man with her stands and holds out his hand. "Not exactly, no," the man answers flatly before introducing himself. "Brett Tinsley, and this is my wife, Greta."

I shake his hand and then hold my hand out to her. The woman licks her lips and stands, offering me her hand. She's carrying extra weight in the midsection, almost as if she could be pregnant, but I wouldn't dare ask. That's one lesson my father did teach me. Never ask if a woman is pregnant. Ever.

The minute my palm touches Greta's, I feel a bolt of electricity zip up my arm. It's not painful, just unusual. Warm. Comfortable, even.

"Grant Winters." I feel Luna come up behind me and touch the small of my back. "This is my girlfriend, Luna Marigold. How did you say you know me again?"

"It's okay, sweetheart. Go on. You said you would if you saw him again. Now's your chance," Brett urges vaguely, his eyes on his wife's.

"You would do what?" I question, feeling that weird prickle stabbing at my neck, a deeper sense of foreboding coming over me.

Luna must sense my mood, because she moves closer to my side so I can wrap my arm around her, her hand coming to rest on my stomach as if she's lending support.

"I promised I would introduce myself to you." Greta's voice is shaky when she speaks.

"I'm not exactly following. You said you know of me. How?" I repeat, tendrils of irritation starting to weave their way through my mind at the oddity of this greeting.

"Well, you see...um..." She pushes a lock of hair behind her ear.

"Yes?" I urge.

"We have the same mother."

Those words are quite possibly the last thing I could have ever, even in my wildest dreams, imagined would come out of this woman's mouth.

"I'm sorry." A fire burns in my gut instantly. "What the fuck did you say?" My tone is harsh and demanding an answer.

Brett moves around the table and pulls his wife back to his front. A protective gesture if I ever saw one.

"Gretchen Winters is my mother too."

CHAPTER FOURTEEN

CROWN
C H A K R A

When a person is closed-minded, they may
have a blocked crown chakra.

L U N A

Oh snap. This cannot be good. Grant had already made it known to me he was an only child and his mom had abandoned him. He hasn't shared his thoughts on this tragedy or told the tale of what happened. And here a woman stands, claiming to be his...sister.

I rub my hand up and down Grant's back as his entire body goes ramrod straight.

"I don't know who you are or what kind of game you're trying to play, lady, but you're not getting a dime out of me." He points his finger at her, and she cringes.

Her husband's eyebrows rise up toward his hairline, and shock blankets his features.

"Um, Grant, maybe you should try to talk about this..." I attempt.

He scoffs. "There's nothing to talk about. People have tried to blackmail me before. It happens in my position. You should be ashamed of yourself."

"I'm not lying!" Greta chokes out on a half sob.

Brett holds her in his arms. "You don't know what you're saying. We're not trying to blackmail you." He sneers. "We don't want anything from you or your dickwad father. Bunch of scumbags, the whole lot of you." He shakes his head as he pulls a now fully crying woman into his arms.

Grant's head jerks back, and then an eerie calmness overcomes him. "Right. Gotcha. Have a nice dinner. Luna, we're out of here."

He turns on his heel, pulls out a stack of twenties, and tosses them on the table. Far more than enough for our meal and drinks.

"I don't know what to say. He obviously didn't know about you."

"No, he wouldn't. But we know *everything* about him." Greta looks out the window, her eyes following Grant as he storms to the car.

I make a split-second decision. "Do you have a card? I'll talk to him. Perhaps I can have him reach out when he's digested this information. You see, his mom is a hot-button item for him. She abandoned him..."

"Yeah, when she was pregnant with me. A baby not created through love or the man she was married to."

Oh, yowzers. This is not good. Not good at all. "Uh, the

card?"

I rush back to the table, grab my purse, pull out a free yoga session card, and hand it to her. "It's the only thing I have with my information on it." I smile and hear a double honk coming from Grant's Aston Martin.

Greta hands me a card from her purse with a shaking hand. "I've never wanted anything from Grant, other than to know my brother. Please tell him that for me."

I nod and stop, at a loss for words. "It will be okay. Eventually."

"Eventually," she repeats. "Thanks for trying, Luna."

"Yeah, bye." I wave and rush out the restaurant, around the building, and to Grant's car. The second I get in, he backs out and stops abruptly.

"Seat belt," he grates through his teeth, as if he's seconds away from losing his mind.

I stop, get out of the car, and walk around to the driver's-side door.

He pushes open the door. "Luna, what the fuck! Get in the car."

"Get out. I'm driving. You are in no state." I cross my arms, prepared to wait it out if I have to.

"I am perfectly capable of driving my goddamned car, with my goddamned woman sitting in the passenger seat where she belongs."

I shake my head. "Nope. Not happening, buster." I open my palm and close it, gesturing for him to give me the keys.

His eyes are like ice daggers ready to strike at any moment as he stares at me. "You're not going to let this go, are you?"

With a firm shake of my head, I respond, "'Fraid not. We protect each other. That's what you do when you're in a relationship with someone you care about."

He curses under his breath and maneuvers his big body out of the car, takes a wide berth around me, and then gets into the passenger seat.

I get into the car, adjust the mirrors, and move the seat up a half a foot.

He huffs and sighs as I put the car in drive and head out of the lot. "Do you want me to take you to your apartment tonight?"

"No."

"I could give you some space, let you sleep in your own bed?"

"My bed sucks," he snarls.

I nibble on my bottom lip and head toward my loft. "Okay, will you talk to me about what happened in there?"

"You heard what happened. Some nutjob thinks she's my sister and probably wants a free ride on the Winters' money train. Won't be the first time someone's attempted something outlandish."

For a minute, I allow myself time to think about how I want to respond. He's upset, possibly even angry, and downright hurt. Anything regarding his mother is a sore spot for him, but he's got to talk about it.

"Can you tell me about your mom?"

He sighs and puts his fingers to his forehead. "Not much to tell. We were a happy family. At least in my five-year-old brain we were. I honestly don't remember much about her now. Just that she had beautiful red hair"—he turns in his seat and fingers one of my curls—"like yours but much darker. Maybe more auburn, whereas you're far more copper colored."

I enjoy the attention he pays to my hair, has always paid

to my hair, and maybe I know a bit more now about why he adores it. Because his mom was a redhead. He hinted at it at the charity dinner when he bickered with his father, but he never confirmed anything one way or the other.

"She also has light eyes. Same color as mine."

"Same color as Greta's," I toss out to see where it lands.

"Her eye and hair color did not escape my notice, lamb. That does not make her my half sister."

"No, no it doesn't. Continue with your mom."

He groans. "I don't know. One day she was there, and life was good, and the next she was kissing me goodbye, told me she'd always love me and would write to me."

"Did she?"

"Not one letter."

"What did your father say?"

He shrugs. "At first, that Mommy went away. Later, as I got older and demanded more information, he said she'd abandoned us. Just up and left, never to return."

"That's it? He didn't try to find her, with all his riches?"

Grant lays a warm hand on my thigh. "Lamb, when someone doesn't want to be with you, leaves you and your five-year-old child..." He shakes his head. "I get why he didn't chase after her."

"What about you?" My heart hurts as he squeezes my thigh, his fingers digging in, as if he's anchoring himself to me.

"What about me?"

"Did you chase after her? Um, later, when you were, you know"—I wave my hand in the air—"master of your own domain and all that jazz."

Grant inhales, long and deep, as if the weight of the entire world was just laid upon his shoulders. "No, I didn't."

Without being accusatory, I gentle my words but know I need to ask the question in order to get to his frame of mind. "Do you mind if I ask your thoughts on why you came to that decision?"

He licks his lips, and I put my hand over his on my thigh in a show of support.

"I thought about it. A hundred times over. I came to the same conclusion each and every time."

"Which was?"

"If she didn't want me at five years old, she most certainly wouldn't want me at twenty or twenty-five or thirty or even thirty-five."

"Honey, you don't know that."

"Lamb, nothing has changed in my world. My father still lives in the same house he brought my mother home to when they married. The same home they brought me home to a year later. I lived in that house my entire life, until college, but he still lives there. If she wanted to reach out, she could have a million times. She chose not to. We didn't leave her. She left us."

"Fair enough." And it was. He made a solid point. Why go chasing after someone who didn't want you? Still, it begs the question, what about Greta? The second I laid eyes on the woman, it was like looking at a female version of Grant, only...well...female. There were other subtle differences. Her skin was really pale, almost ashy. Her nose a bit smaller, more rounded, perhaps like Gretchen, Grant's mother.

"Can I ask you another question?"

"You can ask me anything, lamb." This time he turns his hand over so our fingers can interlace and our palms touch. He lifts my hand to his mouth and presses it to his lips, staring out at the traffic on the freeway as we glide back toward Berkeley.

"What if she is your sister?"

His jaw firms, and he kisses my hand.

"When you stormed out, I got my purse, and we exchanged business cards. Just in case." He moves to speak, to chastise me, but I rush my words so he can't. "I had to. At the very least, if she is your sister, you'll want to know, right?"

"Of course. I just... I can't believe it. Why wouldn't I know of her existence, but she knew of mine?"

"She said your mother was pregnant with another man's child when she left you."

He snorts. "What else?"

"I didn't get much, but she said she knows everything about you."

"Yeah, I'll just bet. How much money my company brings in..."

I clear my throat. "I didn't get that impression. She seemed genuine. Made it sound like she'd been watching you, or at the very least following your life, for a long time. I don't know... It's worth investigating."

"You got her card? We know their names, Greta and Brett Tinsley. I'll have my security officer look into her first thing tomorrow."

"That's a good plan." I smile. "It would be nice to find out you have a sister."

He sighs and looks out the window once more. "Yeah, I guess. I don't know...maybe."

"Family is everything," I whisper.

Grant squeezes my hand. "Not mine. Though the one I one day want to make with you...yes. That will be the day family is everything."

A rush of happiness coated in this dreary mood has me blinking back the tears and focusing on the road.

I love you.

In my head the words are so clear, but now is not the time to share them.

★ ★ ★

A full week passes before Grant brings up his possible sister. He tosses his jacket on his boring couch, and it instantly disappears, the black blazer on the black couch.

He moves mindlessly into the kitchen, releasing the buttons at his cuffs and rolling his sleeves up his forearms. I can hear him pulling out wineglasses and the distinct sound of him searching through the bottles in his wine fridge.

"White or red tonight?"

"I'm feeling red this evening. There was a chill in the air today."

I go over to my two bags, both of which he didn't utter a word about. Which is awesome because I pull out some of the loot I bought him at the thrift store. Four new throw pillows, two a sunshine yellow, two a muted yellow, gray, and white. The multicolored ones have a pattern of arrows running in vertical lines. As I suspected, they look fantastic on his pristine couch, but they also add a touch of color. I have a bunch more colors to add before I'm done.

"What does a chill in the air have to do with red versus white wine?" he hollers from the other room.

"When it's warm out, I prefer white. It's cool and refreshing. If it's colder out, a warm red just feels better going down the throat and into the tummy."

Grant enters the room as I'm arranging the pillows. He hands me a glass of red. I toast his glass, but he looks away.

"Wait!"

He turns around abruptly as if I'd just screamed. I mean, I kind of did.

"You have to look me in the eye when you 'cheers' me before sipping, or you'll have seven years of bad sex."

He chuckles and eases into the white leather lounge chair about to lift the glass to his lips.

I frown.

"You know that's absurd, don't you?"

"You want to risk it?"

His eyes shift to half-mast. "*Touché*," he says before holding out his glass.

I touch the edge and listen to it sing and then lift it to my lips while my eyes are focused on him. "You were about to tell me what you found out about Greta Tinsley?" I turn for my bag and pull out a chenille throw in a masculine hound's-tooth print of red and black. Once I've shaken it out, I lay it over the back, folded neatly but lengthways so that it adds some color to the boring couch.

Grant watches me work but doesn't comment.

"Greta?" I urge, going back to my bag and riffling through it to find yellow, red, and white vases in varying sizes and a gray, leaf-shaped bowl.

"Oh, well, her birth certificate was verified. She is my mother's daughter."

"And how can they confirm that?" I place the leaf-shaped bowl in the center of the glass table, dig through my bag, and pull out a variety of circular decorative balls. A couple of them are like twine, another speckled black glass, a mirrored one, and a couple yellow paisley ones to offset the throws.

"Social security numbers match both mine and Greta's birth certificates for the birth mother of record. The father's name on her birth certificate was blank."

"Either way, she's your sister," I confirm, grabbing the three vases and putting them on one corner of the boring, plain white marble fireplace mantle that matches the white boring walls. I adjust them until they are in size order, the tallest being farthest from the edge.

"Appears so." He takes a long sip of his wine as I go back to my other bag and dig through to find the stained-glass candle holder I had at home. I was sure it would look way better at his place. It's a variety of red tones and absolutely stunning. I set it on the other side of the mantle, back up, and survey my work.

"What are you going to do?" I ask, trying not to make a big deal out of it, even though it has to be destroying him on the inside.

Back to my bag, I pull out the last item I brought to liven up the place, at least for now. It's a photo of the two of us, taken at the charity event we first attended. Technically, our first date. Also, the first night we slept together. Even though we just slept.

A photo of us appeared in the Sunday newspaper, and one of the yogis brought it to my attention. Me being a dork, I contacted the newspaper, hunted down the reporter, and had him send me the picture. He did, and now we both have one. Of course, he doesn't know that, but I like knowing he has a piece of me in his home. A piece of us.

"I don't know. Can you sit down? Besides, what are you doing?" He finally looks at the pillows, the coffee table, and the mantle. He stands and walks over to where I'd just set the picture of us in the center of the mantle, the lights above providing the perfect illumination.

"Do you like it?" I hold my hands at heart center, hoping and praying I haven't overstepped his boundaries.

"Like?" His voice is low and gravely.

"Yeah."

He turns around with a smile. "I fuckin' love it." He sets his glass on the coffee table and pulls me into his arms, where he kisses me breathless. "Feel free to spruce up the entire place."

"You mean you noticed you have no color in your life?" I chuckle and trace a line with my finger, starting at his forehead and along the bridge of his nose to his lips.

"Not until you showed up, no. Now, I've got all the color I need...in you."

I grin and kiss him silly, giving back as good as I get. When I pull away, I hold on to his face. "Really, though, what are you going to do about Greta?"

"Call her into my office. Talk to her. Hell, I'm not sure how to go about this."

"Are you going to tell your father?"

"Fuck no!" he says harshly.

"Okay, well, whatever you need from me, I'm there. If you'd like me to sit in, I'd be happy to. If you want to meet her out, maybe for a meal, or have her over here, and I'll cook. Whatever you want to do."

"You would do all that for me?" he whispers, his eyes misting over as he swallows.

"I'd do anything for you. I love..."

"You love?" He cocks an eyebrow.

I lick my lips and chance a glance at the now pretty mantle. He moves my chin with his thumb. "Oh no, you don't. Eyes on me. You love what, lamb?"

"These pillows?"

He grins.

"The centerpiece?"

Grant tips his head sexily, lasering me with his gaze. "I don't think that's what you were going to say," he teases.

"The mantle with the sexy picture of me and my man?"

He hums. "It is awesome, I will admit." He taps against my mouth with one finger. "However, I do not believe that was what you were going to say. Just tell me..." he murmurs against my lips, his tone almost pleading.

"I love...."

"Yes. You love..." he reiterates.

"Grant." I squirm in his arms. "I'm afraid," I whisper against his mouth, my eyes closed so I don't have to look into his eyes.

What if he doesn't love me back?

"Be brave, lamb. I'm right here with you. I won't let you down."

His words pierce the fear inside my soul, and I open my eyes. I focus on his sapphire gaze, eyes I could happily swim in for days on end.

"I love you."

He smiles huge. I'm talking super-duper ginormously wide. His entire face lights up as he runs his hands down my back, over my ass, and lifts me up so I have to circle my legs around him, and we're nose-to-nose.

"I've been dying to hear you say those words," he admits dreamily, as if I'd stunned him.

"Why?" I nuzzle his nose and kiss the tip.

"Can't you see, Luna? I've been in love with you since you uttered your name the very first time I laid eyes on you."

CHAPTER FIFTEEN

CROWN
C H A K R A

*Meditation is the cornerstone of bringing a mental
and physical balance to your crown chakra. Taking
a meditation class can help you feel more at peace,
open-minded, better rested, and less stressed.*

GRANT

I have a sister. A flesh-and-blood living relative beyond my
narcissistic tyrant of a father. The thought of having actual
family shreds my insides. She may have been pretty, seemingly
nice, but I don't know much about her. There's also the little
issue of my mother. Is she around? Does she live in the area?
The mere inkling of that particular possibility has my already
tender stomach tightening like a vice. I flip the business card
for Greta Tinsley over and over in my hand, reading it for the

hundredth time.

Greta Tinsley
Pediatric Occupational Therapist
UC Davis

My sister works with children as an occupational therapist. A woman like that would have her own money, and there hasn't been any further request for contact or money of any kind. Neither Brett nor Greta have reached out to me in the past week since our random meeting at the Thai restaurant.

Was it even random, or do they know what my usual haunts are?

Did they follow us there?

I shake my head. If I remember correctly, they were already seated when we walked in. God, I hate that I'm so suspicious, but my father trained me to be.

Everyone wants something out of you, son. Never trust anyone. People are always looking for an angle.

What I should have been asking my father back then was what was his angle? Training a tyrant. His replacement in the Winters Group. A man who could be as ruthless as he is. Only, I don't think I've succumbed to his teachings. At least not completely. And now, Luna's influence is making sure of that.

Thinking of my beautiful redheaded fairy princess, I rustle up the courage to pick up the phone and dial Greta's number. It rings several times before I receive her voicemail.

I consider hanging up but decide it might be best to force her to reach out to me directly.

"Greta, this is Grant Winters. I've confirmed the information you stated is correct. You are my sister." My voice cracks, and I clear it. "If you'd like to meet up to discuss,

I have many questions I hope you can answer. I will say, I'm sorry I was rude the other day. I'd like to make it up to you with coffee or a meal of your choosing. Please contact me if you are interested. I look forward to hearing from you."

With nothing left to say, I hang up, leaving the ball in her court.

A restless energy sizzles at the tips of my fingers and toes, so I pull out my cell phone and text Luna.

It's done.

She'll know what I mean when she sees the message. I glance at the clock and figure she should be between classes right now.

Her message pops up right away.

Did you talk to her? Set up a time to meet?
Are you okay?

I smile and inhale a full breath. My lamb is worried about me. It's a new feeling to know that someone else *genuinely* cares about my feelings and how I'm faring with contacting my estranged half sister. It sure makes the days easier to face, and the nights... Well, the nights are fantastic. Falling asleep next to her is unlike anything I've ever experienced before. It's chocolate-covered strawberries and whipped cream all together wrapped in the most comfortable bed in existence. When I figure out a way to get her to move in with me, we're taking her bed. Period. No discussion necessary. I answer her message before glancing back out at the skyline. I really do have an incredible view, but nothing is as stunning as Luna's face and looking into her blue eyes.

Left a voicemail.

Good. Ball's in her court. Come to the studio dressed to take a class. Tonight, we're doing a special meditation class. I think you could use it.

Already worked out today. Dinner? Pasta. Pizza. Sushi.

Fucking meditation. She's crazy if she thinks I'm going to meditate. Instead, I'll appeal to her stomach. It's usually the easiest way to get her to do what I want. Offer to feed her, and she falls all over herself ready to eat.

Good thing meditation is a workout for your MIND and not your BODY. And it's my turn. Stop trying to distract me with food.

Before I can respond, another bubble pops up.

Pizza. Definitely pizza AFTER meditation.

Damn it. Why does she have to be so damn cute? I can never deny her. I respond that I'll meet her there at six p.m. and head over to my home across the office to change clothes and grab a suit for tomorrow.

★ ★ ★

Luna isn't at the front desk when I arrive, so I use my key card to get in and walk down the hallway. The artwork is truly incredible. It's going to be rough knowing it will all be demolished when we rebuild the towers. I just hope Brando can come up with something that not only saves my girlfriend's business location but also saves my ass with my girlfriend. I love her too much to see her hurt, and I know her legacy means the world to her.

As I'm thinking of my girl, she pokes her head out the last door at the end of the hallway.

"There you are," I say.

She waves and smiles.

I'd walk a thousand miles if her smiling face was at the end of the journey.

"I'm glad you're early." She lifts her hands in front of her in a placating gesture. "Okay, this had to happen, and I'm sorry if you feel as though I'm dumping this on you, but she's my best friend in the whole wide world, and I can't bear to have the two of you not friendly. You both mean so much to me."

I frown, and my hackles rise. "Spit it out, lamb."

She tilts her head and worries her bottom lip. "Dara is the meditation teacher. But don't worry, I've already talked to her and smoothed the way. Trust me on this. Please?" She lays her hands against my chest and looks up at me pleadingly.

I curl a hand around her nape. "I trust you with anything. I just hope you're right and this goes as you wish."

She grins, lifts up on her toes, and kisses me hard but, unfortunately, closed-mouthed. She pulls away before I have the chance to deepen the kiss. Her hand wraps around mine, and she leads me inside.

There's a couple bickering to my right, and I realize one of them is Trent Fox. Second time I'm seeing him at the studio. A thrill of excitement at seeing my favorite baseball player once again fills my chest. I squeeze Luna's hand and dip my head to hers.

"I knew you knew Trent from when I took your class, but you *really* know Trent Fox. Why are we not doing dinner with him?" I'm absolutely thrilled with the possibility that I could break bread with the celebrity.

Luna chuckles. "I had no idea you were so interested in baseball."

I level a playful glare at her. "Lamb, most men are. Especially if you live in the Bay Area. You're either a Ports fan or a Stingers fan. Even though I work in the city, I'm all about the Oakland Ports."

"Huh. You just didn't seem like the sports type. I haven't watched any baseball games with you."

I chuckle. "No, because I've been spending all of my free time with you. When I'm in your presence, I don't want to be distracted by my favorite sport."

She frowns. "I like sports. I don't know much about them, but you could teach me."

"Deal." I wink.

"At the very least, I can surely share my friends with you." She grabs my hand and tugs me over to the couple.

Trent has his big paw on a tiny blond woman's rounded belly. "I mean it, gumdrop. No more vinyasa flow for you. I'm talking to Luna and Mila. You're hitting five months. No more. Promise me."

The pretty blonde purses her bright-red lips. Add her dark eyes and she's a doppelganger to music artist Gwen Stefani. She moves her hands to her hips. "I'm fine, Trent. *Pregnant*, not sick. Remember!" She groans and then turns her head, noticing us. "Hey, Luna. Can you talk some sense into this brute? He thinks I should stop doing Vin Flow because I've hit the five-month mark with our daughter."

Luna gasps. "Sweet Shiva! You're having a girl!" She claps and then rushes to hug the blonde.

"Hey, man, I remember you." Trent holds out his hand, and I shake it, smiling. "We took a class together not long ago. How goes it?"

"Good, good. Grant Winters. I'm Luna's boyfriend."

His eyes widen. "Yeah? Cool. Trent Fox, and the gushing, frustrating, gorgeous preggo is my wife, Genevieve. Viv for short."

Genevieve backs away from Luna and wipes at her suddenly teary eyes. "I know. I thought for sure his testosterone would overcome any possibility, but nope, we're having a girl."

"Already bought a shotgun." Trent lifts his chest with pride.

I chuckle, knowing what he means.

Luna frowns and shakes it off. "Genevieve, this is Grant Winters, my boyfriend."

I shake her hand. "Congratulations." I don't know what else to say.

"Thank you. Now, back to the matter at hand..."

"Red, please knock some sense into her. All I'm asking is that she slow down on the more advanced practices in her second trimester. She's a hop, skip, and a jump away from her third."

"I'm fine!" Her voice rises, and those hands of hers go right back to her hips.

"Gumdrop...it's dangerous."

Luna lifts her hands between them. "If I may." Both quiet down and look at her. "Technically, as long as Genevieve is feeling well and not having any pain, she should be able to continue her practice as normal until she becomes uncomfortable...."

"See!" Genevieve cuts her off, and Trent visibly bristles.

"*However*...Viv, if it were me, I would start to ramp down my practice choices to those more suited to a pregnant woman's body and the welcoming of the new little life. Your beginning classes are fine, the prenatal, and of course, meditation. I'm certain Mila would agree. It's not that you have to stop; you should start to think about the positions and level of advancement that best suit your pregnancy at this stage and into the next."

"Thank you, Red," Trent announces with a huge smile.

"And, Trent, I'll say to you that Genevieve knows her own body. She's been pregnant once before. Now is the time to celebrate, but be considerate of her feelings and perhaps a bit gentler with your approach to her. You might consider making *suggestions* when it comes to *her* body versus demands."

"Her body is my body." His gaze goes straight to hers. "It's my job to protect you."

Genevieve turns into a pile of mush right in front of us, moving into her husband's arms. "I love you, and I don't want you worrying about me or our girl, so I'll stop doing Vin Flow... if you make me pancakes for dinner."

He chuckles, dips his head, and kisses his wife. "My girls want my famous pancakes, you get my pancakes."

Luna beams with happiness watching the two exchange their apologies and vows of love.

I wrap an arm around her waist and whisper in her ear. "Maybe we should find our spot and leave them alone?"

She nods and curves her arm around me as we turn away

and walk right into Dara McKnight. Her mocha-colored skin is a majestic contrast to the Caribbean ocean blue of her eyes.

"Hey, girl," she says but then glances at me, her lips compressing into a thin, flat line.

"Dara, I believe you have something to say to my boyfriend, Grant."

Dara's gaze narrows. She looks me up and down and then tips her head. "I see your battle has changed."

"You see what?" I'm confused.

"Well, for one, you're clearly in love with my best friend. It's written all over your green aura. Though there are flickers of silver, which prove you're skeptical of me, of this class, or the situation at large."

"Dara, you said you wanted to talk to Grant. Clear the air." Luna's tone has become guarded.

Dara looks Luna up and down and points her finger from Luna's head to her toes. "Don't go all muddy red on me with your anger coming to the surface. I'm just stating it like it is."

"What are you *stating* exactly?" I ask, still lost.

Luna sighs. "Dara is reading our auras. It's like her personal litmus test."

"Why not just ask what you want to know directly?" I skate right over the aura reading because I don't know anything about it, nor do I give it any credence either way.

"I can't help what I see. Besides, what I see is good. He clearly is head over heels in love with you. Every time your hand gets close or you look at him, his green aura brightens, glowing like a brilliant emerald surrounding his entire form. Means his heart is filled...with *you*."

Luna gifts us both a cheesy smile, totally taken off her grumpy tone and back to being happy-go-lucky Zen hippie. "I love that." She sighs.

I chuckle and put my arm around her shoulder and nuzzle her forehead. "Don't need an aura reader to know I love you."

Her cheeks blush so prettily I want to kiss them, but I don't while under the watchful eye of her best friend, whom I haven't exactly won over yet.

"I love you more."

Dara butts into our little love fest. "Okay, okay. I can see the two of you are in deep. I'll make this short and sweet, Grant."

"Appreciated." I wait for her to respond.

"Luna is my best friend. She's important to me and my family. As is this facility and my bakery—frankly, the whole damn street. And you are the man who could be taking all of it away."

I could stop her right there, but she continues.

"Now Luna tells me you're working to figure out a solution, and she explained the details behind the decision. I get that your hands are tied, and I'll be over the moon if what you're working on saves the street and our businesses. More importantly, though, I don't want you breaking my friend's heart."

I tighten my hold on Luna's shoulder. "Not going to do that. In a very short amount of time, Luna has become the most important thing in my world. Her heart is safe with me. And as she mentioned, I'm working on doing what I can for Lotus House and the street. Still, she will not go without a home or a place to work. That I can assure you."

Dara's lips form a small smile, and her eyes continue to assess me. "I can see the truth in your statement, and I'll accept that...for now."

"Much obliged."

She nods and looks at Luna. "You're right. He's ridiculously hot."

"I know!" Luna says with apparent awe. "And you're seeing him fully clothed. Naked, he's... I can't even," Luna admits.

"You both realize I'm standing right here."

Luna grins and rubs her face against my chest. "You are."

Dara chuckles. "Get set up." She glances at Trent and Genevieve as other patrons start to roll in. "Need to set some mental balance up in this place. Dang. Emotions and shit flying all over the place."

"I'm glad we talked. I hope to get to know you and your family better in the future," I offer, mostly because it's true. If she's important to Luna, then I'm willing to make an effort.

Dara winks. "Come have some treats sometime at the bakery. I'll hook you up. All the people I care about come in and out of my shop on a daily basis. You'll get to know everyone very quickly."

Luna leads me over to a spot to the side where we can see the riser but also lean our backs up against the wall behind us.

"Okay, for meditation, you need to get as comfortable as possible while sitting," she instructs and then hops up and heads over to a closet, where she pulls out a few cylinder-shaped pillows and then comes back over.

I cross my legs, and she places one pillow under each of my knees. When I rest them on the pillows, I'm much more comfortable. She grabs both of my hands and maneuvers them palms-up on both of my knees.

"Having your palms up and open allows you to be open. Energy can flow through your palms and into your form as you meditate."

"I don't know how to meditate."

She grins. "Which is why you're here. Tonight's class is guided meditation. All you have to do is follow her instructions and listen to her voice. I'll be right next to you. As a matter of fact, I'm going to press my knee up against yours so our energy can circulate between us."

I smirk. "You just want to touch me."

"This is true." She winks and gets settled next to me, putting the bolsters in the same position she did for me but under her knees. Then she scoots right next to my side so that our knees touch. She rests her hands up and open and then closes her eyes.

"All right, class, thank you all for coming. To start, I'm going to dim the lights even more and come around with some essential oil. The oil will activate your sense of smell and help you breathe into your mediation more easily."

Dara comes around the room and stops in front of me. "Do you like this scent?"

The woodsy smell immediately reminds me of the oil Luna used on me when I had a bad headache and first slept with her. "Very much."

"You should. Luna made it for me." She winks and then puts a fingertip just under my nostrils and above my lips.

She doesn't ask Luna about the scent, just places it under her nose and then pushes her hair off her forehead in a loving gesture. Luna smiles but doesn't open her eyes. They really are best friends. I mean, I can't image Clayton touching me so tenderly, but he does clap my shoulder, pound on my back in greeting. I guess that's the male version of the sweet gesture.

"Close your eyes, everyone, and breathe in the scent. I want you to start by imagining you're standing in the center of a forest. Trees all around you. The wind is blowing softly around your skin, making the branches above your head tinkle and sway. There is a dirt path under your feet. You are comfortable, calm, and know you are in the exact place you are supposed to be...right now. Breathe in the serenity. Exhale any unwelcome thoughts that come into your mind."

I imagine exactly what she says. A forest building all around me, and I'm standing in the center of a wooded path. I can smell the trees and hear the branches moving around me.

"Before you are two paths. One is dark, almost pitch black. The other filled with sunlight and chirping birds. Take the path that is light. The dark is your past. Everything you don't want to relive. Stay in the moment. Walk in the warmth of the sun."

I move to the right, the lighted path. The sun is shining through the leaves, making a myriad of interesting shadows on the dirt path. Even so, the dark path is calling to me, making me curious about what lies at the end.

A sensation of unease slips through my form, and I grunt, my body feeling heavy and weighted. Out of nowhere, a sense of calm fills the air, a soothing energy flowing over me, and I realize Luna put her hand into mine, connecting our energy in the physical plane, which connects our souls in the mental one. With her energy surrounding me, I turn right and start to walk the lighted path.

As I walk, I forget about Dara's voice. It seems to blend into whatever I'm seeing, which is nothing but beauty. The tree-lined path comes to an opening, where a fifty-foot, pristine waterfall plunges into a clear pool below. I walk toward the water and see my reflection in the rippled surface. In it, I'm happy, smiling, my face free of stress.

A noise startles me, and I look to the right of the pool, and there Luna stands on a giant rock, her naked body ethereal against the sun and rushing water. Her red hair flows in waves behind her as the wind blows.

She blows me a kiss and dives into the pool.

"Wow," I say to myself, waiting with bated breath to see her form pop up from the crystal clean surface of the pool.

"Big man, wake up." I feel my body jolt, and I open my eyes to find I'm back in the yoga room. Luna's pretty face hovers in front of me, her hands on my knees. "You fell asleep." She giggles.

"Damn." I run my hand through my hair.

"Did you at least see the forest?" she asks, removing the bolsters as I shake off the images.

"Oh yeah."

"The waterfall?" she continues as I stand up and hook her around the waist, pulling her to me.

"Totally."

"The deer in the meadow?"

"What?"

"The deer in the meadow near the waterfall."

I curl my fingers into her hair and tilt her chin up with my thumb. "No."

She frowns, her nose crunching up prettily. "Then what did you see when she said to imagine a majestic creature, like a deer?"

I kiss her forehead and then focus on her gaze. "Lamb, once I got to the waterfall, I saw *you*. Nothing but you. Naked. Stunning. Diving into the water. The most perfect image. I'll never forget it as long as I live."

"You imagined *me*?" Her voice shakes when she reiterates her question.

"To me, Luna, there is nothing more majestic than you. Your body, your heart, your essence is my happy place."

CHAPTER SIXTEEN

CROWN
C H A K R A

*Individuals led by this chakra tend to experience
extreme clarity and enlightened wisdom above those
who are not in tune with their crown chakra.*

LUNA

Two weeks have flown by, and no word from Greta. With each passing day, Grant is becoming more and more agitated. It took him a while to come to terms with the possibility that he had a sister, and when it was confirmed and he reached out, he expected her to follow up with him. However, this has not been the case. To say that her lack of response has surprised us would be putting it mildly.

I'd looked into Greta's eyes at the restaurant. She wanted a relationship with Grant. I could see it in her gaze and straight down to her very soul. Which is why her ignoring his attempt is so strange.

"I just don't understand why she hasn't returned either of my calls. The first time, I waited a week before leaving another message. And still, no call back." Grant paces back and forth in his office.

Everything is monochromatic here too. I make a mental note to add some color to this space as well. Bring in a couple pictures, another couple sets of toss pillows. Liven it up a bit. He loves the changes I made to his apartment, but more often than not, he's sleeping in my bed.

I reach out on his tenth pass and grab his wrist. He looks down at me where I sit, his expression filled with sadness. It guts me straight down to my bones.

"Maybe I angered her when I didn't believe her originally?" His words are thick, filled with an emotion I only hear when we're alone, usually with our arms and legs wrapped around one another after one of our epic lovemaking sessions.

"Not sure, but I got the distinct impression she wanted a relationship of some sort with you, regardless of how upset you'd been at the restaurant. Besides, it was the first you'd heard of having a sister. She had to know it would cause a bit of an outburst on your part." I try my best to assuage his frustration.

He inhales, fully and deeply, and removes his hand from mine so he can place his hands on his waist. His blazer fluffs out behind him. "It's strange. I didn't know she existed before, and now I can't get her out of my head."

I hate that my big man is feeling defeated and less than. It hurts my heart and wounds me on his behalf. There has to be something I can do about it.

Just when I'm forming a plan, Grant's desk buzzer rings.

"Mr. Walters is on his way back. He refused to let me escort him." Annette's cool voice slithers through the line, betraying her irritation at whoever is coming to see Grant.

"Excellent!" Grant claps his hands. "This is why I asked you here this morning."

I smile and lean back in the chair. "And I thought you just wanted me here because you like having me close."

He dips down and puts his hands on both sides of my chair, caging me in. "That too." He nuzzles my nose and then kisses me briefly. "It's a big moment, and I wanted you to be the first one to hear the news and see the plans."

I frown. "What plans?"

"You'll see." The door opens, and a tall young man enters. He's wearing a pair of khakis and a polo, his dirty-blond hair tousled every which way. Over his shoulder is a black cylindrical carrying case, the contents of which I can't begin to guess.

"Brando! Thanks for coming down, man." Grant reaches his hand out to Brando, his architect and close friend, whom I was told about recently.

"Always love to give Annette a run for her money. She gets prettier and prettier every time I'm here. I wish she wasn't so icy, though." He pretends to shiver.

I grin, remembering back when I first met Annette. His observation is dead on. Except now that I've gotten to know Annette, she's a lovely woman with a staunchly professional work ethic. However, she can be friendly when given a chance.

Grant smiles. "She has to get used to you. She'll warm up."

"Guess I need to start a fire under her hot ass," Brando jokes.

Grant just shakes his head and chuckles before glancing at

me. "Brandon Walters, this beautiful creature is my girlfriend, Luna Marigold."

Brandon smiles wide and checks me out from head to toe the moment I stand up. "So, this is the beauty who has wrangled my buddy, positively domesticating him." He winks.

"Good to meet you," I offer, enjoying his good-natured smile and personality. I hold out my hand for him, and he shakes it with an easy smile.

"Yeah, you always did have a sweet spot for redheads. Looks like you've chosen the prettiest one this time."

Grant's chest lifts with what I can only hope is pride. "Damn straight. Now get your hands off my woman. I believe you have something to share with us?"

Brandon chuckles and heads to Grant's long desk, where he sets the black cylindrical bag. He unzips the top and pulls out tubes of white papers, which look like rolled-up posters. Methodically, he spreads the sheets out and places Grant's coffee cup on one corner and a paperweight on the other. He holds the top left corner with his hand.

"Come check it out," he tuts, a hint of excitement in his tone.

Grant leads me to the desk, his hand warm on my back.

We look down at the paper, and I see a street. Four big squares in all. Two on one side, two on the other. "What you're seeing is an aerial view of your street, and these four squares are the Berkeley Four."

Grant has explained to me that the development and buildings to be built on my street have been named the Berkeley Four. Each tower will simply be numbered Berkeley One, Two, Three, and Four.

"Okay, I see the buildings, what looks like a play area for

kids, and some fountains. What about the businesses?" I ask.

Grant loops his arm around my waist and tugs me close.

"That's the best part." Brandon allows the first sheet to roll up on itself before showing the next. "Here's the ground level of each tower and the breezeways which will connect two towers to one another. Look what's in the breezeways."

Berkeley One shows the lobby of the tower, but to the right of the tower is another door.

"Lotus House Yoga. And the best part"—Brandon is practically leaping out of his skin with exuberance as he points to the breezeway—"nothing in Lotus House changes except the color of the front of the building and maybe some additional windows along with a second story addition for expansion."

"My idea..." Grant rumbles near my ear, and my stomach clenches.

Brandon keeps pointing. "Instead of having a huge garden area like the one across the street with the pool and playground, this tower will have Lotus House and Sunflower Bakery. Completely intact, zero changes to what you have now with the exception of the expanded space and a paint job."

I open and close my mouth, not sure what to say or how to even form the words to express my gratitude. It washes over me, and tears prick at the back of my eyes. "I'm not losing Lotus House..." I choke on the phrase.

Grant turns me to the side and cups my cheeks. "You love it, right?"

I nod as twin tears fall down my cheeks.

He swipes them away with his thumbs. "And I love you." He leans forward and kisses me softly.

"A-And— A-And Sunflower stays the same? D-Dara doesn't have to move either?"

He smiles wide. "No, lamb, your best friend's flagship store stays. Both of those locations will be excellent contributions to the towers. And with a different scale of wealth hitting the neighborhood, you can raise your prices. Maybe allow the folks already in to have a grandfathered set price and new clients the brand-new rates. Possibly offer Towers residents a ten-percent discount. Something that makes them feel welcome."

"Oh, my God...I will. I'll do whatever it takes to make this work!" I jump up, wrap my arms around Grant's neck, and lay a big, fat, wet kiss on him. He takes my head and slants it the way he wants as he plunges his tongue, tasting me deep.

I give him everything I'm feeling in this kiss.

Gratitude.

Relief.

Love.

I know he went to incredible lengths to make this happen for me and my best friend, and it just solidifies how much he loves me and is committed to our relationship. My heart swells as I pull away. He nips my top lip and then my bottom lip, wiping at my tears as he goes.

"Guys, can you stop making out long enough to see the rest of the plans? Not all of it is as exciting. There were several businesses we couldn't save, I'm sorry to say."

"Oh no." I suck in a quick breath and straighten my spine, ready to take the hit.

"This entire street of businesses is gone. Unfortunately, an antique store, smoke shop, and thrift store don't fit anywhere near the master community plan and would not be a draw for the type of clientele we're going to secure in these million-dollar apartments."

The tears come back as I see my friends' businesses wiped

off the street. "What's going to replace them?"

"Well, as you may have noticed, The Tattered Pages Bookstore was not on the same street as Lotus House and Sunflower."

My heart sank. The bookstore is always packed, and the couple who own it have owned it as long as I can remember. It's their dream business. They plan to pass it on to their children one day.

"As you can see in this image, we've moved the bookstore across the street to the breezeway section between tower three and tower four. We've also left room for two upscale businesses to move in."

"You're keeping the bookstore?"

"Yeah, baby, it's a great place, and it's always packed. Plus, even though they are used books, when we talked to them and told them we're giving them more space, they promised to add brand-new books and bestsellers as well as host some reading hours for kids and book clubs."

"Oh, my God! They will love that! They were already bursting at the seams as it was."

Brandon nods. "Yeah, and now they'll have two stories to work with and a much wider section where we're going to build a little platform for author signings, poetry readings, book reveals, the kids' hour, and more. We will also be replacing all of the bookcases and making them perfectly matching and dialed in so it suits a higher-scale area. The entire front will be window so patrons walking by can see the rows and rows of books."

I run my finger along the look of the bookstore, already excited about visiting and buying new books and attending book club meetings.

"This is incredible. And Rainy Day Café? You didn't mention that. Are you getting rid of it?"

Grant grins. "Lamb, they have the best soup and sandwiches I've had in my life. Their salads and the to-go egg breakfast burritos, bagels, and croissants are to die for. People want healthy, well-made food and tasty to-go options when they've got to get to the city or just got back from a hellacious day at work."

"So that means..."

"We're not getting rid of it. We discussed it with them, and we're expanding it, giving them the patio they want, turning it into two stories, new bigger kitchen, etcetera. They'll have to hire a lot more people to help with the influx they're going to get. It will end up being two to four times the size when it's all said and done."

My heart starts pounding, and I swallow against the tears that threaten to fall. "Coree and Bethany have been notified?"

"Yeah, Luna. Everyone on the street has had a sit-down with Brando and me. Even the businesses we couldn't save. Turns out those weren't doing well anyway. We offered them an additional hundred thousand dollars on top of their eviction for their troubles and to help them rebuild or start over."

I gasp. "You did? I can't believe Winters Group would do that. It had to be a blow to the books..."

Brandon laughs. "Winters Group. The old man would never allow that kind of money out the door. Grant took the dent to his bank account. It was all him...."

Grant's gaze flashes to Brandon's, daggers replacing the happiness of moments before.

"Dude, your woman should know you were the one who made it right and out of your own pocket. Not the company.

Definitely not your old man." Brandon shivers dramatically. "Man gives me the creeps. He's so mean."

I turn Grant to look my way. "You did this? Made it okay for everyone?"

"Lamb, I told you I was going to work something out. I'm just lucky that Brando is a genius architect and worked his ass off to make it work. We're also adding a boxing gym to tower one that will be an expansion of Sal's Boxing Gym & Fitness Center, as well as three different entertainment clubs on the tops of towers two, three, and four."

My eyes are swimming with tears again, but I try to hold them back. All of this is good, too good to believe. "Um..." I swallow down the lump and inhale deeply. "Why is tower one not going to have a club on the top?"

Grant turns to Brandon and effectively ignores my question. "Thank you for coming, Brandon. I'll be in touch. Again, appreciate it, man."

Brandon claps Grant's shoulder. "No problem. Glad we could make it work for you and your girl, as well as most of the businesses. This is going to be a great community."

Grant and I watch as he rolls up the plans, ties them with a rubber band, and leaves them on Grant's desk. "For the board meeting next week."

"Perfect. We'll get together soon for a beer."

Brandon's eyes widen. "Looks like Luna is changing more than just your business acumen. You're more approachable, casual. Gotta say, I like what I'm seeing. And I'll await that call for a brewsky. Great meeting you, Luna. Glad to see Winters so happy."

Grant nods and Brandon heads out, offering a short wave.

"Bye, Brandon, and thank you again for the incredible

work. I'm truly grateful."

He waves once more, opens the door, and exits.

Grant turns me in his arms, and I place my hands on his chest.

He glances down at me, eyes filled with love and loyalty.

"What's going on the top of tower one? You evaded my question and then abruptly dismissed your friend. That's not like you."

He curves a hand around my nape and sets his thumb on my cheeks. "Because I didn't want Brando here for this part. It's private, between you"—he kisses my lips—"and"—he deepens the kiss with a little touch of his tongue before pulling away—"me."

I hum and grip his chest, digging my nails into the breastplate of his shirt, loving the feel of his hard, muscular chest under my fingertips. "Grant..." I mewl, heat building between my thighs. "You didn't answer me."

One of his hands leaves my back and slides down to my ass, where he starts to inch up the hem of my flowy dress. When he has it high enough to where he can run his hand along my panty-clad ass, he grunts and pushes his hips against mine.

I can feel the long ridge of his manhood pressing into me. Unable to hold myself back any longer, I wedge my own hand between our bodies and slide it down his sizable length. He grunts, dips his head, and lays a line of open-mouthed kisses along my neck.

Grant slides both hands under my dress, lifts me by my ass, and sets me on the top of his desk. He leans over, pushes a button, and all the windows go frosty. I hear the lock on his door click into place. While he bathes my neck in kisses, he multitasks, gripping my panties in one hand, lifting my body with the other, and tugging the panties down my legs.

"Wanted to fuck you on my desk the second I saw you the first time you visited. I can't get the image out of my mind."

"Mmm..." I sigh and tilt my head up, letting him work my neck and push down the top of my dress along with the cups of my bra so he can get at my breasts.

He wraps his lips around one aching point, and I cry out. He hums in his throat and flicks at the erect nipple before sucking it into the warmth of his mouth.

"Grant..."

"Love your tits, lamb. So pink and pretty." He snuffles his nose along my chest to the other breast, which he gives equal attention.

I arch into his lush kiss, loving his mouth on me but needing more. So much more. I open my legs wide so he can get even closer and I can reach his belt, button, and zipper, which I make quick work of getting open until his erection falls into my palm. He's velvety smooth and hard as steel.

"Fuck, Luna," he growls and takes my mouth in a searing kiss. His tongue tastes every angle of my mouth while I work his length in my fist.

He pulls away on a harsh breath. "Lie back. I want to see your body sucking me in while I take you on my desk." His tone is firm and grating, like he can't wait a second more to have me.

I lie back, my breasts exposed and cool to the air. He looks at me, my bared breasts, and the space between my thighs with intense reverence.

"Love you, Luna. So damn much." He clenches his teeth, centers his penis at my opening, and enters me, one steely inch at a time.

The moment he fills me is nothing short of nirvana. Being

connected to Grant is the best feeling in the world.

He's sunshine and warm winds.

Dark chocolate drizzled over ice cream.

Sunday mornings in bed.

Wood-burning fireplaces and toasted marshmallows.

He's everything I could ever need or want...and he's all mine.

Grant spreads me open farther with his thumbs, thrusts as deep as he can go, tips his head back, and groans loudly into the empty room. "You're so tight. Warm. Everything in my life that's good, Luna. I'd do anything to have you, have this for the rest of my life."

I run my nails down his forearms, bringing his gaze back to mine.

"I love you. Now make me come." I remind him of where his penis is planted.

"Your pleasure is my pleasure." He smiles sexily, grips my hip with his free hand, and proceeds to make love to me thrust after blessed thrust, on the top of his desk, with his entire office running around outside his locked door like buzzing little bees in the hive.

★ ★ ★

Content, thoroughly sated, and back in his apartment for a fantastic round two of incredible sex, I watch Grant pull his armor—the black suit I took off—back on, one lovely bit at a time.

He pushes his arms through the dress shirt and faces me with the sides open, gifting me a sexy swatch of my man's golden chest and six-pack.

I sigh and snuggle up to his pillow and watch him, with no intention of moving anytime soon.

He smirks. "You're going to lounge around all day or head back to the studio?"

I stretch out my arms and legs and snuggle back into the pillow. "I think I'm going to lounge for a bit and then head back. You?"

He frowns. "I have a meeting with my father today. I'm going to show him the plans Brandon made. Make sure he's on board with the decision before I present it to the board of directors."

I nod. "Do you think there's a possibility of him changing the plans?"

He shakes his head. "No, not that I can imagine. It's a perfect master community, and originally, we only planned on the towers, not the rest of the street, but with this influx of plans, it will only help us secure wealthy buyers. They want to live in a nice area, with a short commute and a location that suits their wives or husbands, as well as kids, for those who have them."

"Well, I love it and you for making it so wonderful and incorporating me, Sunflower, Rainy Day, and the bookstore. And helping out the others...incredible."

He grins. "Glad I scored some points with my woman. You never know when you'll need a get-out-of-jail-free card."

"This is true. Now, are you going to tell me what the plan for tower one's top floor is? If it's not going to be a swanky club or restaurant, what is it going to be?"

This time Grant smiles huge, crawls onto the bed, and cages me flat on my back. "It's going to be my new apartment."

"The whole floor?" I open my eyes wide, knowing this

building has three-fourths or more as his office building, and this small corner as his apartment, and it's really big as it is.

"I'm going to need to be close to Lotus House."

I frown. "Why?"

"Because that's where my woman lives, and if she likes to live near her work, then she can lay her head in our new home... together."

I'm pretty sure my eyes bulge out of my head. "You want me to move in with you?"

He nods. "I want us to start together there, brand-new with every room planned and decorated by you. All of the appliances, cabinets, bathroom tile—all of it—chosen by the lady of the house..." He pecks my mouth. "You."

"Wow. That's..."

His gaze turns serious and his jaw hardens, as if he's preparing for me to respond negatively about moving in together.

"Freakin' awesome!" I wrap my naked arms and legs around his clothed body and kiss him hard.

He dips in his tongue, making the kiss a whole lot hotter a whole lot faster.

Our tongues tangle, our hands grope, until I literally can't breathe because he's kissing me so completely.

"Yeah?" He pulls back, his eyes dancing with happiness.

"Oh yeah. Totally. I cannot wait!"

"There's only one rule," he murmurs.

I raise my eyebrows up toward my hairline.

"You have to bring your bed. We'll use mine as a guest bed."

I snicker and rub my nose with his. "You love my bed, big man."

"I do. Almost as much as I love you."

"Deal!" I squeal and kick my feet. "We're moving in together!"

"Yes, we are. Of course, it won't be done for a long time, so for now, I think we should start by me moving into your place."

I let my arms fall and then cup his cheeks. "Really? You want to live with me?"

He pets my cheek with his index finger. "Lamb, I told you, I want to be wherever you are. Plus...I really love your bed."

I close my eyes and start laughing.

"Can I assume your laughter is a yes, I can move in with you?"

I run my thumb along his bottom lip. "Yes, Grant. I'd like nothing more than for you to move in with me. However, I have no idea where you're going to put any of your stuff."

He chuckles. "Lamb, I'm not taking anything with me right now, maybe not at all. We'll keep the apartment available in case I need to be in the city or have out-of-town businessmen and women who need a place to stay. Only thing I'll be bringing are my clothes and moving our picture on the mantle to my office desk. Nothing else matters."

"You're right, nothing else matters. And you know what, big man?"

He hovers over me, waiting. "What?"

"I can't freakin' wait!"

CHAPTER SEVENTEEN

CROWN
CHAKRA

*A couple driven by the crown chakra are
fiercely loyal to one another in all things.*

LUNA

Once we finished making out after our second round of lovemaking, Grant left to meet his business obligations for the day and said he would return to me later in the evening for dinner.

Internally, I squealed with delight. We're going to move in together. The entire floor of tower one of the new buildings would be our home. He assured me there would be many bedrooms for not only our overnight guests, but our home would grow along with our love. Which meant he planned on us having our children there one day.

Swoon!

The thought of bearing Grant's child has me wanting to spin in circles where I stand, arms out, wild and free. On top of that, he's found a way to save most of the businesses on my street, including Lotus House, Sunflower Bakery, Rainy Day Café, and the Tattered Pages Bookstore. I could not be happier.

I hop into the elevator and wave at Annette, an exuberant skip in my step. She returns the wave and smiles softly. See, she can totally be nice! She even scheduled a car to take me wherever I wanted to go. Grant doesn't like me taking Uber, even though I think it's perfectly safe. It sure does cut into the monthly bills, though, except now that I've been dating Grant, he's paid for everything aside from my apartment and the meals I have on my own, which admittedly, aren't many.

I exit the elevator and wave at the doorman, who rushes to open the door for me. As I step out onto the sidewalk, the driver is parked out front and holding the door open.

"Ms. Marigold, Winters Group has hired me to take you wherever you'd like to go today."

I smile. "Thank you." I tip my head and get into the car. He waits until I've gathered my maxi-dress inside before shutting the door and coming around to the driver's side.

"Where to, ma'am?"

Lotus House is on the tip of my tongue, but after sitting through my man's pacing and hearing the hurt in his voice that his sister has not returned his calls, another address spills form my lips unexpectedly.

"UC Davis Medical Center, please."

I bite into my lip and think about this decision. Visiting Greta Tinsley at work is absolutely going to mean I'm getting into the middle of the situation with Grant and his estranged half sister.

Is it a wise decision?

I don't know. All I do know is that I cannot watch my man be torn apart by the time she's taking to return his overtures. Even if she no longer wants anything to do with him, she should, at the very least, tell him as much. Don't keep him dangling like a puppet on a string or lying in wait for her next scrap of affection.

I shake my head and firm my resolve. No, this is exactly what a woman does to help her man. She wades in, regardless of the consequences. Perhaps I can talk some sense into her, explain that Grant genuinely wants to get to know her. Understand how she came to be his sister and everything in between.

In the meantime, this might take me past the time I intended to be gone, which would mean I'll need a substitute for my class this afternoon.

I pull out my phone and text Dara.

Can you sub for me tonight? I have something important to do that can't wait.

I sigh and watch the cars weave in and out of San Francisco traffic as we go up and down the hilly streets. According to my world-traveling boyfriend, San Francisco is unlike any city in the world. Downtown is full of large hills and valleys, with multicolored Victorian row houses intermingled with big businesses. Streets cross parks and what seems to be an endless number of piers, including the most famous, Pier 39, which brings countless tourists each day.

While I stare dreamily at the beauty around me, my phone beeps, signaling Dara's reply.

*Sure. I missed taking a class today because
Jackson was fussy, so this works out great.*

I type out a quick thank you message and promise to call
her tomorrow and ask her to give baby Jackson some snuggles
from his auntie. Before I can even put my phone back into my
purse, the driver is pulling into the parking lot of the hospital.
When he stops in front of the medical center, I get out, feeling
more certain of my decision than I was before.

Grant deserves some answers. Besides, Greta was the
one who shared their sordid history first, breaking the cone of
silence after all these years. She can't take it back once it's been
revealed.

"I'll park close. Call the number on this card when you
want to leave." He hands me a business card.

"Oh, I didn't expect you to wait. I can Uber back."

The driver grins. "Strict order to see you wherever you
want to go until you are home for the night, which I have as
being on a street in downtown Berkeley proper."

I shake my head. "Was this Grant's doing or Annette's?"

He tips his hat and offers me a beaming smile. "Just call
the number on the card when you're done. There is no time
limit. I'm at your service."

"Thanks. It appears my overprotective man and his
overprotective secretary have spoken. I'll call." I flick the card
and put it into my purse, where I can easily pull it out.

Without another word, he gets back into his car and drives
away.

Sighing, I think about Grant and how much he has
changed. He's an entirely different man than the one I first
met when I entered his office a couple months ago. It's so

strange how much a person's life can change when they meet the person they're meant to share their forever with. And that's what this is between Grant and me, the beginning of our forever. I know he's the one. I have absolutely no doubt. The good news is he's made it very clear to me I'm his forever too, part of which is having a clean slate. He's cleared the path for any potential animosity we could have had by taking care of my business and my street. He's shown great compassion and strength in his willingness to make changes with the buildings and incorporate most of the current companies, mine included. When all is said and done, it's going to be a vastly different area but one that I think will be good for us.

More people, more clients. It means we all get to expand our businesses, and that is a blessing in disguise. My mind is already spinning with the possibilities of a second level. I may discuss this addition with Crystal and my mother. A long time ago, they had mentioned they would have loved to have a space where they could teach the art of yoga to up-and-coming yoga teachers. Offer a training school accredited by the National Yoga Alliance and offer new yogis the opportunity to earn their Registered Yoga Credential. I had looked into what offering that might look like, and the biggest problem was the space. We already have back-to-back yoga classes in the four main rooms along with private sessions in the smaller ones. We also have a reception area and a tiny office. We don't even have a breakroom.

With Grant's new plan, that will change. I'm going to reopen the idea and think about having a much larger space where we can teach regular yoga workshops to enrolled students. A school of sorts. Each of the current teachers could take a session a month to teach their style of yoga and help expand the community with more yogis. The options are endless, and I can't wait to talk to my teachers about all the different ideas I have. Collectively, I'm sure we'll come up with the best possible plan.

The sounds and smells of a hospital hit me pretty quickly when I walk in, and UC Davis is no different. It may be a world-renowned medical facility, but that doesn't change the fact that sick people come here to get treatment. People also die here. I shiver.

I'm not a fan of hospitals.

It's not that I'm scared of people who are sick or have an aversion to people fighting their medical condition; it's just that the feeling of doom and gloom, the zap of energy, is so potent here. The negative waves smash into me like an invisible ocean, slamming against the tide. Mindlessly, I follow the signs to the pediatric section of the hospital.

When I get to what I think is the right place, I see a bunch of nurses dressed in a variety of multicolored scrubs. One lady has dancing cats holding umbrellas. Another nurse has a shirt with candy covering every surface as if the candy was emptied out on the floor and no longer contained the wrappers.

As I approach, a hand touches my shoulder, and I turn around quickly.

"I thought that was you, Luna. What are you doing over in my side of the world?" my friend Amber Alexander says, smiling.

A huge sense of relief washes over me, and I wrap her in a big hug.

She returns the hug and pets my hair. "Hey, what's the matter, honey?"

I inhale fully and exhale before speaking. "I'm just glad

to see a friendly face. I'm actually looking for someone who works here."

Amber's green eyes sparkle as she pushes a lock of her hair behind her ear. She's the epitome of the girl next door. Long, thick brown hair parted down the center. Green cat eyes, a dusting of freckles across her nose and cheeks, and perfectly natural pink lips. She's also thin and tall, with an athletic build that suits her well.

"Who is it? I'm sure I can help you. I know everyone in Peds."

I twist my fingers together. "I'm looking for Grant's sister, actually. Greta Tinsley."

Her eyes widen momentarily. "Greta is your boyfriend's sister? Wow. I had no idea." She blinks a few times and then purses her lips.

Instead of spreading the sordid details around about how little we really know of his sister, I choose to keep them to myself.

"Yes, I was hoping I could catch her in her office for a few minutes, unless of course she's too busy."

Amber tilts her head down toward me. "Too busy. Um...no. I can... I'm not quite understanding why you would think she'd be at work right now. She's still waiting on treatment. Been out of the office for over two weeks. She's got a room down in the Hematology Department. Come on, I'll take you there."

I nod and swallow the immediate fear that crawls up my throat.

Amber glances at me as we walk quietly back to the bay of elevators. We get on, and she presses a button to go up. I'm not really paying much attention because my mind is swirling like a vortex with a million feelings I don't know how to manage at this moment.

"You seem surprised to know about Greta being admitted to the Hematology ward while she awaits treatment for her aplastic anemia."

"Honestly, Amber, Grant just found out he has a sister a couple weeks ago. The reason I'm here is because he reached out to her, and she hadn't returned his calls. I came down in order to possibly talk to her about reaching out to him." I shake my head as my heart squeezes. "We had no idea she was sick."

Amber pauses and inhales. "If Greta hadn't already given me permission to speak about her condition openly to her friends and family, I wouldn't ethically be able to discuss her condition, even if I'm not her doctor, but I'm sorry to say, honey, she's very sick. She needs a bone marrow transplant."

The elevator doors open, and I follow along like a little lost puppy. Taking the turns without really seeing where we are or where we're going.

Randomly, she stops, turns to me, and smiles brightly, as if the lighting above just bathed her in a pretty white glow. "Perhaps that's why they reached out to you in the first place," Amber states matter-of-factly.

I frown. "Why?"

"Because of her condition, of course."

"Is it life threatening?" I reach up and grab my crystal necklace, bring it up to my lips, and say a little prayer for Greta and her family.

"It can be if not treated. I know she's been battling this for a while. Grant can be tested to see if he's a match. The most likely match would be a blood sibling."

Too much information. My eyes tear up with sadness. Grant has no idea his sister is battling a medical condition which has prevented her from reaching out. Moreover, he could have the cure.

"Sweet Shiva, this is not what I expected when I came today."

Amber frowns and puts her hand on my shoulder. "I'm sorry, Luna. I'd have to read her chart to see where she's at with her treatment, but the last I heard, she hadn't found a donor yet. I'm surprised they didn't reach out to Grant right away. As I said before, the only reason I'm even talking to you is because you're family, and I know Greta personally, and she's given me permission to speak freely. The entire pediatric department knows all about her condition. We all take turns donating blood, sitting with her, even bringing over dinners to her husband and her two kids."

I suck in a huge breath. "She has children? Oh my..."

Amber nods. "A four-year-old son and six-month-old girl."

I close my eyes. The blow of knowing Grant has extended family hits me like a tornado to my soul. Grant is going to be devastated. He hasn't even been able to have a relationship with his sister, and now he's going to find out she's sick with a life-threatening condition. On top of that, he has a niece and nephew.

Family.

A *real* family.

Amber holds out her arm, gesturing to a closed door. "Room two oh two. I'm going to check in with her doctor and see what more I can find out. See if there's anything I can do. You go on in."

I reach out and hold on to Amber's hands. "Thank you. I really appreciate you updating me. If you could keep Grant's relationship to yourself, that would be excellent. I want to discuss all I've learned with him so he can process as he needs to."

Amber squeezes my hands and pulls me into a hug. "Of course. Anything you need from me or Dash, you know where we are."

"Thanks."

Amber offers a sad smile and then walks away.

I look at the door, do a full minute of Pranayama—yoga breathing—before I work up the courage to knock on the door.

"Come in," says a sweet-sounding voice I don't recognize as Greta's. Her voice was far deeper at the restaurant.

I open the door and peek my head in. "Hello, it's Luna Marigold to see Greta." I stop with my hand on the door.

Greta is sitting in the bed, looking like death is knocking at her door. Her skin is paler than mine, her eyes gaunt, lips seeming dry and cracked, and her hair is a dank color. Though that's not what stops me in my tracks. No, it's the redhead with sapphire eyes who is holding Greta's hand and smiling at me. The same smile I get every time I please my man. Grant's smile. The smile he so obviously got from his birth mother.

At first, when I saw Grant Senior, I thought they were replicas. And they are. Only with this woman, I can see the similarities too, the softness Grant has that his father doesn't have. The softness he got from the woman who just stood up.

She stands tall, raises her chin, and approaches me. "You're Luna, my boy's girlfriend."

I open my mouth to speak, but nothing comes out. I'm stunned stupid.

"I'm Gretchen Winters. Grant's mother."

The stunning redhead holds out her hand. I place mine

in hers on autopilot. Her hand chakras jolt mine instantly, the same way her son's do.

Gretchen pats our clasped hands with her other one. "I can see you are taken aback by my presence. As am I. When Greta told me she'd seen her brother, spoke to him face-to-face, I was scared at first and then overjoyed she had that moment."

I nod, still not knowing how to respond.

"I'm going to leave you alone with Greta so you two can talk. Though I'd like to have some time with you as well, if you don't mind."

Yep, all I can do is nod.

She smiles, pats my hand again, and lets my hand go, moving around me to the door.

"Baby girl, I'll be back soon."

"Thanks, Mom," Greta responds, her voice scratchy.

I shake myself out of a stunned stupor and walk to Greta's side. "I... I had no idea. Grant...he's been trying to call you."

Greta smiles. "Really? He reached out?" There's hope filling her tired gaze.

"Yeah. And he's been a mess not knowing why you didn't respond. All we had was your work phone number, so he's called and left voice mails."

Greta closes her eyes briefly, but when she opens them again, they are filled to the brim with tears. "He confirmed the truth of our sibling status."

I bite my lip and nod. "Yes. He's going to be shocked when I tell him about this."

She shakes her head. "Don't tell him..."

"But Amber says..."

"Amber? Amber Alexander?" she questions.

"Yeah, she's my very good friend. Her husband works at

my yoga studio, Lotus House. She brought me down and told me you have a bone marrow condition and since you have a sibling..."

Greta puts her hand on my wrist and squeezes. "No. I will not use Grant. He's been used all his life by that vile man. And this isn't why I contacted him. Actually, I didn't plan on meeting him that night. Brett was taking me out for my last meal before I was admitted to the hospital. God brought Grant to the restaurant that day, and I'm so grateful I had the chance to talk to my brother for the first time, but I could never use him to help me now."

"I can't keep this from him, Greta. I won't. Our relationship is based on honesty. I'm sorry."

Greta takes a deep breath and looks away, a tear slipping down her cheek. "This isn't how I wanted to finally have a relationship with my brother. I've been watching him from afar for so long. All of his lacrosse games in college. Mom and I went to every game. Stood in the stands and cheered him on, even if he never knew we were there. His graduation from high school and college the same. We had to avoid Grant Senior, but Mom and me, we were determined to see him walk those stages. So proud."

More of Greta's tears fall as my heart breaks in half. She'd watched him from afar? Rooted for him when his own father tore him down?

I grab Greta's hand. "He's going to come here. He's going to be angry. I can't help that. I will try to ensure he doesn't share that anger with you. I don't know what's going to happen when he sees his mother after all these years."

Greta nods. "Everything is so messed up. If I wasn't sick..."

I lift her hand and kiss the top of her palm. "You didn't

mess up anything. I'm sure there are two sides to the story. Right now, what's important is you getting better. What's your prognosis?"

Greta licks her dry lips, and I look around for her water cup, find it on the side table, and place it on the table in front of her. She takes a sip. "Thank you."

"Of course."

"I'm waiting for a donor."

"What condition do you have, if you don't mind me asking? What happened to make you sick?"

She sighs and dips her head to the side, glancing outside the window. "I had my daughter Gabriella six months ago. Shortly after her birth, I started to get these on and off flu-like symptoms followed by nosebleeds, dizziness, and shortness of breath. I went to the doctor, and at first, they just assumed it was a bad flu. Then I started to get bruises and skin irritations, headaches and..." She takes a labored breath. "And the symptoms worsened. Eventually, I had some additional tests done, where they found out I had a bad viral infection. Was hospitalized for a while, pumped full of fluids, and they thought it was over. We all did."

She looks at me, her gaze piercing. "It wasn't over. All the symptoms came back a couple weeks later, and once again, they progressed. Eventually, blood was drawn, and I was found to be severely anemic. Then it was discovered I wasn't producing healthy red and white blood cells. I was getting sicker. They gave me several rounds of blood transfusions, which only helped for a short time. Not long after, I was diagnosed with severe aplastic anemia. The only permanent cure is a bone marrow transplant. Two weeks ago, I was admitted."

"I'm sorry you're going through this, Greta."

"Me too."

"Amber says Grant has a huge chance of being a donor match because you're siblings."

Greta closes her eyes and looks away.

"Greta, is this true?"

She nods. "Yeah. But like I said, I can't use him. He deserves better. He deserves a real sister. Not one who only comes into his life because she wants something."

"You didn't! You didn't even tell us. I found out on my own. Don't you think that's divine intervention? A sign from the universe itself?"

She shakes her head. "I don't know. I do know I'm really tired, Luna, and I, uh, need to rest before my mother comes back. Thank you for coming. It was really lovely seeing you again. Send Grant my...um, well, just tell him I would have called him right back."

I rub my hand over hers. "Okay. Rest. I'll see you soon."

"Yeah. Thanks for stopping by." She sighs and looks off into the distance where the window is, effectively shutting me out.

I exit the room and see the flash of red hair down the hall. The woman may want to talk to me, but there is no way I'm talking to her without Grant. I've got enough to tell him about when I get home. Moving fast, I make it to the bank of elevators and press the button for the main level.

Pulling out my phone, I press memory dial number one.

"Lamb..." His breathy, sexy voice eases the ache pressing down on my heart after seeing Greta and hearing her story.

"Grant, we need to talk. When can you meet me at home? I'm going to hit the grocery store and make dinner in for us tonight."

"Sounds good. I can be home in a couple hours."

"You can't make it sooner?" I grind my teeth, hating myself that I can't even wait for him for a couple hours, but this information is burning a hole right through my gut as it is.

"Luna, is something wrong?" I can hear the alert, concerned tone, and it opens the hole bigger.

"Yeah, honey, I'm afraid I have some uncomfortable news to share." I swallow around the emotion clogging my voice.

"Are you okay?"

"Yes, I'm fine. Just, meet me at home as soon as you can. I'll be waiting. I love you."

"I love you too. I'm having Annette cancel my last meeting, and I'll be home within the hour."

"That's a good idea. I'll see you soon. I love you."

Grant's voice shakes when he responds. "Lamb, you already said that. Fuck, you're scaring me."

"Just come home safely to me."

"Always. Soon."

"Soon."

CHAPTER EIGHTEEN

CROWN
C H A K R A

*Those individuals led by the crown chakra are considered
to be ruled by planet Jupiter and are known to have
a mystical and out-of-this-world type of love.*

GRANT

I break every speed limit as I race back to Berkeley and my woman. I can't begin to guess what uncomfortable information she has to share, but it's definitely bad news. She wouldn't have bothered me at work or requested I come home had it not been important.

After parking behind Sunflower, I use my key, type DARA into the security system, and take the back stairs up to Luna's place two at a time.

When I get there, the door is unlocked, soft music is

playing in the background, and the smell of grilled peppers and onions wafts in the air.

"Luna?" I call out, rushing to the bar counter of her small kitchenette. I stare, looking her up and down, from her bare feet and red-tipped toes, up her calves to the hem of her sleep shorts and camisole, over her perky handfuls, along her neck and arms to her face. There's nothing I can physically see on her that would warrant any concern. "You okay?"

She tips her head to one side and then the other. "Yeah. But...here." She sets a bottle of Patron on top of the counter and pours two shots.

Tequila.

I've been with Luna two months now, and not once have I seen her drink hard liquor. This news must be bad if she's bringing out the strong stuff.

She turns down the burner under a pan of green, red, and yellow peppers and some onions she'd been cooking. A stack of corn tortillas are next to the stove, and cut-up steak seems to be ready to sear in a silver metal bowl. The entire room smells delicious, and my mouth waters. If I wasn't so fucking scared out of my mind with whatever it is Luna needs to tell me, I'd be sneaking bites of her homemade meal.

Luna walks around holding out a couple wedges of lime and some salt. She grabs my hand, brings it to her mouth, and licks the space between my thumb and forefinger. My dick stirs in appreciation at her blatant sexual gestures.

"Lamb..." I warn through clenched teeth.

"Just go with it," she says while shaking some salt onto the wet spot.

She does the same to her own hand and then hands me the shot and one for herself. "Namaste."

Together we hold one another's gaze—for fear of the seven-year bad-sex rule—lick our hands, slam the drink, and bite the wedge of lime. The sour taste floods my tongue along with the burn of the alcohol.

"Sit. If you'd like, have another."

"You need to tell me what the fuck is going on."

Luna nods, rises on tiptoes, kisses me, and then focuses her gaze on mine. "I will, but honey, when I'm giving bad news, I need to be able to do something. Today, I'm going to be making the man I love some fajitas. Do you like fajitas?"

"Yeah."

She rubs her hands along my chest. "Okay. You sit there, and I'll talk."

I'm not prepared for what she says.

"I went to UC Davis Medical Center today to see your sister. Greta."

Instantly, a pang of irritation strikes my heart. "Luna... you shouldn't have done that."

She drops the meat into the pan with the veggies and pours a little more olive oil in with it. Immediately it pops and sizzles. "Yes, I know. I just couldn't see you upset anymore."

"And did you see her?"

"Yes." One word. Nothing more.

"Don't keep me in suspense. Why didn't she return my calls?"

Luna pushes a lock of hair behind her ear. "You see, that's the thing. She wanted to call you. And she would have Grant, I promise."

"I hear a but coming on."

Luna inhales, closes her eyes, and turns toward me. "She couldn't call you back because she's in the hospital. She's been admitted. Grant, honey, your sister's really sick."

I grip the arm of the stool so hard my knuckles turn white. "Okay. How sick?"

Luna swallows, and her eyes tear up. "Very. She has aplastic anemia."

"Forgive me, I have no idea what the fuck that means. I went to business school, not medical school."

Luna stirs the meat and veggies, her eyes stuck on the stove. "It means her body is no longer creating red and white blood cells. She needs a bone marrow transplant as soon as possible."

"What?"

"Yeah, apparently she got really sick after she had her second child..."

"She has children?" I gasp, my heart pounding a rock beat in my chest.

"Yeah, honey, she does. A four-year-old boy and a six-month-old girl. When she had her daughter, she got what she thought was the flu. The symptoms got worse from there. Now they're at the point they need a donor."

I run my hands through my hair a few times, allowing the strands to fall through my fingers. "Fuck. She's sick."

"Yeah, but...um, she's on a donor list. They've been waiting for two weeks. She's been hospitalized this whole time. Apparently, when we saw her, that was the last night she was feeling well enough to really go out."

I focus on the Patron bottle, grab it, pour myself another shot, and toss it back sans the salt and lime. It scalds a trail down my throat, which suits my mood.

"What are the odds of her getting a bone marrow donor match?"

Luna purses her lips and turns to me once more. "Well, you see, that's the thing. It's not that easy. She's been living off transfusions for the past few months. And the most likely donors are..." Tears fall down Luna's cheeks as she looks at me.

"The most likely donors are what? Tell me!" My voice rises right along with my ire.

"Siblings." She mutters this like it hurts for her to even say the word.

A bullet to the chest would have been the only thing that could shock me more. "Are you telling me I could be a bone marrow match?"

Luna nods, more tears falling down her cheeks.

Well, this is too goddamned much! I practically fly out of my chair, the stool falling to the ground. "Fuck!" I tug at the roots of my hair and start pacing. "You mean to tell me my sister is fighting a life-threatening disease that could kill her, make her children motherless, and I could be the one to fucking save her?"

I clutch at my chest as my heart burns like fire. Shivers rack my frame, and I'm on my knees. Tears pouring down my face as the sobs tear from my throat.

Luna's arms come around me from the side. "I'm sorry, Grant. I'm so, so sorry this is how you're finding out."

Years of being alone swim over my battered mind.

My mother hugging me the last time.

Her red hair flying in the breeze as she leaves.

Her rounded belly...

I never recalled that last part in my memory; I was always so focused on the fact that she left. Walked right out of my life and never came back. Apparently she took my sister with her.

"Fuck! I need to be tested. *Immediately.* I have to go there now!" I attempt to stand, but my knees fail, my body ravaged with heartache.

Luna's right there, her loving arms holding on to me. "Visiting hours are over. There's nothing you can do tonight. Tomorrow we can go there. Together."

"I just found out I had a sister, and now she could be taken away?"

"I know..." Luna's voice is soft as she runs a hand up and down my back in soothing movements.

"Why didn't she come to me sooner?" My voice cracks, filled to the brim with sorrow.

"When I asked her the same thing, she said she didn't want you to feel used. Said you'd been used your whole life, and she never wanted to be one of those people."

Her answer pounds against my mind and heart. My long-lost sister was protecting me. Sacrificing...for me. The only other person who has ever done that in my lifetime is Luna. Definitely not my father.

"I don't even know what to say."

Luna nods, helps me to a stand, and wraps me in a hug. I hold her for a few long minutes, breathing in her comforting scent, reveling in her love.

"Come. Sit at the bar. Eat. We need to talk some more. There's a few things that didn't add up during my conversation with Greta."

I blink tiredly and let her urge me into my seat at the bar. She goes back around, pours me another drink, which I toss back in a second flat, before she continues cooking her dinner. Luna lights the burners once more and finishes up the meal efficiently and with her normal Luna flare. Which means there's all of the fixings, everything you could ever possibly want on a fajita and then some.

A steaming, mouthwatering plate of meat, peppers, and sides is set on my plate with a tortilla holder between us.

Luna comes around, sits her pert ass on the stool next to me, and grabs my hand. "Eat. You're going to need it."

I watch her eat as though the food could disappear off her plate at any moment. Makes me wonder if she was poor or had little to eat and that's why she's so quick to eat her meals and loves food so much, but I know her mother and father were middle class and food on the table couldn't have been a problem. Like anything with Luna, it's a wonderful mystery. Something uniquely her. One of the many things I love about her.

When I've finished my first full fajita, she turns toward me. "I met your mother today."

I can feel my eyes widen unnaturally in their sockets. "*What?!*" I roar.

She jerks back and then swallows. "I, uh, met Gretchen Winters today. She was in Greta's room when I arrived."

"You mean the woman is still here? As in, the San Francisco area?"

Luna shrugs. "Grant, I'm not sure. She alluded to knowing who I was, even said, 'You're my boy's girlfriend.' As if she was meeting her son's girlfriend like any other day of the week. I can't say I wasn't taken aback. It was weird."

"Fucking hell."

"And there's more."

"Jesus Christ. I'm never letting you out of my sight again. All hell breaks loose," I growl, but I try to remain as playful as I can, even though my insides are knotting up with every new admission.

Luna sips her water and wipes her mouth. "When Greta and I were talking, she made a comment that she and your mother used to go to your lacrosse games in college, and they both watched you walk the stage from high school and college. Cheering you from afar."

On that admission, I toss the fajita to my plate and push it away. There is no way I'm getting one more bite down my gullet now that it's churning with straight-up acid.

Luna clasps my hands. "You need to talk to your mom."

"You think?" I shake my head, and her expression falls into one of sadness. I squeeze her hands. "I'm sorry. I'm not mad at you. I'm frustrated by the situation. One thing is piling on top of another. Two weeks ago, I found out I had a sister. Today you tell me she's sick with a life-threatening illness I can possibly help cure. On top of that shit storm, you met my mother, whom I haven't seen in thirty years."

She cups my cheek and leans forward so our foreheads are touching. "I know this is a lot to take in. Just remember, you're not alone, Grant. Not anymore. It's you and me now. I'm here to support you through every step. I've already called subs for my classes tomorrow. You can call Annette and have her clear your day. Heck, clear the next few days, if you can. Whatever it takes."

"Yeah. Tomorrow we'll go down first thing in the morning."

"Visiting hours don't start until ten a.m."

"Fuck! How am I supposed to wait that long?"

Luna runs her fingers through my hair. "It will be okay."

"She has children. A boy and a girl?" My voice shakes at the thought that I have a niece and a nephew. Real blood relatives. Ones I hope I can get to know.

"Yeah, honey. She didn't say what her boy's name is, but

the baby is Gabriella."

"Gabriella. Pretty," I murmur, committing the name of my one and only niece to memory.

"Yes, it is," Luna agrees.

"I can't eat any more. I'm sorry. My stomach is tied up in knots."

She lifts my plate and takes it into the kitchen to dispose of the half-eaten food. "Go take a load off. Watch something mindless on TV."

I nod, kick off my shoes, and remove my suit and kick it to the side. I don't even care if it gets wrinkled. It doesn't matter. Nothing matters right now other than getting to my sister and figuring out how I can help. I flop onto the bed in only my boxer briefs and undershirt. My mind is spinning a mile a minute, but the same simple fact keeps popping up again and again.

I can't bear to lose my sister. I just found her.

* * *

Luna is squeezing my hand as I practically drag her through the hallways of UC Davis Medical Center.

"Room two oh two," she says, pointing in front of us.

I had the evening to sit and stew over everything I found out. None of it good, aside from the knowledge that I might be able to help.

As we reach the door, Luna tugs on my hand, stopping me in my tracks. "Grant, you need to calm down. I know you're eager to see her, but the woman is still battling a very serious illness. Try to be calm, okay?"

I close my eyes, clench my teeth, and nod curtly. She's right, of course, but that doesn't change the vortex of emotions hammering me at every angle.

She taps on the door and then opens it. "Hi, Greta, it's Luna, and I, um, I have Grant with me."

"Come in," I hear from beyond the door.

I follow Luna inside and find Brett sitting next to his wife, brushing her long brown hair. He stops and glances at us, his jaw firm, his emotions on his sleeve.

Anger.

Pride.

Grief.

I can only imagine what he's feeling, knowing his wife's condition and not being able to help. On top of that, I was a dick to them at the restaurant weeks ago, which I'm sure is not helping the current waves of distrust and agitation I'm sensing in the room.

Luna walks over to Greta and grabs her hand. "How are you doing today?" she asks sweetly, her voice like a song even when she's asking something as mundane as finding out how someone is.

Greta offers a small smile. "I've had better days," she answers.

I grind my back molars in an attempt not to burst with the war of questions and thoughts I have inside me.

Greta's blue eyes shift to me. "Brother." She smiles a bit bigger and reaches out a hand.

A single word, and I'm figuratively brought to my knees. My spine stiffens, the hairs on the back of my neck prickle, and my nerve endings fire with the desire to move, to do something. *Anything.* I take hold of her hand and stand near her bed, staring into eyes so much like my own. Her hand is warm and dry but still.

"Greta, I'm sorry you're unwell. Luna has informed me of the details behind your condition."

"I'll be okay."

I raise my eyebrows up. "Then you've found a donor?" I deadpan, getting right to the heart of the matter.

She closes her eyes. "No, but I will. I'm sure I have many years left on this earth."

I clench my teeth. "I'm scheduled to be tested later this morning," I announce.

There's a definite benefit to Luna being best friends with a well-respected doctor at this facility. We were able to call Dr. Amber Alexander last night and inform her of my desire to be tested. She promised to notify the appropriate parties first thing. She kept that promise. Not an hour before visiting hours were to open, I was called by a staff member in the Hematology Department to schedule my test.

"Grant...you didn't need to do that—" Greta starts to object.

I cut her off. "Yes. I. Did. For once in my life, I have family. We may not know each other, but I'll be damned if I'm going to let you die and not get my chance to get to know you."

Tears fall down Greta's cheeks. "I didn't want you to come into our lives this way..." She hiccups and sobs.

Brett takes her other hand and brings it to his lips, kisses it, and comforts her. "Pookie, you have to let him get tested. This could be your best chance for a match. You know they told us siblings were the most likely source for a bone marrow match that would produce new cells after transplantation. There is also the least chance of rejection."

More tears fill Greta's eyes. "Grant, I wanted you in my life. Not to have to save it."

I grab her other hand and smile. "That's what big brothers are for, right?"

She laughs and grips my hand with both of hers.

"I'll never be able to repay you for this, especially if you're a match." She sucks in a shallow breath.

"Then you'll owe me one someday." I grin. "Maybe when Luna and I have children, you'll babysit for us."

Her eyes shine with happiness. "I'd love that. And you have to meet my kids, Gavin and Gabriella. Gavin looks exactly like you. Brown hair and blue eyes. Gabriella is her daddy's girl. Blond hair and light eyes. We're not sure of the color yet, but I want you to meet them soon."

Luna runs her hand down my back and curls against my side. I loop my arm around her waist, appreciating her warmth and solidarity. "I look forward to that day."

A nurse enters the room and greets Greta and then informs us she needs to take some blood samples and other medical things she needs privacy for. I nod and then lean over Greta's bed and place a single kiss on her forehead.

"I'll let you know the results of the test. I'm slated for eleven a.m. They said it would only take a few hours because they have hematologists on hand here to run the necessary tests. We'll know this afternoon."

Greta nods. "Thank you, Grant. I'm not sure there are words that can express my gratitude for what you're doing."

"Just live... That's all that matters."

I turn around and head out the door, Luna by my side, until I hear Brett call from somewhere behind us.

"Grant, hey, wait up." He jogs the twenty odd feet to us. "Look, man, I know we got off on the wrong foot..."

"All my fault." I raise my hands in a gesture of surrender.

"I wasn't expecting to hear the information your wife told me. Having a sister wasn't even on my radar."

Brett rubs at the back of his neck. "Yeah, well, I didn't take your response well. It's just with Greta being sick and a new baby... The house of cards is falling down around me."

I reach my hand out and cup his shoulder with the most supportive gesture I can muster. "It's okay. I understand. Any man in your position would lose his mind. If it was Luna..." I shake my head.

Brett nods and swallows, his voice scratchy when he responds. "What you're doing could save her. Truly save her life, and I'm thankful. So, thank you. For what you're about to do."

"Man, we don't even know if I'm a good match." My own voice cracks, and I cough to clear it.

"No, but the fact that you want to try means a whole helluva lot." He pulls out a business card. "This is my contact information. It has my cell phone on it too."

I reach into my own pocket and pull out one of my cards and hand it to him. "Same here."

He pockets the card and smiles. "Okay, well, keep us posted."

"Will do."

"Thanks again. Good seeing you, Luna."

"You as well," Luna states, looping her fingers with mine.

We both watch as he walks back to his wife's room, his shoulders down and his head forward.

Luna leans her head against mine and runs her free hand up and down my arm. "You're a good man, Grant Winters."

I look down and kiss her forehead.

"Let's go see about the test. I hear it's a bit painful."

"Oh...I'm sure I can nurse you back to health," she says suggestively.

"Lamb, are you suggesting some sexy role playing where you're the hot nurse and I'm your patient?"

She giggles. "Maybe. Why? Does that excite you?"

"Hell yes! Come on, Nurse Marigold, I know how we're going to kill a few hours while waiting for the results after my test."

"You're a bad boy."

"Just a minute ago I was a good man. Now I'm a bad boy?" I knock her shoulder with my own.

She chuckles, and the sound lifts my mood. "You've got me."

"Oh, I have no doubt I'm going to get you...right between your pretty thighs."

"Shhhh! Grant!" she scolds, and we laugh all the way to my appointment with the lab.

Please, God, make me a match.

CHAPTER NINETEEN

CROWN
C H A K R A

*When you have a perfectly balanced crown
chakra, you will feel grounded, in control of your
emotions, connected to God, and intuitive.*

LUNA

After the test was complete, we went home and made love.
Grant was quiet on the way home, but the second we entered
my loft, he was pushing me against the wall, his hard body all
over me.

Now we lie in bed, his face resting against my chest, one
finger drawing circles over my breasts, down my rib cage,
around my naval, and back up.

"Are you scared?" I ask, worried he's not expressing his
feelings through words.

He blows out a puff of air, and it warms my nipple. "Yeah. I want to be a match."

I cup the back of his head, holding him closer to me. "I want you to be a match too."

"It's strange."

"What is?"

"Before meeting Greta, I had nothing in my life to live for besides you and work. Now the possibilities are far grander. A sister, brother-in-law, and a niece and nephew. I've never had a family before. And Luna, I want it. So bad I can taste it. It's like I've been presented with this new life, one with you and a family, and I'll stop at nothing to have it. Does that make sense?"

My eyes water, knowing this is hurting him. Understanding the ache he must have. I had it when I lost my father. Before his passing, my family of three was everything. Now my mother is traveling with her best friend, and I'm here alone. Except I'm not. I have Grant now and the studio and everyone in it.

"It makes perfect sense. And I have a feeling it's all going to be okay." I kiss the crown of his head.

He sighs and goes back to tracing my shape with his fingertips. I don't know if it comforts him to touch me or if he's attempting to go for round three, but with each pass of his fingertips around my erect nipple, a jolt of arousal shoots through my body and lands between my thighs.

I wrap my arms around him. He lifts up his face and smirks before shifting his body on top of mine and kissing between my breasts. Slowly, he moves to one aching tip and then the other, worshiping my breasts and neck, bathing me in kisses.

I sigh and arch into his ministrations, loving every second. He works his way down, nipping at my ribs, licking a circle around my belly button, until he reaches between my thighs.

"Spread your legs for me, lamb. I want my mouth on you."

I do as he asks, opening my legs.

He sits up on his knees and slides both hands down my thighs. His touch is one of reverence, his expression, awe.

"I love every inch of you, Luna. Your pearlescent skin. Your bee-stung lips. Sky-blue eyes. Fiery red hair, but nothing... *nothing* compares to the beauty between your thighs. I'm *starved* for you." He covers my sex with the heat of his mouth.

I cry out and grip his hair as he devours me, taking me higher and higher in mere minutes until every press of his lips and tongue sends ribbons of pleasure rippling through my nerve endings, and I fly apart. Lost to the magic of his dark kiss.

He brings me down slowly, leisurely, as though he has all the time in the world to please me.

And then his cell phone rings right as he's about to enter me for the third time today.

His entire body goes rigid. Each of his beautiful muscles bulging, skin misted with sweat from giving me his all. The erection between those powerful thighs is long, hard, and so thick I mewl with the desire to have him inside, completing me.

He scrambles from between my legs and around the bed where his phone lies.

"Winters," he barks into the phone. "Yes." His once heated gaze turns sharper, more focused, and I watch as my man closes his eyes and then looks up at the sky as if he's sending a silent prayer up to the heavens above. A serene expression crosses his face, and a small smile forms on his lips. "That's great news."

I sit up, tugging the sheet to cover my naked body. His smiles make me smile.

He's a match. That must be the reason for his happy expression. I know it straight through to my soul.

Then, as if water was splashed over his face, he frowns, his eyebrows coming so close together on his forehead they're almost touching.

"I'm sorry. Is that unusual?"

Those same expressive eyebrows seem to have a life of their own as they rise in what I can only assume is shock.

"What exactly are you saying?" His tone is firm and unrelenting.

I watch, my breath caught in my throat, as he starts to pace, naked as the day he was born, his erection deflating at whatever news he's received.

"And that only occurs with full-blooded siblings." He states matter-of-factly. "I see. Thank you. Set up the harvest as necessary. I will take whatever appointment is available."

He hangs up his cell and tosses it on the bed. Grant's hands go into his hair, and he starts to pace again. "Fuck!"

Uh-oh. He only paces when he's trying to work through uncomfortable information.

"Grant, honey, what is it? You're a match, right?"

He nods. "Yeah. Oh, I'm a match all right."

I shimmy out of bed and stop him midstride. "Then what's the matter? This is what you wanted, correct? To be able to donate."

He puts his hands behind his neck, his fingers clasped, elbows parallel to the floor. "I'm a match."

"Okay, that's good." I place my hands on his pecs. "Then what's wrong?"

"I'm a perfect fucking match. None better." His face is turning red.

He's angry.

"Big man, you're going to have to help me out here. I'm not catching on to the problem."

"Apparently, the test they did not only proves your percentage of compatibility, but it confirmed that Greta Tinsley is my biological sister."

I frown. "We already knew that. You share the same mother."

He shakes his head and speaks through clenched teeth. "No. That would make her my half sister. She's my *full* sister because we share the same mother *and* father."

I open my mouth and gawk. "No..."

"Yes," he growls.

Gooseflesh rises all over my skin. "How can this be? Greta said that when your mom left, she was pregnant with another man's baby."

Grant turns around and goes over to the rack of clothing we added for him near my own wardrobe. It's a makeshift clothing alternative for now until we have our new home. He rips off a T-shirt and pair of jeans.

"Means we don't have all the information, and neither does Greta. I spent thirty years not knowing my sister. I'm not spending the next thirty in the dark."

"What are you doing? Where are you going?" I ask as he slips on a pair of underwear and then his jeans.

"To talk to my father."

"Um, do you think that's a good idea when you don't know all the information? Besides, shouldn't we get to Greta first to tell her and Brett the good news?" I'm trying to be the voice of reason. He needs to cool down before he speaks to Grant Senior.

Grant tugs on his shirt, the black material stretching delectably across his muscular chest. I follow his lead, slipping into a pair of underwear and then yoga pants, a bra, tank, and a tunic.

"Fine. I'll call him while we're there. Have him meet us. This bullshit ends today. I want answers, and someone is going to give them to me." His tone brooks no arguments.

I nod and slip into some gladiator sandals before pulling my hair up into a ponytail. Makeup is not an option. Grant is already about to burst out of his skin if we don't get in the car and head to the hospital soon.

He grabs my hand as I cross the strap of my purse over my body. We're out the door and headed to the hospital at lightning speed.

GRANT

The minute we enter the room, the three people already seated stop speaking. Greta is lying in the bed, Brett on one side of her, a redheaded woman I can just barely remember at her other side.

The woman stands up, her hair falling down her back like I recall from my memories. Her hair and eyes have haunted my dreams. And in every last one of them, she still leaves.

"Grant. Son," she whispers, as if my presence is hurting her emotionally.

I narrow my gaze at her as Luna glues herself to my side. I wrap an arm around her shoulders, keeping her close. I'm going to need her fortitude to get through this moment.

Ignoring the woman, I turn my focus to Greta. "I'm a match."

Brett, who stood when I entered, leans heavily over his wife's bed, his shoulders starting to quake. "Thank you, God!"

His wife grabs his hand, but her eyes are on me. "You're a match?" Her voice quavers.

"Yes." I choke down the emotion swelling in my throat.

"You don't have to do this." Her voice cracks, and her eyes fill with tears.

"Yes, I do. You're my sister. I'm your brother. I take care of what's mine."

Tears rain down her cheeks in rivulets.

Brett comes around the bed, arms open wide. Luna releases me, and I let the man hug me. He claps my back hard. "Grant...I can't thank you enough. Shit..." He sobs, and I wrap my arms around him and hug him back as he breaks down.

"Owe you, man. Owe you *everything*." He barely gets the words out on a hoarse whisper before pulling away and rubbing a hand down his face, getting himself back together.

"We're not out of the woods yet," I announce. "Her body has to accept my marrow, though the hematologist doesn't see any problem with that since we're a *perfect* match, which often comes with *full-blooded* siblings. Isn't that right...Mother?" I grate through clenched teeth and glare at the woman standing silently to my right.

Greta clears her throat. "What are you talking about? Mom?" Greta grabs our mother's wrist, and she jolts as if she'd been zapped with electricity.

"I don't know, baby girl..." she attempts, but there is no way in hell I'm going to let her continue to lie to either of us.

"You absolutely do. Stop lying. For once. Tell her the truth. Tell us *all* the truth." My voice rises to the point where I'm almost yelling.

Luna sidles back up to me and puts a hand to my chest. I can feel her touch seep deep into my soul, soothing me like a cool balm over a heated burn.

"Your father didn't believe me!" she says. "I told him the baby was his, but he cast me out anyway. Said I was fooling around on him. Over and over I told him I wasn't. He wouldn't believe me." Her volume turns a bit high-pitched.

I close my eyes as the ramifications of what she's saying slam into my heart.

"Why would he think you were unfaithful?" I say flatly.

My mother twists her fingers and looks down at the floor. A shameful stance if I ever saw one. "There was this man. Chris. Another father at your kindergarten class. We became close. He was a single father, and um, very attractive." She picks up a hunk of her hair and runs her hands over it in what seems to be a nervous gesture.

"Continue." I glance at Greta.

Brett's sitting on the hospital bed, his wife in his arms, her face planted against his chest but her eyes on our mother.

"I was married, and I never went there with him physically. Not really." Her voice shook. "Your father, he couldn't see reason. He was gone all the time, barely ever home, always working, and I was lonely. So lonely."

"And..." I prompt when it doesn't seem like she's going to continue.

"One day he came home early from a business trip. He found us having a play date. Chris and I were on the couch. You kids were playing in your room, and I don't know what happened, but Chris kissed me. It was only ever the one kiss, and your father walked in and saw us kissing and lost his mind." Tears fill her eyes. "A week later, I found out I was pregnant. Told Grant Senior this was our second chance to find happiness. All he could see was Chris. He believed the child was Chris's because he was gone all the time. I tried for four months to get him to believe otherwise. Tried to be the perfect wife. I never saw Chris again, but it wasn't enough."

"He asked you to leave," I surmised.

She shook her head. "No. He cast me out. Said I needed to leave and take my bastard child with me but to leave you behind. If I didn't, he'd ruin Chris's life, mine, as well as that of my unborn child. I was young and scared. I had nothing but your father and you. I believed him. He was very powerful. Had a lot of money and contacts. He'd do as he threatened. So I sat you down, said goodbye, and left. It was the worst day of my entire life. There hasn't been a day that goes by that I don't wish I could have found a way to take you with me or to get your father to believe me. But you know him. Once he gets something in his mind..."

"There's no changing it," I add flatly.

She nods.

"Then why did you tell me my father was from an infidelity from your first husband? You lied to me all these years, Mother?" Greta's voice is filled with heartache.

My mother closes her eyes, more tears falling. "Because I couldn't bear to have you think your own father didn't want you. It was better that you thought I was the one in the wrong."

Jesus, what a clusterfuck. The end result being my father is the biggest prick in the universe and my mother another one of his victims.

"I loved you every day, Grant. Missed you every second. And I wrote you like I promised."

I scowl. "I didn't get a single letter."

My heart pounds against my chest as my body temperature rises, and she takes a step closer to me. I take one back in return, making it clear I do not want her near me. Not right now.

"No. Each one was returned unopened and labeled Return to Sender. Still, every week until you went off to college, I wrote to you. Told you about our lives, wondered about yours. Wished for your happiness. Hoped maybe one day you'd get the mail and open it yourself. Still, we went to your sports games, watched you graduate both high school and college. Those were very proud moments for me," she whispers and wipes at her soggy eyes.

Shivers ripple up my spine, and tears prick against my eyes, but I don't let them fall. Not here. Not now. I focus on the fire in my gut, the tornado of anger building up my chest.

There are too many conflicting emotions battering me. I swallow and reach for Luna's hand. "I need to go check in with the hematologist and find out what the next steps are. Greta, let's focus on getting you well, yeah?"

She nods.

"The rest we will deal with in time." It's the only promise I can offer her right now.

"Okay, Grant." She sniffles, and it sends an icepick into my gut.

"Luna, let's go." I grip her hand.

Without waiting for goodbyes, I drag Luna out of the room.

"Grant, wait, just stop." She tugs on my hand until I stop and spin around.

"What? What do you want to talk about? How fucked up that scene in there was? How my father is the world's most giant prick! Maybe about the fact that my sister just found she has a father, and he's the same one everybody hates!" I roar, not caring about the people bustling around me.

Luna grabs my hand and walks me to the stairwell, where we escape inside.

"Look, I know it was messed up..."

"You think?" I respond, my tone dripping with sarcasm.

Luna scrunches up her nose and glares at me. "Your anger is not helping the situation. You need to calm down and think all of this through. A lot just happened. You have seen your mother for the first time in thirty years. Let's start with that."

I shake my head. "What about it?"

"Well, what are you feeling?"

I groan. "Numb. I'm feeling numb."

She purses her lips. "Okay, I can understand the feeling. It's got to be hard, knowing what she went through. Losing her the way you did."

I swallow around the sudden lump in my throat. "Yeah."

Luna pulls me into a hug, and I curl my arms around her. Her warmth, energy, and love fill up all the emptiness I had before her entry into my life.

"Are you going to be okay? This was a lot to take in, and you're planning to go through the harvesting process, which is a whole other big task ahead."

I sigh and inhale the scent of her strawberry shampoo. "As long as I have you, I can face anything. Just don't ever leave me."

She leans back and cups my cheeks. "Grant. You're never getting rid of me." She stands on tiptoe to kiss me. I take her mouth, and I take it deep. I drink from her lips, sucking in all of her goodness and light, allowing her essence to blanket me for the challenges ahead. And my lamb gives it freely.

I rub my forehead against hers. "I love you."

She hums and kisses my lips briefly. "I love you too."

We stand there for a long time in the empty hospital stairwell, embracing one another and reinforcing our connection.

Luna runs her fingers through my hair. "What's next?"

"We go to Hematology and find out what we need to do."

"And then?"

"Then I pay a visit to my father."

★ ★ ★

The process for a bone marrow donation is unbelievably easy and the hospital top notch. They wasted zero time in getting me scheduled for the next morning. It would be an in-and-out, same-day procedure. I'd go in at eight o'clock and then be released late that afternoon. I'd be asleep for the procedure. The doctors would begin preparing Greta for transplant, and we'd know in the coming weeks if the transplant worked.

I was eager to get the show on the road and restless as Luna held me in her arms in our bed.

"I'm glad you decided to wait to see your father." Luna runs her hand up and down my bare abs.

"Me too. I need to be clearheaded for the procedure tomorrow, and there's too much to say to him. My thoughts and feelings are too raw and disjointed to make any sense. Plus, I'm more worried about getting this done for my sister than anything else. She needs to be my focus right now."

Luna nods. "What you're doing for Greta is amazing. You know that, right?"

I sigh and place my hand on her arm. "I'm doing what

anyone in my situation would do."

Luna shifts up onto her elbow so I can see her face in the moonlight shining into our loft.

"That simply isn't true. Not every man would step up, especially for someone he barely knows."

I run my fingers through her silky hair. "She's my sister," I say, as if that answers all.

She frowns. "Yes, but you didn't know until recently. And with everything going on... I just... I think you need to realize what you are doing is commendable. Honorable. And I, for one, am proud of you."

I grip her around the waist and tug her up and on top of my body so she's plastered to my chest. "Thank you for being here with me. For being you. For not leaving my side. You're my rock, Luna. I could never have maintained my sanity without you in my life."

She dips her head forward and kisses me before speaking. "And you're never going to be without me." She moves to kiss me again, but I cup her cheeks, stopping her forward progress.

"Do you mean it?"

Her nose scrunches up in the cute way I adore. "Mean what?"

"That I'm never going to be without you?"

She smiles wide. "Of course. I love you with my whole heart, with my entire being. You're my one, Grant Winters."

"Then let's make it official." My heart speeds up, and butterflies take flight in my stomach as I wait for her to answer.

She sits up, and I move my hands to her waist as she rests her palms flat against my chest. "What are you saying?"

"I'm saying I want you with me forever. As my woman. As my one and only. As my wife."

She gasps. "Grant..."

"I'm serious. I want to marry you. When all of this blows over and we have some breathing room, I want to make you my wife." The decision was so easy it just came out.

I want Luna as my wife.

"You're not kidding?" She shakes her head, her curls falling over her bare breasts, her nipples poking through the fiery strands like a carnal game of hide and seek.

I shake my head. "No. When I know what I want, I chase after it until I get it, make it mine."

Her voice is low when she replies. "You don't have to chase me. I'm already yours."

I lick my lips. "Prove it. Marry me."

"It's too soon. We've only been together a couple months."

"Luna, you can't put a time stamp on love. I want you with me until the day I take my last breath. I want you to bear my children. Hopefully, sooner rather than later."

"Sweet Shiva. Now you're planning to get me pregnant!" She gasps and puts a hand to her heart.

"Lamb, do you want to be with me forever?" I ask, my heart in my throat, my entire soul open, bared to her, waiting for her to accept the gift.

"Yes," she whispers but loud enough so I can hear her perfectly.

"Then what does the amount of time between us matter? It only matters the amount of time we have left and that we not waste it."

She smiles wide. "I can't believe we're doing this. My mother is going to freak."

I grin. "Does that mean what I think it means? You're going to marry me?"

Luna places both of her hands on either side of my head, plasters her chest to mine, and whispers against my lips, "Yes. Yes, I will marry you, Grant Winters."

I lock my arms around her and roll us both until I'm hovering over her. "I'm going to make you so happy." I kiss her lips and pull back, smiling.

"You already do. Just by being you. Now come here. I want my fiancé to make love to me." She tugs at my back and neck to bring me closer.

"Anything you want, lamb. It's yours."

CHAPTER TWENTY

CROWN
CHAKRA

*The crown chakra couple is said to have a spiritual love that
spans the afterlife. When they die, they will join one another
in the spiritual world to live out their days together, forever.*

GRANT

"Son. To what do I owe this pleasure?" My father stands
from behind his desk in his study and walks over to the
sideboard. He pours himself a whiskey neat. "Drink?"

"Yes." I'm going to need it.

When he's made our drinks and hands me one, he sits
down in one of the red velvet, high-backed chairs near the
fire he has going. The room is draped in luxury and opulence.
Floor-to-ceiling antique eighteenth-century bookcases span
half the room, and the expensive art he's collected over the

AUDREY CARLAN

years covers the rest. He doesn't even like art. He obtained
the pieces to save face with his rich buddies. Those pictures
should be in museums for the world to see, not collecting dust
in a stuffy old man's office, rarely to be seen by anyone outside
of the one percenters he rolls with.

I sit in the chair opposite him and try my best to get my
immediate anger at even seeing him under control.

*Follow what Luna said. Say your piece. Get your answers,
and go back home to her.*

I take a full breath in and let it out before speaking like
Luna taught me. "Father, I've met Greta Tinsley."

My father's face doesn't change or reveal even a hint of
recognition. "Should I know this name?"

"Yes. She's my sister."

This time, Grant Senior's eyes flare, but they do so with
anger, not remorse. He moves his drink to the side table and
leans forward, a filthy scowl marring his face. "Did that bastard
child try to blackmail you by claiming to be your sister and
having some kind of right to our fortune?" he growls.

I shake my head and calmly take a sip of my whiskey,
allowing it to burn a fiery trail down my throat and warm my
gut. "No. Not at all. Apparently, she's known of me for a long
time. We ran into each other at a restaurant."

"Oh, she'd like you to think that. They've all got angles,
son, and they are never genuine."

"You would think so. And at first, I did as well, but I had
my team investigate her. And do you know what they found
out?"

He grabs his drink and takes a healthy slug. I wait for him
to finish the drink. "Well, don't sit on it, boy. Spit it out. What
did they find?"

"She is indeed my sister. Gretchen Winters is her mother."

On the mention of that name, his face turns red and the scowl deepens. "That cheating slut! She was never supposed to contact you. I warned her. If she did, I'd ruin her and the lives of her manwhore and her bastard child." He stands up, walks over to the sideboard, and pours himself another drink. This time, he takes a huge glug.

"Turns out, Greta Tinsley was suffering from a rare disease. One for which she needs a bone marrow transplant."

My father grunts. "And now we're getting somewhere. This being the reason why they contacted you. To get your marrow! Blood-sucking vampires! I hope you told them to stick it where the sun doesn't shine and to drop dead!" he hollers and paces the room.

"No, I didn't. I met with Greta and found her to be a lovely woman."

"Of course they're going to make you think that, son!" He sneers. "They want something from you!"

I shake my head and sip my drink. "Actually, at first, Greta didn't even tell me about her disease. Luna found out about it accidentally and informed me."

He huffs. "You think that because you're too soft. You always have been, even as much as I've pushed to toughen you up. What you don't see, son, is that they planned every last second of you coming into contact with them. I'll bet that bitch Gretchen was the mastermind behind it too."

"Again, you'd be wrong. And I was tested to find out if I was a bone marrow match for Greta."

My father sighs and sits back down in his chair. "Let me guess... You were a match." He rolls his eyes dramatically.

"Yes." I grin, loving that he thinks he's laying into me when

I haven't even dropped the bomb on him. This game of cat and mouse is taking the burn off the knowledge I now know to be true.

"Please tell me you're not going to give her a goddamned thing."

I shake my head. "Actually, I've already donated. I underwent the procedure last week. Greta has received the transplant, and we'll know if her body accepts my marrow and starts creating white and red blood cells to fight her disease very soon." I smile wide.

"Look at your face. You're pleased with yourself. Son, you've made a grave mistake, but I'll clean it up. I'll wipe the floor with them."

"No. You will do no such thing," I say with a raised voice and returning anger.

He frowns. "Don't you dare tell me what I can and cannot do. I am your father. The patriarch of the Winters name. I will protect you even if you won't protect yourself! These people are bottom feeders. The scum of the earth. A bastard child and an unfaithful woman."

"Why didn't you ever tell me my mother wrote me letters?"

He snorts. "She didn't. Left you, left me, and took her bastard child with her."

"Lie!" I roar and slam the tumbler down on the table, the contents sloshing outside of the glass and spilling all over the wood.

My father glances at the drink and then back up at me, his eyes turning to daggers. "What did you say to me?"

"You're a liar and a coward! My mother didn't leave you. You cast her away with threats of ruining her life and the life of her unborn baby. You told her if she ever approached me, you'd set a plan into place that would destroy her and Greta as well as the man you thought she was cheating on you with. Which, by the way, she never did!"

He laughs dryly. "I caught them kissing in this very house!"

"*That* she did admit. And I understand if you couldn't trust her anymore, but you did not have to cast her and your own child out the door with nothing. You could have divorced her and allowed me to still have a mother! I prayed for years, Father...*years* that she would come home."

I stand and rub at the back of my neck. "And you forced her to go, leaving me without a mother for my entire life!"

"She didn't deserve you. And the child she carried was proof of her infidelity. What would you have me do? Raise another man's child as if it were my own, a daily reminder of her treachery?" he grates through his teeth before sucking back more whiskey.

"You are so fucking blind. I had the test done to see if I was a match for her marrow. And you know what they told me...oh, patriarch, seer of all things? They told me Greta Tinsley and I are an exact match because we are siblings."

"Of course you are."

"*Full-blooded* siblings, Father! Thirty-year-old Greta Tinsley is your biological daughter. Her four-year-old son, Gavin, and her six-month-old daughter, Gabriella, are your grandchildren, and you're never going to know them."

"It's part of their lies! They are telling you a tale," he blusters and stands to go fill his drink once more. Fucking old man has turned into an alcoholic.

"No. It's the truth. The tests have been done. I have a copy right here." I pull out the second, more conclusive DNA test I had run by the hospital. "This is the DNA test I personally had done. It's all there, in black and white. Greta is your daughter and my sister. Now, if you will excuse me, I have a family to get to know, without you."

"Son...this can't be true!" he cries out, the information apparently starting to seep in.

"It is the truth. And so is the fact that you are going to die old and alone with no family around you. I'm going to talk to the board of directors on Monday. Either you resign from the board, or I will resign as CEO of the company. You can train a replacement."

"Son..." He gasps. "I have built Winters Group to be the global leader it is. You and this company are my legacy, my father's legacy, your grandfather's legacy..."

"Yes, and I will continue to run it as I see fit, but only if you remove yourself from it. Otherwise, I'll take my shares and sell to the highest bidder, and someone else will be the second-largest investor in the company and you'll have to answer to them. Though I think if I tell the board and the current investors that it's either you or me, they'll choose me. I'm willing to risk it either way. Are you?"

"You can't do this!" he screams. "You're my son! I've taught you everything you know!"

"This is true. However, there is a part of me you haven't been able to touch. My heart. And it's owned by Luna, Greta, and my new family. Now if you will excuse me...I need to spend some time with the woman who gave me life and get to know her."

"You're choosing a woman you barely know over me!" He grabs at his heart, and his form cants to the side, where he catches himself on the back of the chair, his drink spilling down the red velvet.

"Ohh...that's gonna leave a stain. The choice is yours. Resign from the board, keep your shares, and you stay rich in the knowledge that I'm a good leader and will take the company where it's meant to go. Play with your trophy wife; take up backgammon and traveling for all I care. Just do it away from me and my family." I start walking toward the door. "Oh, and by the way, Luna and I are getting married three months from now. You're not invited."

"Grant! Wait...son! You can't do this. You don't want to do this! I'm your father!" he hollers, but I keep walking until I'm out the front door of my childhood home and into my Aston Martin on my way to see my fiancée, who's waiting for me.

★ ★ ★

The moment I enter my apartment, Luna is rushing to me, arms open wide. She slams her body into mine in a fierce hug. She squeezes me hard before pulling back, cupping my cheeks, and staring into my eyes.

"Are you okay?"

I smile wide and wrap my arms loosely around her waist. "Yeah, lamb. I am. More than okay. I'm free."

"Free?"

"Yep. Free of his reign, the power he holds over me."

"Wow. That sounds life changing." She blinks prettily, but her focus is all on me. The house could be burning down around us, and her entire focus would be on me.

"I gave him an ultimatum."

Her eyes seem to widen. "Really?"

"He resigns from the board of directors, or I resign from

Winters Group as the CEO and sell my shares in the company to the highest bidder."

Her mouth drops open. "No, you didn't!"

"Oh, but I did."

"What did he say?"

"He was angry, of course. Livid. I didn't react to it. I breathed calmly like you said and told the truth."

"The whole truth?" She pets my lip with her thumb.

"Yeah." I let out a breath of air. "Everything. About Greta being his daughter, about how we are getting married, and he isn't invited..."

She frowns, and her entire face turns sad. It's like kicking a puppy. She's so very expressive. I always know where I stand with her and how she feels about something. "Are you sure about that?"

I curl my hand around her cheek and tilt her chin with my thumb. "Positive. He's not going to sour the most important day of our lives. Speaking of sour... How's that sweet and sour pork you're making for dinner? It smells wonderful."

As if I flipped a switch, her face lights up, and she bounces in place. "It's going to be awesome, and they'll be here soon! I also made some homemade macaroni and cheese for the kids. Greta says they love mac and cheese." She claps. "I can't wait to meet my niece and nephew! Eeek! It's so exciting!"

As if on cue, the buzzer to my door rings. I would have liked to have them over to the loft above the bakery, but it's far too small. I thought about taking them out but figured it would have been awkward since we're trying to get to know one another and meeting the kids for the first time.

I head to the door and pull it open. Greta smiles huge when she sees me and rushes into my arms. Her head lands on my chest.

Behind her, I find Brett, who has a diaper bag in one hand and a child carrier in the other. Next to him is Gretchen, holding the hand of a dapper little boy who is the spitting image of me at that age. Wild layers of brown hair and dark-blue eyes. He's clinging to his grandmother's leg and assessing me.

I get down on my haunches and smile at the boy. "Hey there, little guy. I'm your Uncle Grant."

"Yeah, I know. Mommy tolded me."

"And that pretty redhead behind me is your Aunt Luna. We'd love to have you come in and spend time with us. Would that be all right?"

"I have presents!" Luna squeals behind me.

I chuckle and shake my head. "Of course you do."

"One for every birthday we missed!" she adds, her voice hitting mass volume with her exuberance.

Gavin's eyes bug out a bit. "Presents. For me and Sissy?"

"Looks like it, bud. You want to come in and check it out?"

He taps his mouth the same way I do when I'm thinking hard on something before he smiles. "Okay!" And then he runs in toward Luna.

"Hello, son. Um, I mean, Grant." My mother holds out her hand in greeting.

I lick my lips, look down at her hand, clasp it, and tug her toward my chest. I let her go, and she wraps her arms around me, hugging me close. Her body trembles in my arms. "You have no idea how long I've wanted to hug you." Her voice is coated in heartache.

I pet her hair, close my eyes, and breathe in her fresh linen scent. It whirls around my senses, reminding me of summer long ago, laughter, and a whole lot of love. Everything I'd forgotten over the years, having been so young when I lost her.

"Me too, Mom. Me too."

She chokes on a sob when I call her Mom.

"Hey, you two, the kids are about to open their presents. Something you didn't need to do, by the way!" Her tone is conciliatory but playful too.

I hook my arm over my mother's shoulder and lead her into the living room, where Gavin is tearing through brightly wrapped packages.

"I have zero control over my woman. She owns my soul, and if she wants to buy our niece and nephew presents, far be it from me to stop her."

Greta rolls her eyes, and it looks exactly like how my father did earlier in the day. A prick of pain pierces my heart, but I look around the room and let the new love of family fill it up and make me whole again.

"We have something for the two of you as well," Greta announces, handing Luna a package.

Luna sits on the couch and pats the side next to her. I let my mother go and sit down next to her. "What have we got?"

"I don't know. Do you want to open it?" she offers, but I can tell she's dying to open it herself.

"No, lamb, you go on ahead."

She lifts her shoulders to her ears and squeaks adorably. I'm going to have to buy her gifts more often because I love hearing the multitude of excited sounds she makes when she's happy.

When the paper is torn apart and the box lid lifted, she pulls out two silver framed photos. The first one is a picture of Brett, Greta, Gavin, and little Gabriella in her mom's arms. Etched into the bottom of the frame it says *The Tinsleys*, but it's the next frame that puts a vise lock on my throat, making it instantly dry and scratchy. In the next silver frame is a picture of just Gavin holding his baby sister, Gabriella. On the top of the frame it says *Uncle Grant & Aunt Luna* and the bottom says *We love you. Gavin & Gaby.*

Luna sniffs and pets the picture over her title of Aunt Luna and then brings it up to her chest as if she's hugging it. "We love it. Don't we love it, Grant?"

"Yeah, awesome gift. Thank you."

Luna pops up, taking the frames over to the mantle. "For now, we're going to set them here. Then, when we get our new home, we'll put it back above the fireplace so we can see them every day."

I stand up and hug my sister and then shake Brett's hand. "You want a beer, brother?" I ask.

Brett squeezes my hand and claps me on the shoulder. "Yeah, brother, I do."

I wink at him and then find out what everyone wants. Gaby is sleeping, and Gavin is already playing trucks on the table with his new toys.

As I enter the kitchen, Greta follows me.

"So I met with my hematologist today, and the good news is, he said my body is not rejecting your marrow. He thinks it's working, but we need to wait a little longer to really tell if my red and white blood cells are regenerating. With the last few rounds of blood transfusions, you can't really tell, but since I'm having no side effects suggesting rejection, we're on a positive path."

I smile wide and lean into the counter. "That's great, Greta. Good news. A definite positive first step."

"Yes, it is."

I turn around and pour a glass of water and hand it to her. Then I go back and get a beer for Brett and pass it to her to give to her man. After she takes it, I pour Luna, Mother, and myself a glass of Rombauer Zinfandel and bring it out to them.

"A toast," Luna says and looks pointedly to me.

"To family. There's nothing more important," I say.

"Hear, hear!" Brett says.

"Absolutely," Gretchen agrees.

"Yay!" Luna cheers, cuddling into my side.

"To my beautiful family. To Greta and Brett, my son, Grant, and soon-to-be daughter-in-law, Luna, and my lovely grandchildren...I love you all."

The five of us raise our glasses to each other, and Luna and I look one another right in the eye and sip at the same time, smiling.

After dinner, I find myself sitting on my couch, a four-year-old against my side, my arm around his little body as we watch a cartoon I was able to get via On Demand. In my other arm, Luna is holding baby Gabriella, or Gaby as I've found the family calls her. She's asleep and has all of Luna's attention. Greta is watching the godawful cartoon with rapt attention cuddled beside her husband, and my mother is sipping her after-dinner decaf and Bailey's while watching her children, a serene expression on her face.

I nudge Luna from her staring contest with a sleeping baby. "You ready for one of those?" I grin.

She smiles wide, and it steals my breath. My woman is by far the most beautiful woman I've ever known.

"How's about we start trying on our honeymoon?"

She purses her lips, thinks about it for all of two seconds, and then smirks. "You think you can get me pregnant that fast?"

"Oh, lamb, when it comes to being with you, I'll take on any challenge. I'm the right man for the job." I blow her a kiss, and she giggles.

"Yes, you are. The perfect man for me." She leans over to kiss me.

"Ew, gross. Not posta kiss while watching toons." Gavin bats at my leg.

"Do you see how pretty Aunt Luna is, bud?" I hook a thumb toward her body.

He puckers his lips, taps on them with his first finger, and focuses all his attention on her. "Yes. She's pretty. I wike her hair. Wike Grandma's, only more redder."

"So you see why I can't help wanting to kiss her."

He tilts his head and then shakes it. "No kissing during toons." He says it as an admonishment, not a statement, sounding very much like his Uncle Grant during business dealings. Apparently, he takes his cartoons very seriously.

"All right. All right, bud. I'll be good." I rock his shoulders, and he giggles and smiles up at me. With that one smile, I've fallen in love with a four-year-old boy. I glance to the side and take in my niece's serene face. Okay, maybe I'm a little in love with a six-month-old girl too.

"Um, Grant, could I speak to you privately for a moment?" My mother stands and walks over to her bag, where she pulls out a wooden box about twelve inches long and four inches tall. It has a chunky black latch holding it closed.

"Sure." I hold my hand out toward the hall leading to my bedroom.

She follows me inside, and I shut the door when she's in.

She turns around and presents me with the box. "When

I had to leave you back then..." Her voice cracks and shakes before she clears her throat. "I made you a promise. One I kept. I'd always hoped one day I'd get you back and would be able to give you these." She hands me the wooden box.

"What is it?"

"All of the letters I've written you over the years that your father returned. I never stopped sending them. Every time I mailed one, I would pray and hope that it would finally make its way to you."

I open the box and see what seems like endless stacks of unopened letters, dated and in order.

"Gretchen...uh...Mom, I'm not sure what to say."

She pats my arm. "You don't have to say anything, son. They were for you, and I'm glad I can finally make sure they went to the person for whom they were intended."

CHAPTER TWENTY-ONE

CROWN
CHAKRA

It's the night before I marry the woman I breathe for. Without her, the Grant I've become, the one I'm proud to be, would not exist.

Luna.

My love.

My life.

My everything.

I make myself comfortable in my lonely bed. Luna's mother demanded tradition, so my lamb is staying with her this evening. It took a lot of begging and a stellar blow job on Luna's part to get me to agree to such an archaic tradition, but in the end, I'd do anything for her. Even without her beautiful lips wrapped around my cock, although I'll admit I made out like a bandit. She sucked me, and I fucked the hell out of her. I wanted her to remember me there, between her thighs, all night. Hopefully, she'll dream of me.

Knowing I've been putting off the inevitable, I pull out the box Gretchen gave me months ago. The box contained all the letters she'd written to me over the years. Up to this point, I didn't feel like I was strong enough to read through them. With Luna's love, and the fact that I'm going to make her mine for eternity tomorrow, I feel strong enough to take on the burden of my past.

I pull out the first one. Dated the day after she left me. I'll never forget it because it was Valentine's Day. A day that should be filled with love was the worst day of my life. Since then, I've never celebrated it. This year, I will fill my soon-to-be wife's world with flowers, chocolates, a fancy dinner, and jewels. Not that she cares about those things. She'd be just as happy if not happier with a picnic in the park, but I want to bestow all beauty on her. Perhaps I'll take her to the park and gift her a pair of gemstones the color of her fiery hair. Yes, she'd like that much more.

Opening the first envelope, I take a deep breath and start to read.

Grant,

Yesterday was the worst day of my life. I left you behind. Walked away. My God, it feels as though my soul has been ripped right out of my body and replaced with an emptiness nothing will ever fill again. Every step that I took sent a knife through my heart, baby. You must know that.

Grant, your father is a difficult man, my dear boy. I loved him dearly but apparently not enough for him to trust me. I'm sorry I failed. Failed you and myself. I keep replaying everything that happened over and over, trying desperately to find a place

I could have done better, tried harder to explain. Your father refuses my calls. He won't listen to reason, and he won't back down.

I'm scared, Grant. Scared of what he'd do to me, your unborn sister, and the man he thinks I've cheated on him with. Right now, I can only hope and pray I'll be able to get through to him...find my way back to you.

I love you, my beautiful boy. Forever and ever.

Mom

My heart cracks, and tears fill my eyes as I pick another letter at random.

Grant,

You turned ten years old today. Happy birthday, my beautiful boy.

Greta and I made you a cake, even though we know you'll never see it or taste it. Still, it's our way to stay close to you. We bake things we think you'd like, imagine that you're happy, though I worry you're not. How could you be, without a mother to help guide and nurture you?

I miss you.

Greta is doing well in preschool and eager to start kindergarten next year. Like you, she's so smart. Both of you got that from you father. He was always the smartest man I'd known. Part of what made me fall in love with him all those years ago.

I'll write again soon. Just know that I love you and pray every night that one day I'll be able to see and hug you again.

All my love, forever and ever,

Mom

God, what she must have been going through. Absolute
agony. If Luna and I are blessed with a child one day, I know I'll
want to participate in every moment of my child's life. Since
I've gotten to know Gretchen over the past few months, I see
how the decision my father made all those years ago broke
her. I'm happy we're repairing that relationship now. Family
dinners every week...Luna's idea. It's worked like a charm to
bring me and my mother and sister closer. It's amazing how, in
such a short time, these women I'd never known have become
so important to me. Now I can't imagine my life without them.

My father, on the other hand, is a completely different
story. Luna tells me that I'll have to set aside my anger
and forgive him someday. She says it's unhealthy to hold
resentment in your heart. Only, I can see no other way. He
stole thirty years I could have had with my mother and sister. I
don't know how to forgive him for such cruelty. Perhaps Luna's
right. Regardless of what he's done, I still love and care for him.
It's just different. At this time, I'm not capable of being in his
presence.

Since he resigned in his position on the board of Winters
Group, the company has thrived. None of us realized the hold
he had over the decisions being made. Now that he's gone,
I'm able to truly lead, and so far, our profit margins have
risen in spades. The board members are happy. The staff are
ecstatic, and the construction of the Berkeley Towers is going
smashingly. We should be moved in by next year as long as new
problems don't arise.

Sighing, I pull out another letter farther along in the stack.
Based on the date, it looks like around the time I graduated
high school.

My beautiful boy,

Seeing you walk across that stage was a dream come true. You're so tall, a foot above your sister, but incredibly handsome.

Your valedictorian speech made me weep. I know, I know, I'm a sappy mom, but in that moment, I knew you'd be okay. Sure, I could see the cocky confidence your father has bestowed on you, but in your eyes I could see your soul, son. And, baby, it's beautiful. You are beautiful. I can't wait to see where you end up.

A mutual friend of your father's stated you were going Ivy League. What an honor. My son, Valedictorian and an Ivy League college attendee. You must be spinning with excitement.

Greta and I are cheering you on from afar. She's very proud of her big brother and sad, too, that she doesn't get to know you. I have to keep talking to her about approaching you. She wants more than anything to have a relationship with you, but alas, I fear for her safety and well-being as well as yours. We're not a part of your life, and I fear we never will be. At least I know that my son is going on to bigger and better things. Hopefully, leaving all of this behind.

I wish you all that life has to offer and more.

I love you dearly.

Your mother,

Gretchen

Without even taking a breath, I grab another in the stack. Tears pour down my face and wet my shirt. My heart is pounding out of my chest.

Grant,

I am so proud of you! Greta and I cheered so loudly when your lacrosse team won the championships. We've attended every home game and have loved seeing your skills grow along with the man you're becoming. You're a natural sportsman. Fair, strong, and calculated. Keep up the great work, my beautiful boy.

I love you, forever and ever.

Mom

Wiping my nose and clearing my throat, I suck back a huge gulp of my whiskey I'd poured earlier. The alcohol burns the back of my throat, but it wakes me up. Brings me back to the here and now. This is not a decade ago. It's the night before my wedding. The night before the rest of my life. Still, I grab the very last one in the stack. I need some closure. The rest I'll read with Luna. Allow my connection to her to help heal the wounds of the past as we go through them together. For now, I'll end at the end. The very last one in the box.

My dear son,

Today you graduated college. I have never been happier in my entire life. My son, graduating with honors. I know this is the last letter I will write to you. I now know you are not getting them, and each one returned breaks my heart all over again. Plus, I can't bear to spend another year receiving no responses. Just know, my beautiful boy, that your mother loves you. Always. Forever. And through the rest of my life, until the day I take my dying breath, I will think of you. Often. Fondly. With more love than I can ever bear to share in person.

I wish you the most beautiful life, Grant.

With everything that I am, I love you.

Your mother,

Gretchen

EPILOGUE

LUNA

Today is the first day of the rest of my life. Grant reaches for my hand, and we turn to face the small congregation together.

I see everyone I could ever want or need in my life standing up and cheering.

Dara and Silas McKnight, with their daughter, Destiny, on her daddy's hip and almost one-year-old Jackson on his mommy's. Dara is beaming with joy. "Your auras are beautiful, baby!" she cries out with glee. Silas just shakes his head and kisses his daughter's temple.

Next to them are Atlas and Mila Powers, her large pregnant belly protruding on her small frame. Atlas is holding his daughter, Aria, around the waist as she stands on her chair and claps wildly.

Behind them are Trent and Genevieve Fox and their entire brood, including her brother, Rowan, who has almost finished college at Berkeley State and about to go into the majors alongside his brother-in-law. The Ports want him badly, and he wants to be on the same team as Trent. Mary is standing sweet as can be next to her new boyfriend. Trent keeps giving the boy the stink eye, one arm around his wife, the other around his child, William. Genevieve looks like the mother of fertility as she cradles their newborn daughter, Amberlyn, named after Viv's bestie Amber.

The next row down are Amber and Dash Alexander. Dash is holding his wife in both his arms, his hands protectively cradling her still-flat belly. They just announced their pregnancy to the crew last week, much to everyone's delight. Amber will continue to be a busy pediatrician at UC Davis while Dash scales back some of his tantric writing and speaking engagements to be an at-home dad. Aside from the yoga classes, he'll write books when he can, but his kid is taking front and center while his wife becomes the breadwinner. Her brother, Brian, and his girlfriend are sitting with them, clapping away.

Standing with them are Nick and Honor Salerno and their twins, Hannon and Nick Jr. There has been no announcement of another baby, but the couple has agreed to start trying in the near future. Work has started on the Berkeley Four towers, and along with that, Nick and Honor are busy preparing their second location, which will occupy an entire floor in tower one. Gracie is sitting in the aisle with them, along with her fiancé, Victor, who happens to be one hundred percent Italian, much to the Salerno matriarch's delight. Nick has even given

Victor his approval and hired him to work at their gym. Nick plans to have Victor and Gracie oversee the new gym once it's up and running.

Across the aisle is my mother, Jewel, standing arm-in-arm with her best friend, Crystal Nightingale. Both women are crying what I hope are happy tears. My mother is nothing but smiles. When she came back from her trip to India, she went right into wedding planning mode with her cohort, Crystal. Which was awesome because I was so busy working and preparing for the shutting down of Lotus House while work began on our buildings. My mother took to Grant like a baby to a bottle. She loved him instantly. Said she knew when she touched his hand that his heart was pure and filled with love for me. I don't know how she knew that, and sharing did not occur, but I didn't care either way. All that mattered was my mother was happy for me and liked her future son-in-law. Of course, he did sway her pretty well when he told her we're going to try to conceive during our honeymoon. Grandbabies tend to trump all...or so I'm told.

Behind my mother and auntie is Grant's family. His mother, Gretchen, and her date—who we're told has promise—along with Brett, Greta, Gavin, and Gabriella. Greta is holding both of her hands to her chest, and tears are falling down her cheeks. She's such a big crier! And her tears are making me a bit teary too. Brett is fist-pumping the air like a lunatic, happy as a clam we're about to make them an aunt and uncle. Hopefully.

Standing behind them are Clayton and Monet Hart with their daughter, Lily, and son, Knight. Apparently, Clayton's repeated tossing of Moe's birth control pills worked, because when Amber and Dash announced they were pregnant to the group, Clayton and Monet announced they were having their third child too, though she's only ten weeks versus Amber's twelve. Clayton is ecstatic. Moe apparently has put Clayton on full diaper duty with Knight for his sins.

Pulling in the back rows are Bethany and Coree from Rainy Day Café and Ricardo and his now live-in boyfriend, Esteban. Next to Ricky are Vanessa and Devon McKnight and Joan and Richard Fox, as well as Annette, Grant's assistant, who brought a date. Cannot wait to grill her about that!

The rest of the attendees are some well-loved clients of mine and business associates of Grant's, but for the most part, we've kept our wedding very small. No bridesmaids or groomsmen, just us and our loved ones as witnesses.

"It is with great honor that I present to you Mr. and Mrs. Winters!" the minister announces.

The crowd claps even louder, whoops, and hollers.

Grant squeezes my hand and leans toward me, his lips brushing against my ear. "Are you ready to walk through life as Mrs. Luna Winters?"

I smile up at him. "Absolutely!" I swing his hand, and he leads me down the aisle.

When we reach the end, he turns me around and kisses me deep. The crowd goes wild once more. Once he's had enough, he presses his forehead to mine. "I never thought I could be this happy, but you enlightened me to a whole new world. One where I'm loved and in love in return."

I cup both of his cheeks and look up into his sapphire-blue eyes, hoping our children get those gems one day. "When I first got your letter about Lotus House six months ago, I thought my world had ended, but you, *you*, Grant, *enlightened me* to the possibilities of what we're going to create. To what we have created together with our love. And hopefully, we'll be adding a family to our lives very soon. What we have is never ending. It's only the beginning to our path of enlightenment together... forever."

The End

ALSO FROM WATERHOUSE PRESS

Keep reading for an excerpt of Bolt!

EXCERPT FROM BOLT SAGA: VOLUME ONE

BY ANGEL PAYNE

REECE

She's got the body of a goddess, the eyes of a temptress, and the lips of a she-devil.

And tonight, she's all mine. In every way I can possibly fantasize.

And damn, do I have a lot of fantasies.

Riveted by her seductive glance, I follow Angelique La Salle into a waiting limo. A couple of friends from the party we've just left—their names already as blurry as the lights of Barcelona's Plaça Reial—wave goodbye as if she's taking me away on a six-month cruise to paradise.

Ohhh, yeah.

As an heir to a massive hotel dynasty, I've never wanted for the utmost in luxurious destinations, but I've never been on a cruise. I think I'd like it. Nothing to think about but the horizon...and booze. Freedom from reporters, like the mob that were flashing their cameras in my face back at the club.

What'll the headlines be, I wonder.

Undoubtedly, they've already got a few combinations composed—a mix of the buzz words already trending about me this week.

Party Boy. Player. The Heir with the Hair. The Billionaire with the Bulge.

Well. Mustn't disappoint them about the bulge.

As the driver merges the car into Saturday night traffic, Angelique moves her lush green gaze over everything south of my neck. Within five seconds my body responds. The fantasies in my brain are overcome by the depraved tempest of my body. My chest still burns from the five girls on the dance floor who group-hickied me. My shoulders are on fire from the sixth girl who clawed me like a madwoman while watching from behind. My dick pulses from a hard-on that won't stop because of the seventh girl—and the line of coke she snorted off it.

Angelique gazes at that part with lingering appreciation.

"*C'est magnifique*." Her voice is husky as she closes in, sliding a hand into the open neckline of my shirt. Where's my tie? I was wearing one tonight—at some point. The Prada silk is long gone, much like my self-control. Beneath her roaming fingers, my skin shivers and then heats.

Well...shit.

If my brain just happens to enjoy this as much as my body...I sure as hell won't complain.

Maybe she'll be the one.

Maybe she'll be...more.

The one who'll change things at last.

Even if she's not going to be the one, she's at least *someone*. A body to warm the night. A presence, of *any* kind, to fill the depths. The emptiness I stopped thinking about a long damn time ago.

"You're magnificent too," I murmur, struggling to maintain control as she swings a Gumby-loose limb over my lap and straddles me. What little there is of her green cocktail dress rides up her thighs. She's wearing nothing underneath, of course—a fact that should have my cock much happier than it is. Troubling...but not disturbing. I'm hard, just not throbbing.

Not *needing*. I'm not sure what I need anymore, only that I seem to spend a lot of time searching for it.

"So flawless," she croons, freeing the buttons of my shirt down to my waist. "*Oui*. These shoulders, so broad. This stomach, so etched. You are perfect, *mon chéri*. So perfect for this."

"For what?"

"You shall see. Very soon."

"I don't even get a hint?" I spread a smile into the valley between her breasts.

"That would take the fun out of the surprise, *n'est-ce pas*?"

I growl but don't push the point, mostly because she makes the wait well worth it. During the drive, she taunts and tugs, strokes and licks, teases and entices, everywhere and anywhere, until I'm damn near tempted to order the driver to pull over so I can whip out a condom and screw this temptress right here and now.

But where the hell is here?

As soon as I think the question, the limo pulls into an industrial park of some sort. A secure one, judging by the high walls and the large gate that rolls aside to grant our entry.

Inside, at least in the carport, all is silent. The air smells like cleaning chemicals and leather...and danger. Nothing like a hint of mystery to make a sex club experience all the sweeter.

"A little trip down memory lane, hmmm?" I nibble the bottom curve of Angelique's chin. It's been three weeks since we'd met in a more intimate version of this type of place, back in Paris. I'd been hard up. She'd been alluring. End of story. Or beginning, depending on how one looks at it. "How nostalgic of you, darling."

As she climbs from the limo, she leaves her dress behind

in a puddle on the ground. It wasn't doing much good where I bunched it around her waist anyway. "Come, my perfect Adonis."

Perfect. I don't hear that word often, at least not referring to me. Too often, I'm labeled with one of those media favorites, or if I'm lucky, one of the specialties cooked up by Dad or Chase in their weekly phone messages. Dad's a little more lenient, going for shit like "hey, stranger" or "my gypsy kid." Chase doesn't pull so many punches. Lately, his favorite has been "Captain Fuck-Up."

"Bet *you'd* like to be Captain Fuck-Up right about now, asshole," I mutter as two gorgeous women move toward me, summoned by a flick of Angelique's fingers. Their white lab coats barely hide their generous curves, and I find myself taking peeks at their sheer white hose, certain the things must be held up by garters. Despite the kinky getups, neither of them crack so much as a smile while they work in tandem to strip me.

I'm so caught up in what the fembots are doing, I've missed Angelique putting on a new outfit. Instead of the gold stilettos she'd rocked at the club, she's now in sturdier heels and a lab coat. Her blond waves are pulled up and pinned back.

"Well, well, well. Doctor La Salle, I presume?" Eyeing her new attire with a wicked smirk, I ignore the sudden twist in my gut as she sweeps a stare over me. Her expression is stripped of lust. She's damn near clinical.

"Oh, I am not a doctor, *chéri.*"

I arch my brows and put both hands on my hips, strategically guiding her sights back to my jutting dick. I may not know how the woman likes her morning eggs yet, but I *do* know she's a sucker for an arrogant bastard—especially when he's naked, erect, and not afraid to do something about it.

"Well, that's okay, *chérie*." I swagger forward. "I can pretend if you can."

Angelique draws in a long breath and straightens. Funny, but she's never looked hotter to me. Even now, when she really does look like a doctor about to lay me out with shitty test results. "No more pretending, *mon ami*."

"No more—" My stomach twists again. I glance backward. The two assistants aren't there anymore, unless they've magically transformed into two of the burliest hulks I've ever seen not working a nightclub VIP section.

But these wonder twins clearly aren't here to protect me.

In tandem, they pull me back and flatten me onto a rolling gurney.

And buckle me down. Tight.

Really tight.

"What. The. *Fuck?*"

"Sssshhh." She's leaning over my face—the wonder fuckers have bolted my head in too—brushing tapered fingers across my knitted forehead. "This will be easier if you don't resist, *mon trésor*."

"This? This...*what?*"

Her eyes blaze intensely before glazing over—with insanity. "History, Reece! We are making *history*, and you are now part of it. One of the most integral parts!"

"You're—you're batshit. You're not forging history, you bitch. You're committing a crime. This is kidnapping!"

Her smile is full of eerie serenity. "Not if nobody knows about it."

"People are going to know if I disappear, Angelique."

"Who says you are going to disappear?"

For some reason, I have no comeback for that. No. I *do* know the reason. Whatever she's doing here might be insanity—but it's well-planned insanity.

Which means...

I'm screwed.

The angel I trusted to take me to heaven has instead handed me a pass to hell.

Making this, undoubtedly, the hugest mess my cock has ever gotten me into.

Continue reading in:

BOLT SAGA: VOLUME ONE
By Angel Payne
Coming June 12, 2018

ALSO BY AUDREY CARLAN

The Calendar Girl Series

January (Book 1)   July (Book 7)
February (Book 2)   August (Book 8)
March (Book 3)   September (Book 9)
April (Book 4)   October (Book 10)
May (Book 5)   November (Book 11)
June (Book 6)   December (Book 12)

The Calendar Girl Anthologies

Volume One (Jan-Mar)   Volume Three (Jul-Sep)
Volume Two (Apr-Jun)   Volume Four (Oct-Dec)

The Falling Series

Angel Falling
London Falling
Justice Falling

The Trinity Trilogy

Body (Book 1)
Mind (Book 2)
Soul (Book 3)
Life: A Trinity Novel (Book 4)
Fate: A Trinity Novel (Book 5)

The Lotus House Series

Resisting Roots (Book 1)   Intimate Intuition
Sacred Serenity (Book 2)   (Book 6)
Divine Desire (Book 3)   Enlightened End
Limitless Love (Book 4)   (Book 7)
Silent Sins (Book 5)

ACKNOWLEDGMENTS

To my editor, **Ekatarina Sayanova**, with **Red Quill Editing, LLC**... This is it. It feels like it's the end of an era, though the fact that I'm taking you with me to the next series means our work has only just begun.

To my Waterhouse Press editor, **Jeanne De Vita**, thank you for loving this series as much as I have. Your endless enthusiasm for the Lotus House gang has been such a kick! I hope to work with you sometime again in the future.

To my pre-reader, **Ceej Chargualaf**, this was a wild ride, but we made it through! Your laughter, anger, threats, cheers, daily emails, messages, and "you got this" notes have made this series so much more. Thank you for being you.

Tracey Vuolo, you came onto this project as a pre-reader later in the process, and you busted ass to catch up. I adore the way you connect with my words and am so lucky to have you as part of my team.

Jeananna Goodall, thank you for knowing just what to say when life gets in the way. You are an amazing PA, beta reader, but more than that, you are my friend.

Ginelle Blanch and **Anita Shofner**, my beta extraordinaires, you're like the sprinkles on my donuts. You help make my novels more colorful and sparkly. I appreciate your willingness to always jump in and get the job done. And Ginelle...the crying pictures make my freaking day every time I get one! Means I'm hitting the readers in the squishy parts too. <wink> Love you both.

To the Audrey Carlan Street Team of wicked-hot Angels, together we change the world. One book at a time. BESOS-4-LIFE, lovely ladies.

ABOUT AUDREY CARLAN

Audrey Carlan is a #1 *New York Times*, *USA Today*, and *Wall Street Journal* bestselling author. She writes wicked hot love stories that are designed to give the reader a romantic experience that's sexy, sweet, and so hot your ereader might melt. Some of her works include the wildly successful Calendar Girl Serial, Falling Series, and the Trinity Trilogy.

She lives in the California Valley where she enjoys her two children and the love of her life. When she's not writing, you can find her teaching yoga, sipping wine with her "soul sisters" or with her nose stuck in a wicked hot romance novel.

Any and all feedback is greatly appreciated and feeds the soul. You can contact Audrey below:

E-mail: carlan.audrey@gmail.com
Facebook: facebook.com/AudreyCarlan
Website: www.audreycarlan.com